FOLDED

HUNTER GRANT SERIES

TINA CLOUGH

PART 1
MARIKO AND GRACE

MARIKO

Mariko stops by the lift door and mutters a quiet Japanese curse as she fishes around in her large shoulder bag and thinks, why did I buy a bag with no pockets inside? She kneels, takes things out and puts them in a pile on the polished concrete floor of the landing. Just as her fingers close around the keys, the door to the emergency stairs opens, and two men and a girl with her hands bound together in front of her stop abruptly at the sight of Mariko. She rises quickly to her feet and holds the bag defensively in front of her, unsure of where to turn. The men exchange a few quick words in a language she does not understand, then one takes two swift steps forward and grabs her arm.

'Let me go!' She pulls to the side and tries to reach the lift button, but he drags her towards the door next to her own. Her keys fall to the floor, and she steps on her tablet, which cracks under her foot. The other man pulls the bound girl across the landing, reaches into his pocket and unlocks the door. It is over in half a minute; not until the door closes behind them does Mariko realise that she did not even scream for help. She glimpses an untidy living room, before she is pushed into a bedroom and the door is locked behind her and the girl.

They stand where the men left them, just inside the door. The bound girl holds her hands out and whispers, 'Can you undo this, please? It's too tight.'

Mariko looks at the cable tie around the girl's wrists and shakes her head. 'I can't – it needs cutting. Who are they? Why did they tie your hands?' Her voice is trembling.

'I don't know – they said they would give me a job and somewhere to sleep.' She looks as if she is about to cry. 'I've slept on the streets for weeks. I believed them, but then they …'

'But what?'

'They told me to get into the back seat and one of them got in beside me … I got scared and tried to get out, but I couldn't open the door. He tied my hands and they said they would kill me, if I tried to run away.' Her voice breaks on a sob.

Mariko nods, she has read about human trafficking and how girls are picked up from the streets and sold as sex slaves or unpaid workers. She studies the room; two single mattresses on top of each other along the wall, a couple of fleece blankets and two pillows. The pillows are bare and look grubby. Under the window is a small table and two folding chairs.

My things will still be on the floor by the lift, she thinks, my phone, a couple of textbooks, the pencil case, the tablet – and I dropped my keys. Maybe someone will pick them up and call the police before those men remember. They were in a panic, they didn't think, but they will come in and take my bag as soon as they realise that I still have it. She puts it on the table and looks inside: a physics textbook, her hairbrush and wallet, a tube of hand-cream, a pencil and a packet of chewing gum.

Quickly she opens the wallet and takes out her credit card

and the ATM card, leaving four twenty-dollar bills and some change. She stuffs the cards under the side panel of her bra and pulls her sweatshirt down. The girl is crying now and tries clumsily to open the window with her bound hands. Mariko helps her, but it has a restraint, and the opening is not wide enough for her to even poke her head out. The girl stares defeated at the street far below, leans her forehead against the glass and sobs. Mariko stands back and tries to think of something constructive she can do; enough noise might make someone come to investigate or call the police.

This flat is a mirror image of my flat next-door, she thinks - I saw the kitchen and the living room as they dragged me in, so the bathroom must be back-to-back with my bathroom. It's on the street side, so the wall opposite the door is the only one that has someone else's flat on the other side.

She bangs her fists against the wall and shouts 'help' over and over and the girl joins in. Mariko runs into the bathroom and puts her head low over the basin and shouts 'help, help' as loudly as she can, hoping the pipes will carry the sound to other bathrooms.

Suddenly one of the men is behind her, he puts his hand over her mouth and drags her backwards into the bedroom, where his companion has hold of the crying girl. She is hysterical now, kicking and screaming, and the man pushes her to the floor, kneels and puts his hand over her mouth. She bites him and he jerks his hand away and grabs her by the throat, presses down hard and puts one knee on her thighs, his other hand over her face. Mariko stands rigid, her upper arms held firmly by the man behind her. She is terrified, but she cannot take her eyes off the scene in front of her. The hand over the girl's face covers her mouth and nose, the fingers dig deep into her cheeks, his other hand presses down on her throat. The only sound in the room is the heavy breathing of the man kneeling on the floor and the grunting noises from the girl he holds down.

Suddenly he gets up and stares down at the girl at his feet;

her head has fallen to one side, her mouth is open, her lips are blueish grey. Blue, bloodshot eyes look vacantly at nothing and Mariko knows she is dead. The man holding Mariko lets go of her arms and pushes his friend hard in the chest and shouts in the language Mariko does not understand. Then he turns back to Mariko and gestures for her to sit down at the table, gives her a hard push and she sits down and watches as they drag the girl's body out into the hall. A moment later the man who killed the girl returns and picks up Mariko's bag from where she dropped it on the floor by the window, searches it and puts her wallet in his pocket before he throws the bag on the table.

'You be quiet!' he says in English. 'If you make noise, I kill you too.'

He leaves the room and locks the door, and she sits there for a long time, staring at the damp patch on the carpet where the girl died so suddenly. It seems unreal and remote, like a memory of a photo or a videoclip, not something she witnessed in real life. She is unable to pull her thoughts into order and remains at the table until dusk fills the room.

1

GRACE

Grace is never late for work. One component of her self-imposed penance for past mistakes is unfailing punctuality. The walk from the bus stop to the office takes five and a half minutes when the lights are in her favour; she always takes a bus that gives her a safe margin. When she passes the apartment towers, the lights at the end of the block change and she slows her pace. She prefers not to wait to cross; she would rather walk slowly and just step off the curb and cross, as if the lights were programmed for her approach. The remote possibility that someone in a group of people waiting to cross will recognise her is never far from her mind.

A little movement of something white close to the edge of the sidewalk catches her eye; a tiny, folded shape with sharp corners tumbles towards her in the air stream from a passing car. She picks it up and looks at the angular little shape in her hand. An origami crane, a tiny marvel of perfection and symmetry. Someone with small and nimble fingers made it, took care to flatten each fold perfectly. She drops it into her bag and walks on.

At twenty to one Linda from the accounts department comes past, as she does a couple of times a week.

'I didn't bring any lunch today. Did you? We could go to the café.'

Grace pushes her chair back. 'You never bring lunch on a Monday, so neither do I now. It's called adaptive behaviour.'

Linda grins. 'You're so clever!'

Grace picks up her bag and drops her spectacle case into it.

'Look at this, will you?' She holds out the little origami crane on the palm of her hand. 'I found it on the way to work this morning.'

They sit at their usual table in the corner; Linda on the banquette and Grace on a chair opposite her, as they always do. While they wait for their coffee, Grace takes the little crane out of her bag and puts it on the table. There is something mesmerising about small, perfect things, she thinks and picks it up, turning it in her fingers, while Linda talks about her immature sister and her good-for-nothing boyfriend. There must be a set starting shape, she thinks, a rectangle for one design and a square for another. I suppose the proportions are important, so you don't end up with a bigger wing on one side or not enough space for the beak.

The coffee arrives, and their lunch proceeds as it normally does. Linda turns every story into an amusing minor drama; she shakes her head to emphasize a friend's unacceptable party behaviour and her ponytail swings from side to side. Her brown eyes move around, taking in everyone in the room; she is never completely still. Grace smiles and nods, says very little.

When they leave, Linda takes her arm and gives it a little squeeze. 'It's so *nice* to have a good friend in the office. You came along just at the right time, you funny old thing. There's nobody else I'd rather have lunch with.'

'Funny, old thing? Honestly, Linda – funny, old thing! I'm not funny and not *that* old.'

Linda laughs and tightens her grip on Grace's arm. 'I know, I'm just joking. I love the way you're so different from everyone else I know - you don't go on about yourself all the time. And it's very restful being with you, you don't fidget.'

Grace is twenty years older than Linda, taller, thinner and not in the least inclined to go on about her life. Linda knows nothing about her, or at least nothing that matters. Now she smiles and gently liberates her arm.

'I'm glad I've got you too, Linda – you brighten up my day. I'd be bored out of my mind, if I had lunch in the staff room every day – the conversation there seems to be on an endless loop of trivia and complaints.'

Having lunch in a café eats into her reduced income, but it is worth it. Linda does indeed brighten her life, and Grace knows how to economise; these days she goes to the library instead of buying books, never buys take-away meals and doesn't go to the movies.

Back at her desk she thinks how lucky it is that Linda never pries into her background and just accepts her for what she is, here and now. She knows that Grace is single and lives on her own in an apartment, but she has never asked for details. Would I tell her? Or would a lie be better, in case she was tempted to gossip about me? Their friendship is only active during working hours and it has never been tested.

It is not until later that evening, when the film on TV ends, that Grace remembers the crane. She gets it out of her bag and studies it again. I'll put it somewhere where I can see it – perhaps on the windowsill above the kitchen bench. And there it sits in the sunlight the next morning, and Grace smiles when she sees it, lit from behind so the double layers of the intricate folds show as shadows. And some kind of pattern, she thinks, and picks it up, on the inside – I didn't notice yesterday. But as she studies it, she begins to wonder. With the point of a knife, she carefully levers a fold open, peers into the crevice and turns the crane at ninety degrees; there are lines of tiny writing that continue into the next fold. Intrigued she unfolds the whole crane and tries to read the lines of miniscule words, but they are too small. In the back of a kitchen drawer she finds the little plastic magnifying glass she got in a Christmas cracker at last year's office party. She imagines a little girl, who loves everything very tiny, sharpening a pencil into a point as thin as a needle and writing a story in letters so small she cannot read them once written.

"Help me, prisoner in 403, two men, one girl killed, contact police and John Anderson, Boston, USA, Mariko Goto."

The writing is so miniscule that even the pin-sharp pencil point has filled the hollow spaces of the tiny 'e' and 'o'. The meticulous precision of the writing is not that of a child. Her mind shies away from thoughts of sinister scenarios; the possibility of being forced to act fills her with apprehension.

2

MARIKO

Mariko opens her eyes and looks at the window; today the sky is blue with a few small clouds moving fast. Every day she does the same thing at the same time. Having a routine, however meaningless, helps her stay calm and creates a sense of purpose. She always gets up as soon as she wakes up; lying on the mattress on the floor during the day would somehow imply defeat. She does ten push-ups every morning and every night, and ten sit-ups in the middle of the day. Every second or third day one of the men delivers a carton with food, always things that can be eaten without a knife and fork. Today is the second day; she has enough food until tomorrow.

She used to leave the uneaten food in the box, but for the last couple of weeks she has been hiding things between her mattress and the wall. They never check and don't seem to notice that there are too few wrappings in the box when they take it away. She adds a small carton of long-life milkshake to her secret supply and counts her treasures: four snack packs of crackers, three small, shrink-wrapped packets of cheese slices, three nut bars and one bag of mixed nuts. She thinks for a moment, then she picks up some of the packets and hides them behind the little drawer under the wash basin in the bathroom, where her credit and ATM cards have been since she was first locked in.

She started hoarding the week they did not replace the box for four days. What if they don't come back, she thought then. How long must I wait until I dare shout for help or break the window? I never know for sure if they are here or not; I think they take turns being here and being in my flat – from the bathroom here I can hear them using my shower next door. To be safe I would have to wait a long time and make sure I could hear nothing at all before I tried to attract attention. The memory of the girl they killed never leaves her mind.

If there is another girl in the room with her for a couple of days, their interactions determine how the day proceeds. One of her captors has brought some clothes and toiletries from her flat; every few days she washes some things in the bathroom and hangs them over the towel rail to dry. Every couple of days she writes a new note, folds it into an origami shape and drops it out the window. When she remembered that first night that the pencil was still in the bag, she hid it in the bathroom; it is her only means of communication. She sharpens it by rubbing it on the grouting between the bathroom tiles, then she uses the edge of her ATM card to give it a fine point so she can write very small.

There have been several girls after the one they killed. All have been told that they will be given jobs and accommodation, and that in return, their earnings must be shared with the men. All have been run-aways or street sleepers.

Each time a newcomer is brought in, one of the men pushes the new girl hard up against the wall, side by side with Mariko and stands in front of them, close enough that the girls feel threatened.

'If you make noise or try to attract attention, I will hear you. I will come in here and kill one of you, doesn't matter which one. The other one can watch.'

Each time he pokes his finger into the middle of Mariko's chest. 'This one has seen me do it, she knows I mean what I say.'

This ritual of intimidation has been repeated every time a new girl has arrived, and Mariko has learnt to nod, to show she does indeed know that he means it.

When she was first taken, she was sure she would be missed and found. She has many friends, both in Japan and in New Zealand, and she thought the tutors at the university would report her missing. That first night in the room she heard them talking and arguing long into the night. A couple of times one of them shouted angrily and Mariko hoped the neighbours would come and knock on the door. The next morning, they brought her cell phone and made her send messages to her Auckland friends and to her university liaison person, saying that she must go back to Japan on urgent family business. All her social media apps have been deleted from the phone and the only messages she sees have come by text or email. Now it is a fixed routine; a couple of times a week both men come in and bring the phone. One man stands behind her and the other sits beside her, holding the phone. To her New Zealand friends, she says that she doesn't know when she will be back, but probably not for some time. Her father usually sends a text message every week, and they let her respond to him and to friends in Japan pretending that all is well, that she is still studying and doing well.

The man behind her reads as she types, his hand grips the back of her neck. She knows she would never have time to type anything other than what they tell her or even send the single word 'help'. The first time they brought in the phone she changed the keyboard to Japanese characters, when she replied to a text from Japan and the man standing behind her punched the side of her head hard. 'Stop! Write in English!' She tried to explain that her Japanese friend would think something was wrong, if she replied in English. The men talked rapidly for a couple of minutes in their own language, then one of them held the phone in front of her again. 'You can only reply in English.' Mariko finds it hard to imagine what motivates them to let her type these replies, surely, they could do it themselves and pretend it is from her.

GRACE

Grace gets off the bus and hurries downhill towards the office in slanting rain. Head bent into the wind she holds the hood of her coat together under her chin. When a little white shape tumbles towards a puddle in front of her, she picks it up and the hood blows off her head. It is another origami construction, a different design, slightly bigger. She quickly puts it in her pocket before it gets soaked and pulls the hood up again. When she gets it out and puts it on her desk, it has flattened and lost its shape. She uses a straightened paper clip to recreate the three-dimensional shape. It's a frog, she thinks, or a toad – a very complicated shape. One side of the body is wet and a bit mushy. She puts it on her desk and by lunchtime it has dried. Turning it over she sees writing on the underside of the body; tiny writing, just like the first time and a shiver runs down her spine. She picks it up and holds it level with her eyes, tries to separate the folds to peer into it, to read the words. The texture of the paper has changed, and the folds stick together; she worries about ripping it and puts it down.

For the first time since the start of her friendship with Linda, Grace takes the initiative and walks down the corridor to the accounts department and suggests lunch at the cafe.

'I know it's not Monday - I'm putting the sandwich I brought in the staff room fridge for tomorrow. I thought we might go out, there's something I want to discuss with you.'

As soon as they sit down, she puts the frog and the flattened crane on the table.

'Oh look - another one!' says Linda and picks it up, delighted with Grace's find. 'How cute – it's a frog. Did you find it this morning? It looks as if it's been wet.'

'I want to unfold it,' says Grace, 'but the layers of paper have stuck together. I'm worried I'll tear it. This other flat piece is the crane, unfolded.'

'Why? Do you want to see how they are made? You can find out on the Internet. I bet there are hundreds of YouTube videos of how to do it.'

Grace hands the flattened crane and the little plastic magnifying glass to Linda and watches her face as she reads the words. They stare at each other for a long moment, then Grace picks up the frog and shows Linda the fragment of writing.

'I found this in nearly the same place – there's something written inside this one too. But how will I unfold it?'

'Wet it again,' says Linda with the certainty of someone who always has an answer, or at least imagines she does. 'Just dampen it a tiny bit and then we'll pull it open very carefully.'

They work together, agonisingly slowly. One drop at a time from Grace's glass of water, dripped from a wet fingertip onto the frog. Grace carefully separates the folds with the tip of her unused knife, Linda holds the structure still by pinning it to the table with long dark blue fingernails. A couple of folds tear a little, but in the end, they have a flat piece of paper four times the size of the first one. On one side are four lines of tiny, pencilled words; they take turns using the magnifying glass.

"Help us, two girls, prisoner in 403, tell police, tell John Anderson, Boston, US, one girl dead, two men next door. Mariko Goto."

Linda stares at Grace with a look of disbelief. 'Oh, my God! Is it for real?'

'I think it is. I found both outside those big apartment buildings – you know, just before the Victoria Street intersection? When I saw the writing on the crane, I thought it a probably a game, that some kids dropped it as a joke. But now I think it's serious – someone is in trouble.'

'You must take them to the police station,' says Linda. 'Doesn't matter if they laugh at you – at least you'll know you've done the right thing.'

Before they leave, Linda uses her phone to take pictures of both pieces of paper. 'Just in case the police keep them, and if you find another one – so we can compare. I'll put something beside them as a kind of measure – I know, one of those paper straws of sugar will do.'

They check that the writing shows clearly in the photos, then Grace puts the pieces of paper in her bag. After work she walks on the far side of Victoria Street and stops to look across at the two apartment towers. Balconies and anonymous windows; no signs of life. What did I expect to see? she thinks, these blocks are enormous with wings angled off towards the street behind, there could be a hundred apartments. I must go to the police - it doesn't matter how much I don't want to.

Standing under the tree on the Cook Street corner beside the central police station she pauses and tries to imagine what she will do, if she meets someone she knows. It will depend on who it is; some would be harder than others. She cringes at the thought of being pulled into a conversation, being asked where she works, how she is coping – or someone looking through her, as if she no longer exists. She takes a deep breath, pulls her shoulders back and walks under the canopy and through the main entrance. Fifteen minutes later she is back on the sidewalk; relieved to not have met anybody she knows but frustrated at the outcome of her mission.

Two changes of buses later she lets herself into her flat and kicks off her damp shoes. What did I expect? she thinks. I was hoping they would take it more seriously, but at least they put the notes in an evidence bag and labelled it. Thank God I didn't see anyone I know. I wonder if something about me will come up when they enter my details into the system, even though I have a different name now. If it does, they might think I made it up, that it's a ploy to get attention. She feels queasy at the thought of others discussing her, whether with pity or contempt.

A week later, on a windy early spring day, she finds a third origami message on her way home. It has caught on a rough patch of paving on the inner edge of the footpath, a water lily or maybe a lotus flower with tiny words pencilled on one petal, disappearing in a fold. She unfolds it immediately; inside is a long message written in the tiniest letters so far. The little magnifying glass is still in her bag; unable to wait she stands on the sidewalk and reads.

"Prisoner in 403, Mariko Goto, I have dropped many notes, lots of girls have been kept here and taken away, also two boys, one girl was killed by the men. Go to police, show note, also tell them contact John Anderson, Boston, USA. The men took my phone. They are in my flat next to this one where I am locked up. This is true - not a joke. Please do something!"

She stares at the tiny shape and inside her a feeling of urgency is building, but the thought of going back to the police makes her feel sick with apprehension. She crosses the street and stares up at the tall apartment blocks, scans the rows of anonymous windows that mirror the sky. She remains there for a long time, her hand held out in front of her; hopes that whoever wrote the message can see the little square of white paper in her hand and take comfort.

Grace and Linda sit opposite each other at their usual table in the café. Grace hands Linda the unfolded water lily and the magnifying glass and watches her face as she reads the note.

'Oh God, Grace – why haven't the police found this girl?' Linda's face creases with worry. 'Someone is a prisoner in a flat in one of those apartment blocks and has been there for ages. And they've killed a girl! You must take this one to the cops right away.'

'Could you do it, please?'

She knows this plea could unravel her cautiously constructed new life, open her up to gossip and speculation. She might have to leave the job she found after so much searching and start again. Linda is looking at her with a puzzled frown.

'Why don't you do it?'

Grace hesitates between saying she has an appointment straight after work and just saying 'forget it, I'll do it'. Then she says, 'I'd rather not go back, there's someone who works there that I don't want to bump into. I got quite upset last time, had to steel myself to even walk in the entrance.'

She can imagine the speculations flying through Linda's head: an ex-lover, a stalker, an enemy from a dispute over money.

To her relief Linda smiles. 'Of course, I will - I'll go after work. I can catch a bus from downtown to get home and the walk to Cook Street will do me good.'

Emboldened by such easy success Grace adds, 'Tell them you heard of someone else who has found origami messages in the same spot. I think it's important that they connect the incidents. Don't say you know me.'

As soon as the words come out of her mouth, she knows that was a step too far. Linda looks searchingly at her for a moment, gets her phone out and takes a photo of the note before she puts it in her bag. 'Of course.'

PART 2
HUNTER AND DAO

3

After a long walk in the spring sunshine, Dao says innocently, 'Let's have a coffee here before we go back. I know it's too early for a morning coffee, but we've walked much further than we usually do, and Scruff looks tired.'

'Aha – and am I right in thinking this is the place with the chocolate brownies?'

She laughs. 'The best ones ever.'

We sit at a sheltered outside table with Scruff under it and his chin on Dao's foot. The early spring sun is warm and there is a breeze coming off the sea.

'We should have gone away a month ago like you said,' says Dao and shrugs out of her jacket. 'I mean somewhere tropical. It's too nice now to leave all this behind.'

'We can do a tour of Northland, instead, like we talked about last summer, but we never did. I want to show you Cape Reinga – so long as it's not during the school holidays.'

'OK, let's do it next week.'

We are walking back when my phone vibrates in my pocket. A message from Plum, my much younger sister: 'Called you twice, no answer. Urgent!' Plum's messages always have exclamation marks and are frequently urgent and I put the phone away and ignore it, but as I follow Dao up the stairs to the living room, I take pity on Plum and return her call.

'Oh God, Hunter,' she says. "I'm at work and I can't talk for long, but something really bad is happening and I don't know what to do about it.'

In the space of one micro-second my mind conjures up a variety of scenarios: a crashed car that she forgot to insure, an unwanted pregnancy, having got arrested for some stupid post-party prank. With Plum it could be anything.

'Calm down, Plum. What's wrong?'

'Do you remember Linda – my friend from high school, a couple of years older than me, with long dark hair and she used to wear Harry Potter style glasses?'

'Not really - I was in Afghanistan most of the time you were at high school, and I didn't meet many of you friends, but never mind, carry on.'

'She just sent me a private message on Face Book, she wanted your number, she's read about you – she sounds desperate. I said I couldn't give it to her, but I think it's really serious, Hunter - I'm sure it is. She only told me a bit, but I think you should talk to her – someone's in real trouble and she doesn't know what to do – and it sounds horrible!' Her voice is rising, she is close to tears.

'Plum!' I say in my old army voice. 'Take a deep breath and calm down. Has your friend been to the police?'

'She and her friend have both been, but for some reason the cops aren't listening – and it's a bit like when Hope Barber disappeared. You know how you told us they kept telling Noah that adults can take off when they like, they don't have to tell anyone, and it doesn't mean they're missing or whatever? It's a bit like that, but worse.'

'OK, I'll listen to her, but I can't be everybody's help desk – give her my number, I might be able to give her some advice.'

When I tell Dao what Plum said she looks thoughtful. 'You

never know with Plum – she does exaggerate, but maybe it really is serious.'

We are on the sofa after lunch; Dao is reading a textbook about algebraic number theory with her feet on my lap and I am doing one of the things I do best; while I'm reading my thumb gently rubs the deep scar made by the shackle she wore for years. It goes right around her ankle, and it is brutally ugly, like a branding. She hopes that massaging it will make it better, but it looks much the same as it always did.

I reach for my phone and put it on speaker, just like I got into the habit of doing when Noah's sister Hope Barber went missing a few months ago. It saves time and explanations, and it gives me the opportunity to watch Dao's reactions to whatever is said. Over the last couple of years, I have learnt what to watch out for; I've deciphered the code that most people don't notice.

'Thank you for letting me talk to you!' Linda says. 'I'm really grateful, because I don't know what to do, it's so frustrating. A woman I work with has left without saying goodbye or anything – and she'd never do that, never. She resigned by text message – which is another thing she'd never do. OK, she did – but that's really strange, because I didn't know she even had a cell phone.'

'Have you called her?'

Dao sits up, intrigued, and puts the book face down beside her.

'No, I don't have her number – we go out for lunch together about once a week, but I've never been in touch with her outside work. And I don't know her address either. I know which bus stop she uses, that's all. She's very private, reserved – I only just realised how little I know about her.'

She is speaking very fast; trying to cram in as much information as possible, as if she's worried that I'll end the call. 'And I'm really worried because of some other stuff that's been going on – not at work, but things she found out about. And it's been going on for a while now, so that makes it extra urgent.'

Dao shakes her head and I say, 'Hold on a moment, Linda.'

'Ask if we can meet,' whispers Dao close to my ear. 'She's trying to say everything at once, too fast – let's sit down and get her to tell us without rushing it.'

'Linda, can we meet? It might be easier for us to make sense of this if you to tell us the whole story face to face.'

'Oh, thank you! That would be great, if you have time – it's complicated and I have photos on my phone too and things that I want to show you. I've taken the afternoon off – have you got time to meet today?'

'We can meet any time – where?'

Linda lives in Mt Roskill and has no transport, and we are on the North Shore; after a short discussion we arrange to meet at a café not far from her flat.

'My flat is hopeless at the moment – my brother lives with me and he's studying for exams, but there's a café just nearby.' She gives us directions to the café in Mt Roskill, and I tell her we'll see her there in an hour.

The café is very small, more a place where people pick up coffees to go; Linda is already there, at one of four little round tables which is all the seating there is. She is well-built girl, as they say, with large brown eyes and a worried expression that seems out of place on her face.

'I got here early,' she says, when we have said hi and got ourselves something to drink. 'It's sometimes hard to get a table – I should have picked a bigger place for us to meet.'

'Never mind,' I say, 'Please tell us about your friend who left - everything. Start at the very beginning.'

'She's called Grace,' says Linda. 'Grace Harris. She came to work for us about a year ago – it's a firm of engineering consultants, quite big. We do a lot of earthquake strengthening stuff and bridges, you know - heavy stuff. I do the debtors and creditors ledger and various accounting things, and Grace does general admin. She's very clever, she reads a lot, and she knows loads of interesting things. At first, I paid no attention to her – she's probably about forty-five or maybe a bit more, a lot older than my usual friends. And she's very quiet - she kind of blends into the background and doesn't say a lot in the staffroom, doesn't wear make-up. She looks a bit boring – but she isn't, she's wonderful. I only discovered this when I was going out to get a sandwich at the café near the office one day some months ago. She was just sitting at her desk looking straight ahead, and for some reason I thought she looked lonely, so I said, 'come out for a café lunch with me, I'm having a treat' sort of thing. Just on the spur of the moment, you know?' She blinks a couple of times and I can see how upset she is, but she's got excellent self-control.

'And then you discovered you had things in common?' suggests Dao and smiles. 'And got to be friends.'

'No, it's funny - we don't have much in common,' says Linda slowly. 'I thought about it on the way here – I know hardly anything about her private life. I never thought of it before. We usually talk about people at work, and movies – she loves movies, and she reads a lot. Sometimes she tells me about a book she's reading, not the kind of books I would read, but she makes it interesting. And we talk about my life, but not about hers – I've just realized. I think I do most of the talking, well, I know I do – Grace is very quiet. But she has a wicked sense of humour – you know the kind where someone comes out with something, straight-faced, and it takes you a minute to realise how funny it was. I know she lives on her own, but not where and I know the bus stop she uses, but I don't know which bus she takes. And I don't have her phone number.'

I notice Dao's chin tilt up by a degree and think I know why; this is intriguing; a woman who gives nothing away about her life outside of office hours. It sounds like very deliberate reticence; most people filter stories about relatives or friends and experiences from the past into conversations.

'And you never met outside of work hours? Not even once?'

'No, it seems mad, doesn't it? We've been friends for at least six or eight months, and I know nothing about her personal life – literally nothing!'

'There must be a personnel file,' I say. 'Could you get a look at it and get her address, maybe her phone number – or even the name of her next-of-kin? Family would know how to get in touch with her.'

Dao sucks the last of her smoothie through her straw and gives me a slanting glance; I react to slurping noises the way other people do when they hear nails scratch against a blackboard.

'Sorry Hunter!' She pushes the glass away. 'The vitamins sink to the bottom, and they make that growly noise when you suck them up.'

Linda smiles for the first time, and Dao continues, 'OK, so we know very little about Grace. Did you do a Google search for her, check social media and that sort of stuff?'

'No, but I will - this all happened today, but I don't expect to find anything. I know she's not on any social media, because we talked about it once. I'll have a go at the personnel files. They're in the admin manager's office, so I'll try when she's in a meeting. Or maybe I can persuade the girl who does payroll to tell me.'

I mentally check back through our phone conversation. 'You mentioned photos you have on your phone, and things Grace found. Want to tell us about those?'

Linda's gazes absently out through the window and Dao slants me her sideways 'don't say anything' look and after a few moments Linda turns her attention back to us.

'It all started when Grace found an origami shape on the sidewalk outside a big apartment building that she walks past on her way to work. She picked it up, thought someone had accidentally dropped it from a window. And then over a short period of time she found a few more – well, two more origami and one book. A physics textbook.'

Dao and I look at each other in surprise and then both speak at once. 'A textbook?'

'Yeah, it sounds crazy – I'll tell you how it happened. First, she found an origami crane, and then a frog and then a water lily – and for some reason she unfolded the crane and inside was writing – the tiniest writing I've ever seen. Grace had a little plastic magnifying glass, that she got in a Christmas cracker, and we read the message. It was written by someone who is in real trouble, serious trouble. The origami frog got wet and the layers of paper stuck together when it dried, but we managed to pull it apart – another message, the same as the first one, just a bit longer.'

She pauses again with that far-away look - she is picturing them together, I think, re-living the moment and we wait for her to continue. 'Those messages – it's definitely not kids or some game, it's a real emergency – someone is being held against their will.'

Dao's focus on Linda is like a laser beam now; if the roof fell in, she wouldn't notice. 'Do you remember what they said?'

'I have photos,' says Linda. 'We decided at the start that we wanted to keep a record of them in case the cops took the actual origami – we both think something terrible is going on in one of those flats. I took the photos before Grace went to the cops with the first two. Then when she found the third one, she asked me to go to the central police station – you know, on the corner of Cook Street? She said that was the best place to go, but she knew someone there, someone she really didn't want to bump into, and she just couldn't make herself go back. So I went after work that day and took the last origami with me.'

I'm getting intrigued now; this is far more complex than I had expected. 'And what did they say when you showed them the message?'

'Oh, they seemed interested, but they didn't actually say what they were going to do. They wrote everything down and they put the paper in a plastic evidence bag, just like on TV. I said I hadn't found it, but my friend had, and I told them a lie – I said the person who found it had to catch an early bus somewhere for an appointment, so I'd offered to take it in on her behalf. And I told them she had handed in two messages earlier.'

'Did they ask her name?'

'Yes, they wrote down my name and her name and my contact details. They seemed a bit surprised that I didn't have Grace's phone number, but I said we just work together, I've never had any reason to call her.'

'And you told them this one was found in the same place as earlier ones?'

'Yeah - but they said they couldn't tell me what they were doing about it. Not that I expected them to. And then today after Grace resigned, I was asked to tidy up her desk, probably just because the manager knew we were friends – and I found a few personal things in her desk drawers. Which was odd – she would have taken those if she was planning to leave. And I don't believe she planned to leave, anyway – she would have told me. The physics book was in her top drawer, right on top of her pens and things.'

I'm on tenterhooks and questions are lining up in my head. Linda leans forward, intent on making us take her story seriously.

'Yesterday we were both in the staff room at lunchtime and when we walked out together, Grace said "I know it's not our café day tomorrow, but let's go out for lunch anyway, I've got something to show you." She seemed kind of excited, or nervous. And then this morning the admin manager caught sight of me when I came in and asked me to check Grace's desk! I asked why, what had happened and Monica – that's the manager – said Grace had resigned with immediate effect just then, she had sent a text message saying she wasn't coming back - I just couldn't believe it! When I found the physics book, I was surprised and I kind of fanned the pages through my fingers, you know how you do? And I noticed that the text on some pages seemed much darker, or denser I should say, so I had a closer look. And on some pages, quite a few, someone has written in tiny letters between the lines. Lots and lots of stuff. And the writing is just like on those origami notes.'

'Wow,' says Dao, 'I'd love to see that!'

'I've got it here, in my bag.' Linda gestures to the floor beside her chair. 'I took it and I think it's vital evidence. I spent a couple of minutes when I was back at my desk reading a little of what was written in the physics book, and I got goose bumps. It's nearly impossible to read that tiny writing without a magnifying glass, it makes you go cross-eyed, but even the little I read told me it's really urgent that someone does something.'

She stares out the window again for a moment and then she turns back to us, clearly stressed and anxious. 'It seems unbelievable that it was only this morning – it's been such a mad day. I decided two things right away – I must give the book to the police so they can do something about it. But first I must read it all and document it, like we did with the origami messages. I said I had a migraine headache coming on and I must go home. I ran all the way down to that big bookstore in Queen Street and bought a magnifying glass, a big square one, and then I sat down in a cafe and started reading - and as soon as I had read a couple of pages, I knew it was crucial for the police to have it. I called the police and quoted the number on the receipt or whatever you call it – the one they gave me when I handed in the last origami note. I asked to speak to whoever was dealing with that enquiry and they put me through to a guy, who said he couldn't tell me anything, but he asked me to bring the book in. And then I thought of you, so I went online and asked Plum to call me.'

She drinks the last of her coffee and looks from Dao to me and back again.

'I'm going to get it copied before I hand it in – there's one of those stationery places not far from here where I can copy it – I want to hand it in as soon as I can. I just wanted to talk to someone who … well, someone who understands these things.'

'And what is it you want me to do? It sounds as if you have it sorted already.'

'I don't know – just talk through it with me, I suppose. I remember from ages ago how Plum said you're amazing at sorting things out, so they make sense, and she always asks you what to do. And I knew you had been involved in some dangerous stuff – when you saved Dao, I read about it in the papers later on when that court case was going on. And now I think something awful has happened to Grace and I thought you might help me work through it before I go to the police. It's really because I want to make sure they take it seriously and do something right away – I've wondered a bit about those notes and if the cops believe the messages – maybe they think it's a kid's game or something.'

'Why do you think something's happened to Grace?' asks Dao. 'Is there something you haven't mentioned?'

'Say that Grace found the book the day before yesterday, and she read it at home that night with her Christmas cracker magnifying glass and then she brought it to work to show to me and to ask me to take it to the police. Or maybe she found it that morning on her way to work, yesterday morning I mean. And maybe she was going to ask me to take photos of all the pages with writing. But she caught up with me too late – I was already in the staff room, because I'd gone to lunch early. So she said, "let's go out tomorrow" - and she left the book in her desk drawer, but then she never came back to the office! She resigned - and I can't believe that's what really happened. The more I think about it the more I believe something's happened to her between then and this morning.'

'Would you come back to our place?' I hope she will say yes. I want to discuss some of this in a quiet setting not right next to a line of people waiting for take-away coffees and with music that makes it hard to have even a casual conversation. 'I don't think this is the best place to look at the photos and the book – we can use our scanner at home and then it's all done. Would you mind if we do that? We'll drive you back to town when we're done.'

To my surprise Linda's eyes fill with tears. 'Thank you!' She wipes her eyes. 'I wasn't sure if you were going to help me – you're both so hard to read. I was getting worried that you didn't think it was very important or something.'

4

Back at the house the first thing we do is download the photos from Linda's phone to my laptop. There is a series of images; the first is the unfolded origami crane, lying flat with a paper sugar straw beside it.

'We wanted to show the scale,' explains Linda. 'It's hard to describe how tiny the writing is, but if you compare it with the print on the sugar straw you get the idea. I tried to take it as close and as high definition as I could. All the writing is done with a pencil, and it must have been sharpened into a point like a needle – the letters are so tiny.'

We enlarge the photos on the screen and study them closely. It is nearly impossible to imagine how someone wrote those microscopic letters. The writing is lower case, and very carefully formed.

"Help me, prisoner in 403, two men, girl killed, contact police and John Anderson, Boston, US, Mariko Goto."

The text is less clear where fold lines intersect the words, but we can read it. The second origami is a bigger piece, also shown beside a sugar straw. The note reads: "Help us, two girls, prisoner in 403, tell police, tell John Anderson, Boston, USA, one girl dead, two men next door in Mariko Goto's flat."

The third note is bigger still, and there are numerous fold

lines, but all the text is legible: "Prisoner in 403, Mariko Goto, I have dropped many notes, lots of girls have been kept here and taken away, also two boys, one girl was killed by the men. Go to police, show note, also tell them contact John Anderson, Boston, USA. The men took my phone. They are in my flat next to this one where I am locked up. This is true - not a joke. Please do something."

Dao picks up the physics textbook and opens the front and then the back, holds it up for me to see. 'Look, the blank pages at the start and the end have been pulled out. I wondered where she got the paper. And folding them into origami – I bet she did that so they wouldn't just flutter away when she dropped them out the window. And origami shapes would catch someone's attention, but a flat piece of paper wouldn't. Very clever!'

'Yes, and then she ran out of blank pages – but why didn't she use pages with print on and write in the margins?' I take the book out of Dao's hand. 'There's plenty of room to write in the margins. Did something happen that made her think she must throw the whole book out to get attention? Did she think she had no more time to make origami out of the printed pages? I wish we knew more details about the situation she's in.'

'There's lots more,' says Linda. 'You just haven't seen it yet - it's all in that textbook.'

Scanning the pages where Mariko has written between the lines of printed text is problematic. The book has a firm spine, and the scanned images show only part of each page; the section closest to the spine curves up and the text fades to nothing in the image. In the end Dao takes charge.

'This isn't working, Hunter! We've got to flatten it - just stand on it and break the spine so we can get it flat on the scanner. We've got to do this now, so Linda can take it to the cops.'

So that's what I do; I open the book at each page with writing, put it face down on the floor, stand on the spine and then put it on the scanner. 'You know what's going to happen before we get to the end,' I say to Dao as the book starts losing its stability. 'The whole damn thing will fall apart, and we'll end up with a mess of loose pages.'

But needs must, we are not prepared to let it out of our hands, until we have everything documented in case we need it later. The thought that not enough speed and effort might result, even after the police have been given the book, keeps us going. And as Dao says in her usual pragmatic way, 'So what could they do to us? They can't prove we broke it and if all the pages are there, who cares?'

There are sixteen pages with Mariko's writing between the lines. She has not written on consecutive pages; she selected pages with solid text and no diagrams and graphs. When all the pages are saved as a PDF file on my hard drive, Dao turns to Linda. 'We'll put the book in a zip-lock bag in case it does fall apart. And I'll email the file to you as an attachment. Have you got email on your phone? OK, so when you go to the police station you can give them the book and then you can ask for a police email address to forward the file to - and you do it right there and then. That way there will be no delay while they get organised so they can read it.'

Linda looks doubtful and turns to me. 'Do you think I should? Won't they wonder why I did that? I know Grace has some problem with the cops, but I want to stay in the clear, if you know what I mean? So I can ask for updates or push a bit, if necessary.'

Dao and I look at each other, thinking this over, and then Dao provides the solution. 'Tell them you tried to read the handwritten text in the book, and you had no magnifying glass, so you scanned the whole thing, so you could read it. They don't know if you have a scanner or if you showed it to anyone. Hunter, do you think she should mention us? If they ask, I mean.'

I take my time considering this. We've come into contact with various police officers in the two dramas we've been involved in; we have some contacts and probably a level of credibility. Not enough for what we might need to do; I think we are better keeping out of it.

'Let's stay out of it, at least for now. If it will help at some future stage, you can tell them you talked to us, but it's not going help now.'

'And if they don't know, we can do whatever we like,' says Dao, who shares my belief that it is better to be able to act without interference than being strictly legal. 'We've been through this kind of thing before, and we know how it works. The minute they know we're involved they'll tell us we must leave it to them. It gets very frustrating.'

Linda looks at me with a dubious frown, and I smile to reassure her. 'We won't do anything criminal, but we like to have freedom of action. You don't know about the incident we got involved in six months ago, but we got further than anyone else, and much faster - by doing things our own way and not giving anyone reason to slow us down.'

'Maybe we should write it up the way Tama did with that report for Sinclair,' says Dao. 'It made it easy to get the context and understand how one thing led to another.'

'We were involved in a tragedy six months ago.' I turn to Linda, who has no idea what we're talking about. 'A key person in that drama was a guy called Tama, and he wrote a magnificent report for Inspector Sinclair, who was in charge of the case. He documented everything chronologically. Not just facts and dates, like most people might, but he linked it with paragraphs of text explaining why he had done certain things, what other people told him and what his conclusions were.'

Dao smiles at the memory. 'It was brilliant - the cops got all our reasoning and our motivation for doing things. Because we did a few things that weren't totally legal – well, to tell the truth, we could have got into a bit of trouble. Tama set it out like a story, with facts kind of built in, and all the background – I think it saved us from a lot of hassle. Let's do that! You can fill in the story details, Linda.

It takes a surprisingly short time to write it, from the first origami Grace found to Linda's discovery of Mariko's notes between the lines in the physics book. Then we open the PDF file and enlarge it on the screen and start reading.

Page 19 - The third girl has been taken away. I must record how they do it, I hope someone will read this one day. This is how it started: I was beside the lift, they came from the emergency stairs, 2 men, 1 girl with her hands tied. I dropped my stuff, lost my tablet, phone, keys. The pushed us into the flat next to mine, locked us in a bedroom, one window facing the street. Now I only have a few things; bag, physics book, pencil, hairbrush. We scream and bang on the wall, the men come in, angry, they push the girl to floor, put hand over her face and on her throat. She died. I will record names, ages, details of those who have been here since then, using as few words as possible. They stay one or two days, get taken to my flat next door, showered, tidied up, I go into bathroom here, shared wall, I hear nearly everything. Men promise them work, money, I never see them again.

Page 23 - After girl 3, I started this list, will continue for as long as I can.

Girl 1 - never found out her name, no details, skinny white girl, bleached hair, blue eyes, about 15/16, short, pierced left eyebrow, killed here by the shorter man, choked to death.

Girl 2 - Jess, Maori girl from Rotorua, 17, mother's name Sharon. I never knew her surname. Two brothers, both younger, I think. She ran away when father beat her for getting drunk at a family party. Here one day, said she would try to escape when they moved her.

Girl 3 – Karen/Kerin (sp?) Gordon. Only here 1/2 day,

looked 20-21, very tall, looked anorexic, ran away from people she owed money to in Tauranga, I think for drugs, kept shouting and asking for 'shit' (drugs) and made a lot of noise, men were very angry, they gave her injection and took her away.

Girl 4 – Emily, very pretty, 18, brown hair, blue eyes, from Hamilton (worked in McDonalds there), mother dead, came to Auck with friend called Tessa to look for work, slept on someone's sofa in shared house in Papatoetoe. Was good at netball at school. Here 2 days.

Girl 5 – Lucy, her surname sounds like Mathus, said she was 16, but looked a couple of years younger, street sleeper, got money by sex work, drugs user, from just outside Whangarei, here for 1 day.

Boy 1 - Rick - 13, reddish hair, brown eyes, from Manurewa, tattoo of eagle on front of neck, on the run, would not say why, said he is related to Rugby league star, wouldn't say which one, here 1/2 day.

By the time we get to the eighth page Mariko has recorded seventeen young people over a course of weeks and with increasing detail. I imagine she decided to ask them lots of questions to record everything she could in the physics book. On some pages she writes about herself, you can feel her despair. She thinks she is going to die, that nobody will know she was there or what happened to her, who she was. She chronicles her life in tiny precise letters between the lines of print. It's her legacy; we must find her.

My name is Mariko Goto. I was born in Matsue in Japan 23 years ago. I thought my father was dead. My mother had a small bookshop, we lived in a flat above the shop. I remember my mother's parents when I was little, but they are dead now, they were old when she was born. I thought my mother was a widow, that my father had died in an accident. My mother died 5 years ago of cancer. All my life my mother spoke English to me about half the time, she said it would be useful some time and I must learn it perfectly. We also had language tapes we played on her tape recorder from when she was young. Before she died, she told me about my father. She was two years in USA at university, got pregnant, the boy's parents didn't want him to marry her, and he obeyed them, so she returned to Japan. I never knew this before. She always said I look different because I take after my grandfather's family, who I never met. Which turns out to be true, but I didn't know my father was an American. After she died, I had to sell the shop, I didn't know how to run it and things went wrong, I was losing money. I found some diaries of my mother's after she died, she wrote them when she was in the US. I found my father via the Internet; he is a lawyer. At first, he didn't want to meet me, but then after a few months he came to Japan for three days and we got to know each other and he decided he liked me, he said he was proud of me. He put money into a trust fund for me, it pays for me to study in Auckland to get a science degree, it also pays my fees and my rent and an allowance. He will not let me meet his real family, he has 3 other children, several years younger than me. I don't think they know about me. We talk by text message every few days. I think he is quite fond of me. I have a lot of friends in Auckland, and I love my studies, I am in my second year of a BSc, majoring in physics. I'm doing very well in all my exams.

The flat I am locked up in is next door to my flat. I was kneeling on the landing taking things out of my bag to find my keys when two men and a girl came through the door from the stairs. The girl had her hands tied and they got in a panic that I had seen them. They forced me into this flat and took most of my things. They killed the girl when she screamed and wouldn't stop. I am listing the other girls (and two boys) who have been here since. They stay one or two days, get taken away, I don't know where.

Every 2-3 days the men give me a carton with food, things that are ready to eat without cooking or knife and fork. I used to leave uneaten food in the box, but now I hide things between the mattress and the wall and behind the drawer in the bathroom. They never notice that there are not enough wrappings in the box when they take it away. I now have enough hidden food for several days.

I hear the TV and the men's footsteps every day. I think one is usually here and one in my flat. From the bathroom here I can hear the shower in my flat next door. To be safe I will have to wait a long time and make sure I can hear nothing at all before I try to make enough noise to get help. I don't know where the men are from, it's not a language I recognise. One is called Ivo (or Evo) and the other one's name sounds like Dragan or Dragon.

Each time someone new comes the shorter man (Ivo), the one who killed the first girl, pushes the new person hard against the wall, side by side with me and stands in front of us, really close and says if you make noise, I will hear you and I will kill one of you – it doesn't matter which one. The other one can watch. And every time he pushes me hard in the chest and says, this girl has seen me do it, she knows it's true.

The first night I heard them arguing for hours. They shouted a lot. I hoped the neighbours would come and knock. The next morning, they brought my cell phone. They forced me to send messages to my friends and to my tutor, saying I had to go back to Japan on urgent family business. Now they do it a couple of times a week, they both come in, bring the phone. One man stands behind me, the other sits beside me, he holds the phone. To my friends I say I don't know when I will be back. John, my father sends a text message at least every week, and they let me reply to him and to friends in Japan pretending that all is well, that I am still studying and going out. The man behind me reads as I type the words, his hand grips my neck hard. I would not have time to type anything other than what they tell me. The first time they brought in the phone I changed the keyboard to Japanese when I replied to a friend in Japan and the man standing behind me hit the side of the head hard. Stop! Write in English! I said my Japanese friend will think something is wrong, if I reply in English. They took the phone and talked in their own language for ages, they argued. Then they made me type again and said I must write everything in English, or they will not let me reply.

I keep my pencil hidden behind the bathroom drawer too, they don't know I have it. I make it very pointy by rubbing it on the stuff between the tiles in the bathroom, then I make it even sharper with the edge of my ATM card which I hid in my bra before they took my wallet.

If the men discover I have pulled pages out of the book I will say it was always like that, it is a second-hand book. I wrote a fake name in the front to prove it.

I wish I had someone to talk to, someone I can trust. When I am alone, I talk to myself, sometimes I cry. I think they have tried to work out how to get John (my father) to pay them lots of money, they were shouting one day and for once they talked in English – there was someone else there with them. It was about how to get 'him' to transfer money so it could not be traced. I wonder if they will sell me or kill me if they can't work out how to get John to pay. I told them he lives in Boston and that he's a lawyer - and they have his phone number on my phone. Nobody has missed me, everyone thinks I am in Japan, apart from Japanese friends and John - they think I'm in NZ. My rent and everything is paid automatically, there is nothing to tell people something is wrong. I'm surprised they haven't thought of making John pay a lot of money into my account and then forcing me to pay it to them somehow. I have dropped many origamis with notes out of the window, lots, with tiny writing asking for help. The other day I saw a woman standing on the other side of the street, I think she was holding my origami note. She was looking up at the building for a long time. I will stick my arm out and wave my white T-shirt next time I see her looking up and then I will drop this whole book out. I might wrap it in the T-shirt, so it doesn't smash and fall apart. Before this, I will try to remember John's phone number to write in the book.

We look at each other in silence; somehow words cannot express how we feel. Linda looks shattered, even though she already knew a lot of the story.

Without saying much, we get into the car and head back over the Harbour Bridge in the dusk of the early spring evening.

Linda calls someone: 'No, I'm not coming tonight – too tired. I'll see you sometime next week.'

I'm not surprised that some social event is beyond her tonight. We drop her off outside the police station on the Cook Street corner and she says not to wait, it might take a while and she'll catch a bus home.

'I'll ask the admin manager tomorrow what she knows about Grace,' she says before we drive off. 'I'll say I don't want to lose touch with her. She might even give me Grace's phone number. Not that I ever saw Grace with a cell phone, but she did send the text message from one when she resigned.'

5

During Dao's ten years in captivity with no schooling, she taught herself quite advanced mathematics. In her captor's house there was a pile of mathematics textbooks from some previous owner, and her innate talent for maths involved her in a long and slow course of study. When we went to meet university staff, they offered to provide a tutor to help fill her knowledge gaps to enable her to study further. She considered for a short while and then said "no, thank you". Mainly, I think, because her unasked-for fame after the court case had turned her into a curiosity. Magazines wanted to write articles about her story and about us, news programs wanted interviews and for a time we had a stalker, who found out where I live, and waited outside the house. But she did accept the offer of access to the university library and today Dao wants to go and get some more books.

I make a brief stop outside the university and Dao grabs her bag. 'I'll text you when I'm ready to be picked up.' I watch her disappear into a crowd of students before I drive away; I always do, despite people honking their horns behind me. At the traffic lights I dial Charlie's number and put the phone on the dashboard in speaker mode.

'Have you got time for a visit? I've just dropped Dao at the library.'

'Come on over for a coffee. I've got no flights booked for today so I'm doing the housework – a break would be nice.'

'I didn't know you did housework,' I say and try not to laugh when she opens the door with a pink duster in her hand, dressed in what looks like army fatigues, an unusual combination. 'I know you're a great cook, but I thought Kristen was the tidy one.'

'She is! Super-tidy, but she hates cooking and cleaning – and I'm at home when I'm not flying, so it works fine. Kristen does the gardening – believe it or not she loves kneeling in the dirt picking weeds out of the flowerbeds and staking tomato plants, even mowing lawns is a pleasure for her. Must be because she sits behind a desk all day.'

It's not what I would have guessed; immaculate Kristen kneeling in the dirt is not an image that comes easily to mind, but neither had I imagined she would join Dao on the indoor climbing wall in Dominion Road.

We sit down with coffee and I tell Charlie the long story about Mariko and Grace. When I finish, she looks as if she can't believe what I have just told her.

'That's incredible! How can that be going on in an apartment block without anyone noticing? It's got to be linked to something really nasty – with potential for serious harm. Again. Or am I leaping to conclusions? I suppose we'd better get that Glock out of storage.'

She looks worried, and her offer is reluctant. I can imagine what's going through her mind: things that might hurt Dao, or me getting shot up again, or even worse.

'You are probably right,' I say just as my phone pings with a message from Dao and I get to my feet. 'Look, I've got to go and pick Dao up from the library, but I'd like to have the Glock. I might get the Remington out and keep it handy in the house like last time, too.'

A couple of years ago Dao was the only key witness to a serious crime and in imminent danger of being eliminated by a drug trade mastermind, a particularly nasty piece of work who called himself The Boss. The only way I could keep her safe was to be armed at all times, legal or not. Carting a Remington shotgun around wouldn't allow a fast response in an emergency situation, so Charlie lent me one of her Glock pistols. I gave it back a few months ago; I never thought I would need it again. She opens the door to the spare room wardrobe and there it is, that black monolith of a gun safe.

'Zero five zero seven zero eight,' I say, just as her fingers touch the keypad, and she pulls her hand back fast.

'How the hell do you know that?'

'I watched your fingers that time two years ago. You said it was your and Kristen's anniversary date, so you couldn't forget it.'

Charlie swings around fast and punches me in the upper arm; she hits exceptionally hard for someone her size. Then she blushes. 'Shit, Hunter - I forgot! That was the arm that got knifed and shot, wasn't it? Did it hurt?'

'Your punches are never painless - but no, it didn't hurt any more than it used to before I got shot.'

A couple of minutes later I walk out with the Glock, one magazine and the belt holster; I still have some ammo in my gun cabinet in the garage. Charlie comes with me to the car, still apologising.

'Don't worry, Charlie, my arm's fine - apart from being ugly. I've missed being assaulted by you.' I put the Glock under the driver's seat and head back to the university.

Linda calls that evening; she sounds tired and subdued. 'Here's the news,' she says. 'Some good and some not so good. The cops listened to all I said - I showed them the book and I said, it's nearly impossible to read the tiny writing, so I scanned it and I'll email you the file. They took me behind the scenes and sat me down in an interview room - it took forever. I explained why I had scanned those pages from the book – I said it was so I could read it, because I didn't mention the magnifying glass or you, just like we agreed. And then I emailed the PDF file of the scanned pages to an address they gave me, and they said they would read it right away and decide how to proceed. But when I said, "but this isn't just about what Grace found, the notes and the book – it's about Grace too" they just said there was nothing to indicate that anything had happened to Grace, but they would look into it. I think the fact that I had no private contact details for her, made it easy for them to dismiss it – you know, it seemed like I wasn't really close to her. They probably thought she had all sorts of things going on in her life that I wasn't aware of. It was really late by the time I got home, but my brother had left some dinner for me, so that was good!'

'Did you get a chance to ask that manager about Grace's details?'

'Yeah, and she really surprised me. I said how I wanted to stay in touch with Grace and she just said, "OK, I'll have a look and send you an email later today". She's given me the phone number that Grace sent that text message from when she resigned. And I got her address from the HR records. I'll send them to you now. I tried the phone number and got no reply, and no voice message either. I went to Grace's flat after work – it's just two little flats upstairs in a commercial building, quite ratty-looking, in Railway Street, which I'd never heard of before – it's kind of east of the Domain, that's why I'm so late calling you, I'm on the bus on the way home now. There was a woman coming out of an office downstairs just when I arrived and she let me in, didn't seem to care who I was. I rang the doorbell and knocked on the door to Grace's flat, and I called out and said, "it's Linda, please open the door". In the end her neighbour came out to see what all the noise was about - she said she doesn't know Grace well, and she hardly ever hears any noise from her flat, so she could have been there after she resigned and just gone out. I'll go back tomorrow and check again. I'll text her and call her as well, just in case she's away. Maybe there was some family emergency and she had to leave suddenly.'

There is no point in contradicting her; she is trying to be positive and to find an explanation that is less traumatic than the one I know lurks in the back of her head. She forwards the email she got from the admin manager and Dao looks up the address on Google Earth. 'It's a bit like that street where Hope's flat was – you know, like a little pocket of industry and odd things. I suppose the rent is a lot less in that sort of place than in a big block of modern flats. Let's go and have a look at Mariko's first.'

'If we can get in – it won't be as easy as where Grace lives.'

'I know, but I'm sure we can do it – we'll have to tell a lie, but you're good at that.'

I let this less than flattering statement pass and go to look over Dao's shoulder. 'Very like the area where Hope lived. Let's go first thing tomorrow.'

We start with Mariko's flat in the inner city and on the eighth number we try on the keypad at the entrance we have success; a woman's voice answers.

'Hi, sorry to bother you – I've come to repair a dishwasher in 403 and I've lost the note with the code. Can you let me in, please?'

'How are you going to get into the flat if nobody's home?' she asks, and I have my excuse ready. 'She left a key for me at the reception where she works, so that's not a problem. Her name is Mariko Goto, a Japanese lady.'

'OK,' she says and there's a click from the door. We take the lift to level four and stand on the polished concrete landing, where Mariko was kneeling when the door from the emergency stairs opened.

There are four apartment doors, numbered 401 to 404. We have discussed this on the way into town and decided to only ring the bell on Mariko's door; the one side by side with 403.

'Stand to one side,' orders Dao. 'I don't want them to see you if they look out through that little peep hole. And when I'm finished you must stay here for a while before you head for the lift in case they are looking – OK?'

I obediently stand well to the side with my back up against the wall and Dao gets her phone out and does something which probably means she is going to record this. She rings the bell, waits a few moments and then presses it again. The door opens back to where I'm standing, so I can't see the man's face, but I will remember his accent. Not that I know where he's from, but it's distinctive.

'Yes?' he says. 'Can I help you?' He doesn't sound particularly helpful.

'Hi, is Mariko at home?' says Dao, and suddenly I have a hideous vision of him grabbing her and dragging her into the flat. I put my left hand on the door handle and prepare myself to reach around and grab Dao's arm fast. Bringing the Glock seemed a bit of an over-reaction when I put the holster on my belt before we left home, now it feels good. But nothing happens; he is not at all suspicious.

'She moved - she went back to Japan a few weeks ago. I live here now.'

'Oh no!' says Dao innocently. 'I've been overseas, my grandfather died - I didn't know she was leaving. Is she coming back?'

But he's not about to enter into a conversation; he just says, 'I don't know' and closes the door.

Dao winks at me, gets into the lift and I stand there for a minute before I follow her down to the front foyer where she's waiting. 'Sorry, I only realised they have those spy holes after we got there – I didn't think of it before. I thought it was better he didn't connect us.'

'Absolutely. What did he look like?'

She stops just outside, pulls her phone out of her pocket and taps the screen a couple of times. 'Quite nice looking, I suppose, but he's got an ugly mouth, no lips. Have a look.'

'You took a picture of him? How the hell did you manage that?'

She hands me the phone and laughs, delighted to have surprised me. 'You know how people don't pay attention if you just stand around with the phone in your hand? Remember Inspector Sinclair and how she hadn't realised I recorded her interview with us? People think you're just holding it. I was ready, I had set the camera to video recording and started it just before I rang the doorbell, but I didn't know if I really got him till now – I had to guess the angle a bit.'

'You're too smart for words, you clever little thing.'

'Hunter! You promised not to call me a little thing!'

I look down at the top of her head, and smile. 'Apologies, I forgot.'

'Who would have thought there are so many Americans called John Anderson,' groans Dao and gets up from the table and stretches her arms over her head. 'There are lots on all the social media – oh, I didn't tell you. I set up accounts on several yesterday, so I can search for things, Face Book, Twitter and so on – so we don't have to ask Plum to always look up things for us. I'm not going to post anything ever, but it's useful to have access.'

'Willow belongs to something called Linked In, some kind of career-based networking thing – we could ask her too. Didn't Mariko mention that he's a lawyer in those notes in the physics book? I wonder if there's some way of checking law graduates.'

I go back to the proposal I must complete this week and leave her to it. An hour later she leaps to her feet, 'Yay! Got him!'

'That was quick. How did you find him?'

'An alumni page, whatever that means, from a university called Harvard law school – and there he was. Do you want to see?'

John Anderson is pictured in the centre of a group of lawyers at a twenty-year reunion of their graduation; a fit-looking man with thick dark hair and broad shoulders.

'OK, so now we need to find some way of contacting him,' I say, but Dao is ahead of the game. 'I know where he works, it's on his own Face Book page – Oswald & Blum, conveyancing lawyers and investment advisers. Once I knew what he looked like it was easy – I had Boston and his face to go by.'

I send John an email from the company's website and ask him to 'get in touch urgently regarding Miss Goto', trying to keep it discreet, just giving my phone number.

He calls a couple of hours later; his voice carries a hint of suspicion. 'I got your message. What is this about?'

I tell him the story and try to keep it concise, but he wants proof; he probably suspects a scam of some kind.

'It's after eleven in the evening here,' he says, 'and I'm at home. Could you send the documentation you mentioned to my private address, please?'

I send the photos of the origami messages and PDF file of the pages in the physics book, but I make no mention of Linda or Grace.

'Why didn't you?' asks Dao, when I tell her.

'I don't know – some kind of instinct to hold something back. I'll send an email to Linda and ask her to forward John's details to the cops. Then they have no idea we're involved – unless John Anderson tells them, I suppose. And he didn't think to ask how I got those scans either, which surprised me. He'll probably call back to make sure I'm not involved with those guys who are holding her.'

6

Linda replies the next day. The police have been in touch and thanked her for providing John Anderson's contact details and asked if she will allow them to tell him her name; he's on his way to New Zealand and wants to meet her.

Two days later John Anderson calls and says he wants to meet us; he has talked extensively to the police and to Linda already.

'I'll take a taxi to your place right away, if you tell me your address,' he says. 'Miss Fields was reluctant to give it to me without your permission.'

Miss Fields must be Linda; I hadn't realised we didn't know her full name. Dao is in the courtyard teaching Scruff to count. They are both concentrating and don't notice me; I stand in the door and wait until she looks up.

When I tell her John Anderson is on his way, she makes a face. 'We'll see how he likes me being involved – obviously he was happy to have sex with an Asian girl, but she wasn't good enough for him to marry or even help.'

When John Anderson rings the doorbell an hour later, I recognise him from the photo on the alumni page; he is still broad-shouldered and fit looking, but there is quite a bit of grey in his hair now. He has a firm handshake and exudes self-confidence and power; his suit looks very expensive, and his teeth are whiter than white.

'You must be Mr Grant.' He sounds relaxed, but underneath the façade he is tense, or maybe he's watchful rather than tense.

We sit inside the glass wall at the end of the room, John and I in armchairs and Dao in the corner of the sofa closest to my chair.

'The police have given me a complete update,' he says. 'Those men have left, both flats are empty, and they have no idea where Mariko is. They didn't know you had been in touch with me – hadn't heard of you, in fact. They thought Linda had found how to contact me.' His eyes scan back and forth between Dao's face and mine.

'Linda asked us for help, but we're not involved. We just helped her find you, when she worried the police weren't acting fast enough. It was Dao who tracked you down.'

I want to give the impression that we're not expecting to be involved from now on. If this is just a courtesy visit to thank us, I'll give him no indication that we're trying to find Grace under our own steam; it won't help if he talks to the police about us trying to find her.

'I'm sorry your daughter hasn't been found. Did the police show you that physics book?' Dao's question seems innocent, but I'm sure she's asking for a reason.

'God yes!' His expression is that of a man, whose fingers are clamped in a vice, pained to the limit of endurance and trying to look normal. 'I've read all the stuff you sent, over and over. Seeing the actual book was worse than reading the scanned pages. I can't believe I never understood what was going on! There was nothing in her text messages to alert me - not the slightest thing!'

'They are clever, those men,' says Dao. 'I mean the way they got her to reply to messages and the way they controlled her. But they never figured out how to get you to pay them a ransom.'

John lifts his mug of coffee, puts it down without tasting it and looks at me, completely ignores Dao's comment. 'Is there a reason why the police didn't know you had helped Linda?'

'As I said when I called you – we have no first-hand knowledge. Linda is involved via Grace, and she involved us, but that's all. And Dao found you, but apart from that we have nothing to do with it.'

He looks long and hard at me, as if he's trying to make up his mind about something. 'Why did Linda come to you? I got the impression that she didn't already know you.'

Dao and I look at each other and I can nearly hear her mental sigh, 'here we go again'. She hates her past being talked about in front of her. I start from the witness angle, less personal somehow.

'Dao was a key witness in the trial of a man involved in smuggling drugs into the country. There was quite a bit of publicity about us.'

'Which doesn't tell me why Linda got in touch with you? What is it you do?'

'I'm a partner in an agency that connects employers with personnel who have specific skills. Linda knows my sister.'

I can tell from his eyes that he knows exactly what I do.

'OK - you facilitate contacts between mercenaries, ex-armed forces personnel, with people who need bodyguards, private armies and the like – dictators, drug barons, anyone who can pay.'

'Very much like lawyers, really,' says Dao quietly, as if she's thinking aloud.

John holds up his hand to prevent me interrupting. 'I just wanted to hear what you were going to say. I've done some thorough background checking, Hunter. I wasn't born yesterday, and I needed to know a bit more about you. I also know that Dao was held captive for her teenage years by a drug trader, who killed her mother. I know she escaped and that you rescued her and have made yourself responsible for her ever since – a couple of years, I think? And I know that earlier this year you were instrumental in finding a woman journalist who had been abducted – by a top intelligence agency guy?'

'OK, that's all correct. I don't know how you found about the journalist – there was no trial, because the man who did it is dead, and we were never named in the media.'

He smiles. 'I have some very useful friends, who know how to find things out. That last bit about the journalist I only got by email after I my plane touched down here - it took a bit of time to get the details apparently. You seem to have a slightly unconventional way of tackling things, I must say.'

It's hard to tell if he's disapproving or not, but Dao's chin tilts up and she looks hard at him. 'And what about you, John?' Her voice is calm but uncompromising; she's not asking out of normal social courtesy, she is demanding. 'What kind of legal work is it you do?'

'I work mainly for corporate clients who invest in international property and sometimes in industry.'

Dao's expression changes by a minute degree and I brace myself for what she's going to say. I know that look; Willow says it's like being pinned to the wall by black arrows.

John turns towards me again, but Dao hasn't finished. 'So that's how you knew how to get a flat in Auckland for Mariko. Those messages Mariko sent you – are they all text messages or did she email as well?'

His expression remains neutral, but something has made him very alert; now he is paying attention to Dao. 'We don't email, only text messages.'

'In case your family sees your emails, I suppose,' says Dao coolly, not asking, but stating a fact.

'Correct,' says John. 'I haven't told my family about her – not yet.'

'Why?'

He's in a corner now, he never expected anyone to ask him

this so directly. I think he's on the brink of telling her it's none of her business, but she continues without pause. 'You caved in, when your parents didn't want you to marry someone with slanting eyes, and you let her go away to cope on her own. Are you ashamed of Mariko's race?'

Dao is half Vietnamese and during her years of captivity she was sometimes referred to a 'slant-eye' by the man who held her; she is not going to show John any mercy. I enjoy the spectacle of tiny Dao controlling the conversation with this assertive man.

John's eyes narrow, any moment now he'll lose his temper; he sees her as young and of no importance. But suddenly Dao smiles, head tilted to one side. 'Have you got a photo of her? I'd love to see what she looks like – I kind of feel like I know her, but I've never seen her.'

To my surprise he gets his phone out and Dao goes over to stand right next to him, and after a few moments he hands her the phone. 'This is the latest photo I have – she sent an MMS a few weeks ago from a rugby game she went to.'

Dao holds the phone out to show me; a pretty girl, with her hair up in a top-knot and a big smile. 'Oh, she's lovely,' says Dao, and his face softens. 'So pretty! Have you got some more?'

He reaches for the phone, flicks his finger at the screen and hands it back to her. 'I've saved all her photos in this folder, have a look.'

I'm surprised he kept his temper in check, but I suppose he feels the inquisition is over and now he wants to appease her; her teenage appearance and that smile of hers has disarmed him.

'What are the police doing about it?' I ask. 'Or don't you want to tell us? I know we're not involved, but we both feel a connection to Mariko after reading her notes.'

'They got in touch with the building manager and got access to her flat two days ago – someone has been living there, they said it's messy and dirty and there was a man's electric razor in the bathroom. The flat next door is empty too, apart from some basic furniture. There is a bolt on the bedroom door. Mariko's stash of food and her pencil were still there behind the drawer in the bathroom – and her bank cards. Both flats are closed off now, they're crime scenes and there's a forensics team examining everything.'

Dao is still standing beside John's chair, quietly swiping through photos and I try to avoid glancing at her; I want to keep John's focus on me. Not that I know what she is doing, but she's up to something; that smile she gave him was a trap.

'We went to her flat a few days ago,' I say, and that gets his full attention. 'There was a guy there and Dao talked to him. If he's vanished, we must tell the police we saw him. Dao's got video of him.'

John's expression is one of incredulity mixed with suspicion. 'What!? And how did she manage that?'

He turns to Dao, who puts his phone on the coffee table and returns to her seat next to me. 'How the hell did you manage that?' If it wasn't such an unlikely idea, I would think he was alarmed.

'Oh, it was quite easy,' she says casually. 'I had my phone in my hand at chest level when he opened the door – he would have thought I was just holding it. But I was ready, already filming when he opened the door. I'll show you.'

While she walks over to the dining table to pick up her phone, I say, 'Dao is very clever with devices of all kinds and people often underestimate her – she looks so much younger than she is, they think she's a harmless little girl.'

His eyes flick down to his phone on the table in front of him; now he's wondering what else she looked at, apart from photos of Mariko, but he can't ask her.

'Here he is.' Dao hands him her phone. 'I can email it to you so you can show the police. He had an accent, but neither Hunter nor I recognised it. Perhaps they can work through immigration and customs records and find him, if they use face recognition technology – and it might help if someone recognises his accent. And of course, Mariko noted what their first names were, from hearing them talk to each other.'

John stares into her face for a long moment; his opinion about Dao is undergoing a total revision and for some reason he is worried. Is it only about what she might have seen on his phone, or is my developing instinct about this man right? Does he pose some sort of danger to us, or is he just a controlling bully under that civilised and well-groomed exterior? He's not a man I want to make an enemy of.

As soon as he leaves, Dao's calm deserts her. 'That first photo he showed me – it was sent by someone his phone identifies as Mark G, and I managed to get a quick look at the Contacts folder and from there I looked at Mark G's other text messages, ones without images. The second to last message Mark G sent him was about a physics exam,' she says urgently. 'Mark G is just an alias he uses so nobody will ask who "Mariko Goto" is.'

I groan at the thought of what will inevitably happen now. 'You know what all this means, don't you? I mean the fact that we have that video of the guy in Mariko's flat and now he is no longer there. We'll have to get in touch with the cops, before they demand we come and see them – once John shows them the video, we are in for it.'

The call to the police takes a bit of time. Getting put through to the person in charge of the Mariko investigation is easy, but we go round in circles as Inspector Bakker tries to come to grips with who we are, the connection with Linda, how we found John, why we are involved and what Grace has to do with it. In the end I get tired of explaining one layer after another and say, 'Linda can explain it all. You have my phone number – get in touch if you want to talk to me.'

She calls at the end of the afternoon and it is obvious that John has told her more about me.

'Mr Anderson has shown us the video of the man you

talked to in Miss Goto's flat.' She sounds exasperated. 'I want you to come in to make a statement – not just about the video recording but your overall involvement. Tomorrow at ten, please - if that suits you.' That last bit means nothing, this is an order in disguise.

'We'll be pleased to,' I say politely. 'I'm sure Mr Anderson has told you all about our conversation today. If you need any more information about me, I suggest that you contact Detective Inspector Benson – he can fill you in.'

'Did you notice that John got angry when I asked him about the flat – when I suggested his job made it easy to find a good flat in Auckland?' asks Dao over dinner. 'Now, why would that make him angry? There's something about him, like he's hiding something, like he knows something he doesn't want to talk about.'

'Yeah, I did notice, but it could have been your question about whether they ever emailed. You actually asked him two questions at once and I wondered which one made him angry – or perhaps suspicious.'

'Oh no, it wasn't about the email thing – his eyes changed straight away when I mentioned the flat. It was instant - and then he tried to hide it.'

7

I nspector Bakker turns out to be a no-nonsense woman in her forties, who has long ago discarded small talk as a meaningless waste of time; she has a very direct way of tackling things, no messing around. I could have guessed her personality from her appearance, short flat hairstyle, no make-up and the shortest-cut nails I've ever seen. She looks as if she would be useful in a brawl, provided she was on your side.

'First up I want you to clarify why Linda Fields involved you in this. And why she gave us John Anderson's contact details, when it was actually you who found them.'

I cross my legs and try the old trick of introducing a slightly off-topic angle. I worked well when Inspector Sinclair interviewed us, when we had found Hope Barber dead; it allowed me to say what I wanted to in my own way instead of responding to questions.

'Probably because Linda knows my younger sister, they were at school together – and she just wanted to talk through what she thought was a serious issue. She believed that the police didn't take it seriously and wondered if we knew some way of progressing it a bit.'

Bakker isn't having any of this, and though her expression

remains neutral, it's clear that this interview is going to be on her terms. 'What did she ask you to do?'

'Nothing,' I say. 'She just wanted to tell us what Grace Harris had found and done - in case we could suggest some way of getting it taken further.'

'Did she ask you to find out who Mr Anderson was?'

Dao replies before I have time to. 'As Hunter just said, she didn't ask us to do *anything*. I decided to try to find him after she showed us what was in those notes and in the textbook. He was quite easy to find, and to save her doubling up on the work, I sent her the details.'

'Why didn't you tell us directly?'

'Why would we? We're not directly involved,' I say mildly, trying to sound reasonable. 'We have no first-hand knowledge of anything to do with this. Linda had already been in touch with you twice, so it seemed logical to give her the information to pass on.'

Dao shuffles her chair slightly sideways, as if she wants to see my face as well as Bakker's, but she says nothing.

'But now you *are* involving yourselves – and doing things that might interfere with our investigations.' Bakker points her finger at us, Trump style. 'Like going to Miss Goto's flat, getting into the building by some devious means and possibly destroying our chance to apprehend a suspect.'

'I seriously doubt that. We went to Mariko's flat when it still seemed unlikely that anyone was taking her case seriously. The man in the video was in no way intimidated or alarmed, as you can see for yourself, and he doesn't look as if he doubted her story. He never saw me, only Dao. And the fact that she cleverly took got video of him must be useful now.'

I stop talking and just sit there looking her; it's up to her now.

'He left, though,' says Bakker. 'Or they left, to be precise. And Miss Goto is no longer in the flat next-door. Whether you scared them away or they were already planning to leave is anybody's guess. However, I will concede that the video is a useful thing to have. You are to stay away from this investigation from now on, Mr Grant. I have talked to both Benson and Sinclair about your previous activities, and I didn't like some of what I heard. You see yourself as some kind of hard guy and think the law doesn't apply to you and ...'

I feel obliged to interrupt her. 'You have no idea what I think, Inspector – you don't know me. I seriously doubt either Benson or Sinclair told you that – they know I have sometimes done things that they would hesitate to do, but breaking the law, a hard man? No way.'

'I'm perfectly sure from all I've heard that you are likely to interfere, so you are not to have anything to do with case from now on. This is an official warning Mr Grant - and I'm putting it on record. You are to stay away from this case and if you don't, I'll have you arrested for obstructing an investigation.'

Over lunch in a Japanese restaurant downtown Dao springs the next surprise on me. 'Did you see that paper that was sticking out under the brown folder on her desk?'

'No, I didn't notice – what was it?'

'I could only see the top part of it - I had to move my chair a bit to see better. Something from the City Council – some kind of information sheet about a building owned by White Investments Limited. I bet it's that block of flats – but why are they looking up who owns it?'

'I don't know – maybe those records have details of who manages the building. If they need a warrant or a court order to get access, they'd need to know who to contact. I'm just guessing, Dao – I have no idea how these things work.'

'Let's find out,' says Dao and picks up her chopsticks. 'There's got to be a reason. Perhaps if we can find out who owns White Investments, we can talk to whoever manages the building too – you know, some kind of caretaker person.'

When we get home, I call Willow and for once I get straight through.

'Hi Willow, I've got a minor problem,' I say, trying to sound casual enough to make her think this is just a theoretical issue; hoping to avoid one of her "I hope you're not getting involved in anything illegal" lectures.

'Someone's asked me to help them, but I'm not sure I'm being told the truth. Is there some way of checking who owns a company? I think they own commercial property in Auckland.'

'If the company is registered in New Zealand, I can look it up in the Companies Register and so can you – I think there's a link on the Internal Affairs website, or just Google the words company register, that should do it – why do you want to know?'

'It could be nothing,' I say deviously. 'But events over the last couple of years have left their mark, and I try to background check everything these days – you should be proud of me.'

There's a snort of laughter from the other end. 'Yeah, right! as they say. Let me know some time what you are doing, won't you?'

I call Linda and tell her about Bakker calling us in for a meeting and what was said.

'God! I can imagine it,' she says. 'I had to go back for another session with her too. She's a toughie, that woman. I tried to tell her that I think Grace has disappeared, but she wasn't interested. So I said I wanted to report her as a missing person, but that was a flat no, too.'

'Why won't they let you?' asks Dao. 'Is it because you're not related?'

'I think the main reason is that she resigned before she disappeared – you know, she might have won Lotto and decided to go on a cruise, or something like that. And I've got to admit that it seems flimsy to just front up and say she's disappeared. I haven't got a single thing to prove I knew her well – just that we had lunch sometimes and that she showed me those notes she found.'

The sole shareholder in the New Zealand registered company White Investments Limited is another company registered in the Cayman Islands called Gray Investments. The director of White Investment Limited is named, but there our tracking efforts come to a halt – his name and address bring up nothing when we search, and Dao speculates that it might not be a real person. And in the Cayman Islands there is no requirement to make the names of shareholders and directors publicly available, so we can't find out anything about Gray Investments. The spelling of Gray could indicate that it was registered by an American, but that's guesswork and might mean nothing.

8

At John's request we meet for coffee in the city the next day, and what he tells us is more or less what we expected; Bakker has advised him not to feed us any information. I can imagine her voice; full of disapproval for outsiders poking around in police business, her obvious personal dislike of me and her suspicious nature. The fact that she knows we have been instrumental in solving problems in the past will not change her mind.

'The police sat me down with the building manager and we went through CCTV footage to see what I could find,' says John, who for some reason seems to have decided to disregard Bakker's warning. 'Thanks to that book Grace found, we think we know roughly when Mariko was taken – we worked backwards and tried to pinpoint it. I think we found the last image of her coming in at the main entrance. There's a hell of a lot of videos to go through – the police will continue looking for the men and those other girls.'

'Are they going to use face recognition software?' asks Dao. 'Or didn't they tell you?'

'I'm sure they will, but it might not be effective. They will probably use an image from that video you shot, but it's not as easy as it sounds. Say a guy with a cap gets into a lift, and he's looking sideways at someone he's talking to, and then he turns immediately to stand facing the door - they wouldn't get enough of his face to be useful.'

Dao has noticed something; her expression hasn't really changed, but I can sense it.

'I wish we could look at the video too,' she says wistfully, and her face looks innocent and sad. 'You know how they say an extra pair of hands is good – extra eyes would probably be good too. But that Bakker woman would never let us, she doesn't like Hunter at all. I keep thinking of Mariko and what's happening to her, how scared she must be.'

He thinks only for a moment before he makes us an offer that takes me by surprise. 'I think I can organise that – you can join me tomorrow when I go back to have another look, I've made a date with the building manager.'

The next morning, we wait outside the apartment block in a cool morning breeze while John calls the building manager, who appears a couple of minutes later from inside the building. He's a short, skinny guy with thick black hair, and despite his fierce eyebrows he seems very friendly.

'Mr Silvano,' says John. 'This is Mr Grant and Miss Johnson, who are going to help me to check some more of the video recordings.'

Dao glances at me and I know what caused that glint of amusement. However good John's researchers are, they've missed one piece of information; we got married a couple of months ago and Dao has taken my surname.

Silvano leads us past two lifts and through to the inner foyer, a big space with banks of locked mailboxes on both sides, and from there to the communications room. It's a small room with a long built-in desk and two screens showing live images from several cameras.

'We have six channels.' He points at the screens, 'I'll open channels 1-3 on that screen and 4-6 on the other one. We can use either to look up recorded video – just click on the icon down here for the search form and enter the date and the time – and then select a channel. We have a camera at the main entrance, two in the underground car park, one in each lift and one in the inner foyer where the mailboxes are. As I told Mr Anderson yesterday, we save six weeks of recordings on the NVR – more than most people do, but seeing we've got the capacity, we thought we might as well.'

He leaves us with an admonition to check that the door locks behind us when we go.

'I'll have a look at the main entrance camera again,' says John and sits down in front of one screen. 'I want to double-check there's no further sighting of Mariko after that date we think is the last.'

There are a couple of spare chairs stacked in the corner and I bring them over so Dao and I can crowd together in front of the other screen. We decide to have a look at Lift One and start from what is presumably the last sighting of Mariko. Dao gets a note pad and a pen out of her bag and puts her phone on the desk beside her.

'Did you notice the certificate in the foyer?' she says in a quiet aside to me. 'Some kind of compliance notice – it says the building is owned by that company I mentioned - White Investments.'

'No, I didn't notice,' I say, as one short scene after another comes up on the screen before us. 'But wasn't it Gray Investments?'

Dao laughs and pushes my arm with her elbow. 'You weren't paying attention, were you, when I told you about it the other day – Gray Investments is the Cayman Island company that owns the New Zealand company called White investments.'

I'm pretty sure this little act is to see if John reacts, exactly the sort of thing Dao excels at. She points at the screen. 'Look at that guy there – he came into the lift talking to his mate and turned around right away to press the button, and now he's standing facing the door and all we saw was the side of his face.'

My focus might seem to be on the screen, but I am acutely aware of John. He is sitting less than a meter away at the long desk and I more sensed than saw him jerk when Dao mentioned Gray Investments. After a moment he says, 'It's a company I do some work for – and that's why we can sit here now and look at the videos. Silvano knows I act for the owners.' His voice has a slight edge to it.

'Perfect!' says Dao cheerfully. 'And thank you for letting us come with you, it's very kind of you.'

I hide my amusement; Dao is playing "bad cop/good cop" all by herself. When we part on the street outside, John takes a few steps and then he turns back. 'Would you like to have dinner with me tonight at my hotel? You've been very helpful and I'm not sure how long I can stay – it would be nice to get to know you both a bit better.'

Dao stares after him as he walks away. 'I didn't expect that!'

Neither did I, and I wonder what is behind this sudden desire to get to know us better. He is smooth and pleasant, but I know we have upset him more than once and I suspect he would make an unforgiving enemy.

'I'd better go up and change,' says Dao and puts her book down. 'I suppose we have to leave soon. I'm going to wear the new top that Kristen and I bought last week – you haven't seen it yet.'

She runs up the stairs and Scruff lifts his head, considers the situation and decides to close his eyes and go back to sleep. A few minutes later he's proved right, when Dao comes down and sits on my knee with her back turned. 'Can you please do the buttons up?'

I look at the row of little fiddly buttons, at least twelve or fourteen of them and the little loops that are made to fit over them. 'Are you sure you've got it on the right way? I don't think my fingers can do this.'

'Of course, I have it on the right way around! Wait till you see the front.' I manage the tiny buttons and she stands up and turns around. 'See!'

'Wow, that's very nice - worth all those damn buttons.'

The man behind the reception desk at the Sky City Hotel is expecting us. 'Mr Anderson asked me to apologise on his behalf – he had to go out unexpectedly, but he should be back in half an hour or so. He's ordered canapes and drinks to be brought up to his suite. I'll get someone to take you up there now.'

This is Dao's first introduction to real luxury. We have stayed in expensive hotels, but we've never had a suite like this; a huge living room in tasteful colours and big windows nearly down to floor level with wide views over the city in two directions. The door to the bedroom is open, showing a bed of monster proportions with the mandatory line-up of decorative cushions. I've never understood that cushion-frenzy; it means you can't lie down without removing them, so you throw them in a corner and then the poor room service person has to arrange them in the prescribed order the next day and they serve no purpose aside from making cushion manufacturers rich. A marketing stunt devised by a genius.

'The waiter is bringing the drinks trolley and the canapes,' says our guide before he leaves us. 'Make yourselves at home – he'll be here in a couple of minutes.'

'Beautiful!' Dao tries one of the striped armchairs, but she gets up straight away and laughs. 'Too big – must be Papa Bear's chair,' she says and wanders over to the nearest window. 'Oh, the view! Nearly as good as from the Sky Tower.'

When the room service waiter has come and gone Dao

picks up a canape and disappears into the bedroom; she returns deeply impressed.

'Sorry, that was a bit cheeky, but you know how I love bathrooms. If we had a bathroom like that, I might never come out again – everything is covered in marble and there is a huge bath. We could both get in. And a thing I've never seen before – the water comes out of a slot in the side of the bath. I bet it comes out like a flat jet of water – but I didn't dare try it.'

I sit in the armchair facing the view with a glass of wine in my hand and the edible treats within easy reach, and Dao stands by the huge window looking at the city stretching out below her feet.

'Do you think there's something more to his work for that investment company?' She turns around to face me. 'I mean the way he jumped when I mentioned the Cayman Islands – he was totally surprised. And you know what I saw on his phone when he showed me photos of Mariko and how he had her listed as Mark G? He's full of secrets that man - I'd love to know more about the Cayman company and why it's there and not in the US.'

'Probably just a tax dodge. I read up on the rules for companies and taxation in the Cayman's – you know how wealthy people hate paying tax? Well, the Caymans is one of their favourite places. And you don't have to reveal who owns a company or who is a director or anything over there – perfect hiding place for a lot of secrets and crimes.'

'I know,' she spins her glass of orange juice in her hands. 'Look, I think the glass goes around and the ice cubes stay still – I wonder why. But there's something about him – a couple of times I've noticed his attention ramping up when I've made a comment or asked a question. He nearly lost his cool once, I thought he was going to shout at me.' And then she laughs again. 'And it was fun pointing out that lawyers also earn money from criminals and dictators. But I knew he wouldn't dare shout at me - not with you there.'

'I forgot to ask you what it was you reacted to, when he was saying that face recognition software might not be very useful. I could tell you noticed something.'

Dao says nothing for a moment, then she sighs. 'I might be too wary of him – too ready to see everything as having some kind of meaning, just because I don't trust him. But remember how he described a scene very precisely, like he'd seen it in real life – a man with a cap entering the lift with his head turned to one side, talking to his friend and then turning around and facing the door straight away, so you never see his face full-on. It was like he was describing something he had actually seen – it was so precise. And it's exactly what *we* saw, when we watched the Lift 1 footage from the week after Mariko was taken. Exactly the same scenario – and he had seen that clip too, because he said they had checked the lift channels to see if there were any further sightings of Mariko, and now I wonder if maybe he recognised that man? But I'm probably just tripping over my own prejudice again.'

Half an hour later John enters the suite, full of urbane apologies. 'I'm sorry - that was very rude. I hope you've been well looked after.' He sounds genuinely concerned that he might have been less than a good host. 'To go out and leave a message with the concierge like that, but I had to just run for it – Bakker wanted me to sign some things before I leave, seeing I officially rent Mariko's apartment – my flight leaves at half past eleven tonight.'

He sees our astonished faces and apologises again. 'Sorry, I haven't had time to tell you. I've got to go back – I got an email just after we parted earlier today about urgent trouble with an important client I've looked after for a decade - I've got to be there in person. I'll come back here as soon as I can.'

We have a lovely meal at Bellota, and Dao discovers another taste sensation to add to her growing list of food discoveries: ham made from acorn-fed pigs in Spain. 'Wow,' she says. 'We must come back here, Hunter – this is delicious. Or maybe just go to Spain and eat this every day.'

John is the perfect host; relaxed and charming; now he smiles at Dao. 'Do you eat out a lot?'

'We do! We love going out for dinner,' says Dao and beams at him; at this moment nobody would guess that she is deeply suspicious of him, and once again I notice that however much she has challenged him, he can't resist her when she seems like a harmless girl. A bit of uncertainty won't do any harm, if she is right about him.

'But it's quarter past eight now,' says Dao, sounding quite concerned. 'Will you get to the airport on time?'

'I have booked a limo to pick me up in half an hour,' he says calmly. 'All I have to do it go back to my room and get my suitcase - I'll get there on time. And this meal goes on my bill, they've got my credit card details. There is no need to rush away just because I have to leave.'

When John says goodbye, he kisses Dao's cheek and apologises yet again for leaving us in his suite.

'I enjoyed seeing it,' says Dao and grins. 'I had a bit of a look around – it's a fabulous suite, and the bathroom is a dream with all the marble and the huge bath. I said to Hunter that if we had a bathroom like that, I might never come out again.'

We are just about to go to bed when my phone signals a message. Dao picks it up, 'It's from John, he must be bored waiting for his flight.' She reads it out: "Just want to thank you again for alerting me to Mariko's plight – I might not have discovered for a long time. And it was very nice to get to know you over dinner tonight. Why don't you book a room at the hotel one weekend and let Dao experience the marble bathroom and that flat jet of water?"

Her face is frozen for a moment and then it dissolves into anger. 'See! I was right not to trust him – I never mentioned the "flat jet of water" during dinner, I never said a word about it. I said the marble bathroom was lovely, but I didn't mention that tap thing, if you can call it that. He recorded us when we were waiting in his suite, maybe he filmed us!'

I think back over what was said from the time John returned from his meeting with Bakker until he left, and she is right, that faucet arrangement was never mentioned. 'Do you think it was all arranged – did he make up that meeting with Bakker, so he could listen to what we said, when he wasn't there?'

'He must have – and what better setting to get us talking about him than leaving us alone in his hotel room – where he could plant a camera or a recording device.'

We go to bed still puzzled by John's motives and spend some time talking through what else we might have said. In the end Dao says with great satisfaction, 'Well, it serves him right to hear that I don't trust him – I think he owed us that dinner for being devious.'

'We're devious too, sometimes,' I remind her, but she doesn't agree. 'That's completely different! We only do devious things to stop horrible things happening. John kind of made believe he liked us and realised we were helping, and then he spied on us. I just don't get it – why did he do it?'

I don't understand it either.

9

Over breakfast the next morning we continue discussing John's deceit, but we arrive at no conclusion. 'I think he's genuinely fond of Mariko, and very worried about her disappearance – or he wouldn't have come charging over here like he did.'

'Maybe,' says Dao, 'but what else could he do when he was told that the police were involved and knew about him. He couldn't just send an email and say he was too busy to come, could he?'

She's got a point, but she concedes that he does seem to be fond of Mariko. 'He did have all those messages with photos of her saved in a special folder on his phone – unless that was to make sure nobody scrolled through his messages and saw that Mark G was a girl. It's hard to know what to think.'

'I wish we could see more of the CCTV recordings – if John hadn't gone back, he might have let us in again. There's such a mass of tiny, short bits of video it's hard to keep your focus. It would be really easy to miss something. And if we could go back, we'd have a screen each and cover twice as much ground.'

'I want to go back too. I want to sit there for hours and just

70

work my way through it. I think I might start picking things up, if I could see some more.'

'Did you see something yesterday that you think is important? You didn't say anything.'

She shrugs. 'Maybe – I'd have to look at more to be sure, it might be nothing. And I would like to see if we can spot Grace going into the building, because it would prove she was there.'

'Well, let's have a go,' I say. We'll get hold of that Silvano guy and ask if we can come back. Who knows? He might let us, seeing that we've already been there with John. And he was pretty relaxed about the whole thing, leaving us like that to lock up - not very security minded.'

And then it strikes me. 'You know how we said we couldn't understand why John recorded us, when he must have known we were trying to help? Maybe the reason was us talking about the ownership of that building and the fact that we had identified the Cayman Islands company – because that made him jump. Perhaps it raised a red flag and he wanted to see what else we might have found out.'

Dao stares into empty space for a moment. 'OK, so he invited us for dinner, hid a recording device and set the scene for us to be alone in his suite. But that must mean there's something about the company that owns the building which he doesn't want us to know – which seems pretty weird. Maybe he has one of those new USB sticks that can record audio – I might get one.'

Thanks to his unusual surname we find Silvano's home number in the directory and his wife gives us his cell phone number.

'No problem,' he says when I call him. 'I'm in East Tamaki at the moment, but I'll be back in the city later today, by lunchtime at the latest. Meet me outside - say about one?'

Dao wants to take Scruff with us. 'He never gets to see the

central city - it will be like an adventure for him.'

It also makes the walk from where we park to the apartment take twice as long; the city if full of interesting smells and Scruff wants to sniff everything, but we get there no more than a few minutes late and find Silvano waiting patiently outside.

'Funny coincidence that you called me just when you did this morning,' he says. 'I was at an industrial site owned by the company that owns this block of flats. It's empty at the moment, just a guy living in the little flat at the back. I drive past and check it every couple of weeks – just to see nobody's smashed any windows in the factory part of the building, you know? The owners told me to ignore the place, but I like to keep tabs on things.'

'I'm sure they'd be glad to hear you're looking after it. It must be expensive to have a big site untenanted,' I say, just to make some kind of response. 'You've still got to pay rates and insurance and all that stuff.'

'I know, but they're going to tear it down and build something bigger – they bought it last year and got rid of the aluminium welding guy who rented it.'

He unlocks the communications room and sets up the two screens for us. 'I hope you find something. The cops have copied the lot so they can search through it. But as Mr Anderson said, the more people who look, the more likely they'll find something.'

I can't believe he hasn't asked a single question; all he says is to make sure the door is locked when we leave, and then he's gone. Dao shakes her head. 'I was sure he'd check that John had said we could come back – he's incredibly trusting. But on the other hand, what's the worst we could do? Steal a screen?'

We have already agreed that we'll start with Grace, but we don't actually know what she looks like, so we both watch the main entrance channel from the day Linda told us was her last day at work.

'Bet that's her,' says Dao suddenly; she's studying footage from the main entrance camera from the evening before Grace's resignation text was sent. 'Have a look!'

I move over and she replays it: a tallish woman with short dark hair in a light-coloured coat with a hood enters just behind a couple. Dao points at the screen. 'See, you can tell she says thank you to those people for holding the door for her - she came running up behind them. They think she's a tenant – but look now, they get straight into a lift and she walks forward, as if she's going to check a mailbox, but all she does is wait a minute, then she gets into the lift on her own.'

I turn back to my screen and open the relevant lift channel, enter the right the date and time in the search box - and there she is. She presses the button for level four, exits the lift and that's the last we see of her.

Dao makes a note of the date and time and gets her phone out. 'I'll take a photo of the screen and send it to Linda – I'll tell her we will fill her in later.'

We have the answer within minutes; the woman in the lift is Grace. We start the process of watching each channel, one after the other, from that moment on to see how and when she left. We find nothing.

Two hours later I pause what I'm watching, rewind and watch it again and then one more time; a guy with a handcart heading towards the lift on the car parking level. 'Dao, did you make note of the day and time you saw that scene in the lift with the two guys talking – you know, the one that was exactly as John had described it?'

She flips a couple of pages back and frowns at her pad. 'I didn't make a specific note, but this is where I started, so it can't be that far away - those clips from the lift are pretty short, but of course there are thousands of them.'

Ten minutes is all it takes. 'Here they are, two of them getting into the lift talking.' We compare the piece I'm looking at and the scene in the lift.

'It's the same guy,' she says. 'Look at that badge on his

jacket, on the sleeve – and he has the same cap. Do you think he's the one who was in Mariko's flat when we went there? It's impossible to tell when he's wearing that cap.'

'I wonder why he is taking that dismantled carton up in the lift. If you buy a big item, like a household appliance, you usually end up taking a flattened carton out, not in.'

We track the guy via the lift camera; he gets out at level 4. We continue watching both lift cameras, one each from that time forward. On the following day at 12.32 both men enter a lift and press button B1 for the car park level; on the handcart is an assembled carton with *Samsung 5.5 Kilo Top loader washing machine* printed on the side. On the car park camera, we see them head for the far corner, and a while later one of them re-appears from around the corner and walks back towards the lift, the other one is away for longer. Dao writes the details on her pad and puts her pen down.

'God, Dao - that was either Grace or Mariko - can't have been both, that box isn't big enough. So those guys are the ones from flat 403 and they are the ones John used as an example of why face recognition might not always be useful. You were right again!'

'Well, in this case I'd rather not have been right. It makes me feel sick to think they killed someone and put them in that box. But whoever it was might not be dead, you know. Remember the notes Mariko wrote – someone was injected and taken away. Perhaps it's just a way of keeping them quiet. Let's go forward from there and see what else we can find. Whichever one wasn't in the box must have left somehow – between that time and when the cops searched the flats.'

We find it the morning after the sighting of the washing machine box; the men get into the lift on level 4 with a girl wearing a hooded jacket; her head is drooping. One of them has his arm around her back, supporting her and they get out of the lift at the parking level.

'She looks drunk or drugged,' says Dao. 'Look at her feet, she's tripping herself up – if he wasn't holding her, she would fall over. I bet that's Mariko, not as tall as Grace – so Grace must have been in the box.'

She changes to the garage channel and enters the same date and time, and we watch the man support the girl across the big space until the trio disappears around the corner. 'And see that light-coloured van heading towards the exit ramp now - two guys with caps on. That's their vehicle.'

More notes on Dao's pad, which now has three pages of descriptive notes, each one with the channel number, the date and the time.

'OK, now I'll try to find that girl, the one it all started with, the one who was killed. They must have brought her in by car and we know they are driving a light-coloured van. How far back do you think I should start?'

'I think John said the last sighting of Mariko was thirty-six days ago. But the oldest date you can go back to is six weeks ago, if you want to start from the very beginning.'

By incredible luck we find the first girl, the one they killed, in half an hour. We watch one garage channel each; we fast forward if the clip is of one or two people, slow down when it's three. Dao spots the two men and the girl appearing from behind the corner of the L-shape of the garage. She is clearly frightened and tries to pull away, but her hands are tied in front of her and they have her in a steady grip; one on each side. They don't take her to the lift, but to a door to one side.

'Ah, yes,' says Dao. 'They took her up the stairs so nobody would see her with her hands tied.'

The following evening at quarter to eleven the men enter the lift on level 4 with a large sports bag, carrying it by a handle each; it looks heavy. They get out at the basement level one and head for the corner where their parking space is. They return to the lift a couple of minutes later without the bag; the van does not leave the building until the next day.

It is now nearly six o'clock and the constant concentration is taking its toll. 'Let's go out and get something to eat and give Scruff a walk,' says Dao. 'I need to move around, and both Scruff and I need to pee. And then we'll come back and start looking for the other girls. It might take longer, because they could have come in the main entrance.'

'If we leave, we can't get back in,' I say. 'We can't ask poor Silvano to come back, he's probably having his dinner.'

'Of course, we can get in – I know the keypad code. When we came, he didn't use a swipe card, he punched in a code.'

'No, we can't. 'Every time we go in, we are recorded too. If we don't tell Bakker right away that we have been back here and what we have found today, she'll be furious. And if she finds out we got in again without Silvano's help, it will get even worse and she'll do something terrible to me.'

'Like arrest you?'

'I wouldn't put it past her – she can't wait to find a reason to haul me in. Let's go home and write all this up and send it to her.'

Because we are tired and don't feel like cooking dinner, we decide to have an early dinner in town. We find a bistro just down the street from the apartments and plan our move while we read the menu outside. It works perfectly; I walk in ahead of Dao, and she slips to one side to sit at the first table inside the door with Scruff tucked right into the corner beside her.

'What a good thing it was that I trained this clever boy!' she says when I return with two glasses and a bottle of water. 'I've told him to be silent and stay still.' She takes the glass I just filled for her and puts it on the floor. 'I'll share yours.'

When I get up to pay, Dao and Scruff head for the door behind me and the guy behind the counter does a doubletake; I wait for him to say something, but he just grins and shakes his head.

10

W hile I feed Scruff, Dao writes up her notes on her laptop with explanations of how various parts of it hang together and I email it to Bakker whose details are on the card she gave me. All I say in my message is that we spent some time looking at saved video and have identified some things that might be of interest, including a sighting of Grace Harris. Bakker dismissed Grace as irrelevant, both when Linda wanted to report her as a missing person and when I mentioned her; now she must do something.

It feels good to have achieved something definite and I make coffee while Dao calls Linda. Telling her all we found takes a while and Dao promises to email her the document I just sent to Bakker. I half listen to the conversation and try to think what else we can do, and just before Dao ends the call it comes to me. 'Hang on, Dao – can I talk to Linda for a moment?'

'Linda, it's Hunter – do you think you can access the personnel files at work and get some more detail about Grace? Like her date of birth if that's in there?'

Dao looks surprised and Linda says, 'Her date of birth? Whatever for? But I can certainly try.'

'It's just a hunch, but remember how we could find

nothing about her at all, and you said she never mentioned her personal circumstances? And she was very reluctant to go back to the police station – I think you told us she said there was somebody who worked there she didn't want to see?

'Yeah, she did say that. But what's her date of birth got to do with it?'

'I'm going to have to find out more about this, but it occurred to me that she might have been in trouble with the law, maybe she'd been in prison. And people change their names sometimes, to start again, so her date of birth might be a useful thing to know. Not that I have any idea how to find out if she did change her name, but I'm going to ask a lawyer tomorrow.'

By mid-morning the following day we know that Grace was born on 4 December 1973. 'I had to be very sneaky,' writes Linda in her text message. 'Didn't dare ask the admin manager, so I bribed the payroll girl. I had to promise her a movie ticket.'

I call Willow's office and ask for her to call me back and assure the receptionist that it will only take three or four minutes.

'What *are* you involved in, Hunter? I hope it's legal. First it's about companies and commercial buildings and now it's about people changing their names.'

'I'm writing a crime novel,' I say, 'but don't tell anyone - it's quite hard and I might never finish it.'

Dao, who is in her usual corner of the sofa, presses a cushion to her face to smother her laughter.

'Really?' says Willow in open disbelief. 'I'll believe that when I see it – don't forget to give me a copy when it's published.'

'OK, but how do people do it? Can you find out afterwards if they did?'

'All you have to do to change your legal name is register

a change of name on the Births, Deaths and Marriages register. You can file a non-disclosure request if you have some reason to keep the new name secret – like for your personal safety or whatever. Say you know what someone used to be called – if there is no non-disclosure proviso you can just look it up. Best to know their birthdate of course, or at least what year they were born, lots of people have the same names.'

'And the other way, if you know the new name – you can see the original name?'

'Yes, but the same thing again – not if there's a non-disclosure on it.'

'When do you go away? Is it this week or next?'

'On Monday – thank goodness. It's a race to the finish – can't wait to spend some leisure time in a hot climate with the twins.'

Dao instantly starts searching the Internet for information. By the time I have checked my emails and replied to a couple, she has discovered that Grace Harris used to be Mary Grace Hudson, before she changed her name nearly exactly two years ago. Dao has just started another online search to see what she can find out about Mary Grace Hudson, when the doorbell goes, so I run downstairs and find a courier on the doorstep.

'Has to be signed for,' he says and hands me a handheld gadget to scrawl my signature on. A stiff brown envelope addressed to Mr Hunter Grant and Miss Susan Johnson. Inside is a formal letter from a law firm in the Cayman Islands telling us to immediately 'cease and desist' all activities that concern White Investments Limited or risk prosecution. It also warns us that the writer is in the process of taking out a New Zealand trespass order to prevent us entering any properties belonging to White Investments or interfering in the current police case regarding Mariko Goto.

Dao reads it and looks confused. 'What does cease and desist mean? Does it mean don't do it – is desist a real word?'

'It means stop and don't start again, or something like it – it's a common legal term when you want to warn someone that they'd better stop whatever they're doing – or else. It's a warning – or a threat. I'd better call Simon. I'm sure half of what they warn us about is rubbish and simply can't be done.'

Simon has been my lawyer since he graduated from law school; I've known him since primary school, and he is the one I turn to for serious business. I often ask Willow for casual advice, but I don't involve her in my business affairs and I'm certainly not telling her about this.

'What should I do – if anything?' I ask Simon when I've read out the letter to him. 'Can they cause any real trouble?'

'They can issue a trespass notice of course, but they can't dictate whether you take an interest in Miss Goto, whoever she is. I presume you're involved in something new and you've trodden on some toes in the process?'

'You could say that – a scary woman called Bakker has warned me off already. Let's meet for dinner somewhere so we can tell you about it.'

'We're having dinner with Simon tonight,' I tell Dao when I end the call, 'so we can tell him what we're doing. He can respond to this letter and if anything goes wrong, he's up with the play.'

Dao looks calm, but I know the code; she is worried. 'What could go wrong? Can those people make the police arrest you or something?'

'I don't think they can, but with someone like Bakker you have to expect trouble. What did you dig up about Grace?'

'She has a FaceBook page in the name of Mary Hudson, no privacy settings and it hasn't been added to in two and a half years. Prior to that it was mostly posts about books and films, the odd dinner out, usually with a group of five or six – and a photo from a walking track of her with three other people – I think it might be the Abel Tasman coastal track we did last year. Nearly all the people who have commented on her posts are women.'

She shows me the last photo, the one from the walk and I recognise Grace but not the others. Someone called Henry Chan has made a comment: "Very impressed you finally got your new guy to go for a walk!"

Dao points at the photo. 'And the one on her right, that's her new guy.'

I look more closely, but I can see nothing to indicate a relationship. 'What can you see that I can't? It could be the one on her other side.'

She laughs. 'No, he belongs to the other woman, check their hands.'

And she's right, the other two have their fingers hooked together, obviously a couple.

'I can't find anything else useful,' she says after a few minutes. 'She isn't on Twitter under either name. That Henry Chan who made the comment – he is on FaceBook, but he's got his privacy setting done up tight, so I can't see anything. I could go and look at her other friends, but I don't expect I'd find anything interesting.'

I am in the kitchen, when Dao turns up beside me and stands very close, the way she does when she's worried.

'If you weren't here, what should I do? I'm not joking, Hunter – I really want to know what you think I should do.'

'Depends on what happens,' I say, trying to be realistic without adding to her fears. 'If I get arrested, you have a raft of choices – you can call Simon or Willow for advice, you can call Kristen for a bit of shopping comfort, or you can ask Charlie or Benson for practical help. Benson would do anything for you, he's like a self-appointed guardian. You have a whole network of people now, who will help you if you ask them.'

She goes back to the living room and when I bring the coffee, she is checking phone numbers from my phone to hers.

'Do you think we drink too much coffee? I read that some people are giving up having more than two or three cups a day because they think it's bad for you.'

Dao laughs. 'If that was true you would be dead already.'

Late afternoon Bakker calls, her voice tells me all I need to know. 'Come and see me first thing tomorrow – let's say half past nine.' There is no pretence of giving me a choice; this is a direct order. When I tell Dao she makes no comment, but true to form she has started planning.

'There are a couple of things I want to do before we go out for dinner with Simon,' she says, her expression intent and serious. 'I've found that industrial site in East Tamaki that belongs to White Investments – I found a building that has a sign saying Specialist Welding. Remember Silvano told us they got rid of a welding business that used to be there. It's the only welding place in that industrial area and it seems to be empty.'

'Why do you want to see it?'

'I just do – why would they ask someone who's paying rent to leave before they were ready to demolish it or whatever they were going to do?'

'If the lease was up for renewal it might have been a good opportunity to give the tenant notice, instead of trying to break his lease halfway through a period. I don't know – but if you want to see it, we'll leave early and go and have a look. Anything else we should think about?'

'I'm going to talk to Benson – I'll call him before we go out. I want him to know what's going on now – before …' She picks up her phone. 'I'll do it now – I'll put in on speaker so you can hear what he says.'

Benson answers and says he is in the car with company, and he'll call back in half an hour when he's back in his office. In the meantime, she loads the East Tamaki address in the Navigate app on her phone; she is completely focused on preparing herself for the worst, and I am powerless to make her worries go away. When Benson calls back, she quickly gets down to business. 'I'm sorry to call you at work, but I think Hunter might get arrested.'

'Really? What's he done now?'

'Have you got time to listen for five minutes while I tell you the whole story? Or should we come and see you?' Her voice is taut with stress. 'We're going out for dinner in town tonight, and in the morning we have to go a police station in town and that's when I think this Bakker woman will arrest him. We'll have to leave about half past eight to get to the appointment with her or we might get caught in the traffic. I could send you a really long email, but I'd rather just tell you.'

'Just tell me now, Dao – you know I always have time for you.' His voice is as calm as ever, but I know he will be concerned about how stressed she sounds.

When she starts telling him the story, I realise that she has rehearsed this in her mind, the whole sequence of events: the main points about Grace finding the origami notes, the handwritten notes in Mariko's textbook, Grace resigning, how Dao found John Anderson, our interactions with him and with Bakker, her research into Grace and how we found out her real name. She doesn't hesitate once; every detail is there, and Benson doesn't say a single word until she has finished.

'Hmm,' he says. 'I'll do some checking and get back to you. I'll swing by on my way home or call you, if you've already gone out. Text me when you leave.'

We are nearly at East Tamaki when Benson calls back and Dao puts it on speaker again.

'It's a long story Dao – I want to sit down and talk through things with you and Hunter. Are you going to be late tonight?'

Dao makes a questioning face at me and I say, 'Don't think so, Benson. We'll probably be home by ten.'

'Text me when you get to the Harbour Bridge on the way home - I'll come to your place.'

'He must have found out something really intriguing that needs lots of explaining,' I say when Dao ends the call.

I'm not going to worry Dao further by voicing my suspicion that Benson has got confirmation that I'll be arrested tomorrow, when we turn up for our appointment with Bakker.

11

The factory in East Tamaki sits well back from the street with a large, concreted yard in front and a driveway down the left-hand side. A grey shipping container has been placed next to a tall roll-up door, and there is a six-foot chain-link fence along the edge of the sidewalk with double gates padlocked together.

'The guy living in the flat at the back is out,' says Dao, as I slow to a stop, 'or that padlock would be hanging down on the inside.'

Above the tall roller door is a black and yellow sign in cursive script: Specialist Welding Ltd. There is nothing at all remarkable about it, but Dao studies the site as if she hopes to draw some conclusion about whatever her theory is. Looking down the driveway to the rear I see what appears to be mangroves behind the property.

'Must be sea water down there – wonder where that comes from,' I say, and Dao gets her phone out as I drive away.

'I remember it from when I searched for this place on Google Earth- there's a little inlet from the sea.' She holds up the phone. 'See, it starts up there and meanders inland and one arm of it is behind this place – both sides are lined with mangroves.'

I pull in at the kerb and have a closer look at the image on her phone. 'It's an inlet from the Hauraki Gulf. I am surprised it comes so far inland – not what I expected at all. Have you seen enough? Shall we head back to town?'

'OK – there's nothing to see really, is there? I thought …'

'What did you think?'

'I was hoping there was some connection – if the same company owned both sites there might have been. And you know what that letter said – to keep away from their properties, plural. But we wouldn't see anything from the street anyway – it was just a vague idea and I'm probably wrong.'

Simon is waiting for us at the Italian place near his flat in Mt Albert, where we've had dinner with him once or twice before. Dao warns him that what we want to tell him is a long story with a lot of detail and suggests he records it on his phone.

'It's very complicated,' she says seriously. 'Lots of details that could be important for you to know – later on. If we tell you everything now, you'll have the recording to refer to, so we don't miss anything out next time.'

Simon shoots a questioning look in my direction and I say I agree with Dao. It is complicated and a recording done now will be useful for all of us. He puts his phone on the table between us, and Dao puts hers beside it and we start. With short breaks to order and when wait staff deliver our food, we spend the next hour detailing every single thing. We start right from Plum's call and continue through it as it developed. Dao tells the main story and I fill in details and explanations here and there. Simon asks a lot of questions and as usual I am surprised that telling someone else a complex story can make you see it as a whole; that the questions they ask can bring out additional details and build a complete picture.

At the end, Dao tells him that she has written up her notes about all we found on the security videos, and she will email them to him. 'I put in notes about the reason each segment we identified is important, and how they link to kind of tell a story - I think you should have that as well, just in case.'

'This is incredible,' says Simon when we reach the end. 'It's like some TV drama – notes thrown out of windows, foreign criminals, abductions. If it wasn't Dao telling me, I would believe someone made it up. And well done, Dao, for telling such a coherent story with so much detail – no wonder everyone said you're an amazing witness.'

He picks up his phone and turns the recording off. 'Inspector Bakker sounds pretty grim. I haven't come across her, but I don't do a lot of court work. If she's going to arrest you for impeding the investigation, we'd best be prepared. I'll tell you how it works and what I will do.'

The details of what happens when someone is arrested are quite straight forward, but Dao needs reassurance. 'But what if the police don't give him bail straight off? How will you get him out?' Her eyes are fixed on Simon's face, her face tight and worried.

'If he gets arrested tomorrow morning, which is a Saturday and if Bakker is as tough as you say and hates the look of Hunter, then she can deny him police bail and insist it goes to court – that means he'll be in the police cells until Monday. She might try to get the judge to deny court bail too, which would mean you stay in a cell on remand, or that you can be at home with electronic monitoring. I'll be there if you have to appear in court, Hunter, and I'll get you out on court bail. From the sound of it I don't think she has enough to contest court bail. The ideal situation would be if we could demolish Bakker's reason for arresting you in the first place, and get the charge dropped.'

He looks into the distance for a moment, deep in thought,

before he continues. 'I'll go home now and listen to it all again, very carefully and make some notes – recording this was a great idea, Dao. I'll email you with any questions about details or timelines, when I've gone through it. I hope we have grounds to contest the charge itself – if Bakker does decide to charge you.'

Then he turns to me and says with great emphasis, 'And listen carefully, Hunter! I know you often come so damn close to the edge of what's legal that you just about fall off the cliff, but this is serious. If you do anything - anything at all! – that breaks the law while you're on court bail, if that's what it comes to – then you're toast. You'll sit in a cell until it comes up for trial – and not a police station cell, in prison.'

I don't think he's bluffing to make me behave; I glance at Dao, but she doesn't react. She stares absent-mindedly at her phone, which is still recording and suddenly she looks up; I can tell she's had an idea. I expect her to say something, but she doesn't, instead she thanks Simon and turns to me.

'If they put you in a cell over the weekend, I must be prepared and have my house keys and my remote for the alarm *before* we go in to see Bakker – I'll get someone to come and pick me up, Charlie perhaps.'

'Sorry I can't offer,' says Simon apologetically, 'I have a family wedding in Taupo at eleven tomorrow morning, so I have to leave early.'

'That's OK – Charlie or Kristen will do it. Or I can take a taxi – don't worry.'

When we part outside, Simon hugs Dao and tells her not to worry too much and to make sure to keep him informed. Just before we walk away, Dao says, 'Oh Simon, that letter that asked us to cease and desist – they got my name wrong.'

He looks surprised. 'Did they? Looked right to me.'

'We haven't told you yet, but we got married a couple of

months ago, just very quietly - and I've changed my name, so I'm not Susan Johnson now.'

Simon laughs and pats her shoulder. 'Just a sneaky secret wedding, eh? I'll have to get you a wedding present. And congratulations, of course. But I don't think the way that letter was addressed means anything in practice. If they get a trespass order, you can say that isn't your name and it doesn't apply to you, but they would challenge that, of course – it would only delay things a little. And I'll have to change your will again, Hunter – I'll get on to it next week.'

On the way home I remember the look on Dao's face earlier in the evening; I feel a desperate need to ensure that she won't try to do something dangerous, if I'm locked up. Just thinking of her actions, when the Boss tried to kill me, sends a chill through my heart.

'Will you promise me you won't go back to the apartment block to look at more video, if I get arrested - or try to get into that parking basement? I will go crazy, if I have to sit in a damn cell worrying about you. Really promise, double promise?'

In the back of my mind sits an unvoiced idea that they might have disposed of Grace somewhere in the subterranean levels of the apartment building and this might be Dao's theory too – we haven't discussed it. We know from what Silvano told us, that there are three basement levels. When they took the washing machine carton down, they stayed out of sight on the car park level for much longer than it would have taken to load the box into their car.

To my relief she promises without any hesitation. 'Absolutely, I don't want to go back there. Why did Simon say you have to have a new will?'

'I made a will a couple of years ago, which is mainly in your favour with a chunk going to Plum and Willow – it was just after I found you. There must be something about being married that makes it defunct – or else it's just Simon being very lawyerly.'

I can feel her staring at me and there is silence for a moment. 'I can't believe you did that! You're mad – you hardly knew me then.'

'I knew enough to decide that you deserved it - and I wanted you to be safe for the rest of your life, if the Boss managed to kill me.'

She puts her hand on my thigh. 'That's amazing – thank you!'

'We're nearly at the bridge and it's only twenty past nine. Why don't you call Benson?'

12

'Benson,' says Dao when we are sitting down with a drink, 'I know I told you the whole story over the phone, but I'd like you to listen to the recording of our meeting with Simon – he's Hunter's lawyer. Just in case I left anything out when I was talking to you – and so you can hear what Simon told us.'

She starts the playback and puts the phone on the coffee table in front of Benson. He listens closely, his beer mostly forgotten, his eyes unfocused in the middle distance. Dao sits down on the floor beside my chair with Scruff close beside her and leans against my legs. And while I play with a strand of her hair and listen to the recording it's as if I hear the story for the first time. It's an interesting experience; I hear nuances in Simon's voice that were not so obvious when I was looking at his face while he talked. Now when I listen to him describing the process of an arrest and what happens next, I think he's pretty sure I will be arrested; I can hear it in his voice. It was one thing thinking, "I'll probably be arrested" and quite another to listen to my lawyer sounding as if it's a near certainty.

When the recording ends Benson looks at me with an expression close to despair. 'Bloody hell, Hunter- why do you do it? Haven't you had enough in the last couple of years to last a lifetime? I don't know if you're crazy or just can't resist a challenge. When Bakker called the other day and asked me what I knew about you, I said nothing that would have caused her to over-react like this. She didn't tell me why she asked, but she was angry. I said that in the past you had sometimes done things that verged on illegal, but I also said you'd been very useful on two occasions and made investigations much easier in the long run. I specifically didn't mention the unofficial warning I gave you about driving around with loaded weapons in your car.'

'Oh no, it's nothing to do with what anyone might have told her,' says Dao calmly and sits up straight. 'It's something else, like something inside her. She said that Hunter regards himself as a tough guy who thinks he can do whatever he likes. You should have seen her face when she said that – it's personal.'

'That's interesting – your impressions of people are usually right.' Benson looks thoughtful, as if he's trying to remember something. 'I heard a rumour about something Bakker did a few years ago, when she was a sergeant – it's just popped into my head. She had to apologise to someone, a crime victim or a victim's family, I think. I'll tell you, if I can remember what the story was.'

And then suddenly he turns on me, angry. 'And what the hell made you take such a risk when you went to that guy's flat? Are you mad? He could have grabbed Dao and used her as a hostage!'

'Sorry, I should have mentioned it,' I say apologetically. 'I wasn't just standing behind the door like some idiot playing hide-and-seek. I had a good grip on the door handle, in case he tried just that, and I was ready to grab Dao with my right hand. All systems on high alert, ready to spring into action.' I don't tell him I had Charlie's Glock pistol in the holster under my sweatshirt.

Dao gets up from the floor and curls up on the sofa. 'Sorry,

Hunter - I didn't realise you were worried about it. I had such a good story and I thought being Asian-looking would make him think I was another Japanese student – you know how people can't tell people from Asian countries apart. And I'm half European, which makes it even harder. I wasn't worried at all. He really took my story at face value – there wasn't the slightest hint of suspicion on his face. But Benson, what about Grace? Did you find anything out?'

'It took me a while, but I knew I'd heard something from a mate who works at Central, a guy I play golf with now and then - I was pretty sure he mentioned the name in connection with a case a couple of years ago. I called him after I talked to you this afternoon and he confirmed I had it right. Mary Hudson, as she was then, was a top admin person at Central, very good at her job and highly trusted. She got involved with a fraudster, a conman and she did that age-old stupid thing, fell in love with the guy, gave him most of her savings to invest in a business he said he was setting up - and then he disappeared. He'd given her a false name and she didn't know how to find him.'

Benson shakes his head at the gullibility of people. 'Phil, that's my mate, said that somehow she managed to find out his real name and got a newly promoted detective to search for him in our system, in case he had a previous conviction, which he did – but she didn't report him for fraud. The crime register had an address and he still lived there, so she went to his house with a spray-can of fluorescent pink paint and wrote "conman" and "criminal" and "thief" all over the front of his house and their two cars – he was married and had a family. Next day she turned herself in for causing intentional damage to property and they prosecuted her for unauthorised use of police information as much as for the vandalism - to set an example, I imagine. I don't know what happened to the conman – I didn't check, but presumably he's in prison. Mary Grace lost her job of course, but the judge let her off with a warning for pleading guilty and for the effect it had on her life – and the detective was in trouble too. She never got her savings back - the guy was a gambling addict and went bankrupt.'

'The poor woman, no wonder she changed her name.' I glance at Dao who seems to be deep in thought and makes no comment. 'That's why she changed her name and was reticent about her past life. A total personal disaster. It must have made it hard to get a job – she probably got no reference from the last one.'

'Very difficult to cope with for someone who's basically an honest and decent person, which I think she is,' says Benson. 'And naturally she wouldn't want to go to the place where she used to work when she found the origami messages, and that's why she asked Linda to go the second time.'

'I've been meaning to ask you, Benson - do you think people realise that we are friends?' His expression tells me he has thought about this. 'You've been extremely helpful on several occasions, a genuinely good friend and a couple of times you've bent the rules to give us information, which I know went against the grain. Are you risking some kind of censure, if it becomes known that we see each other? We don't want our reputation to rub off on you, if I get arrested – particularly if I end up in court.'

He doesn't need time to think. 'It's nice of you to ask, Hunter,' he says, and he sounds quite comfortable about it. 'I did think back on the couple of times I bent the rules as you call it, and none of it was serious enough to cause problems. Not in the context I did it – giving you stray bits of information in investigations where you ended up being the key to some great results. It's not in the same class as consorting with criminals - so no, I'm not concerned. And I've never told anyone I warned you about being armed – never mentioned it to a single person. The possibility that you might be carrying a loaded weapon was discussed a few times during the drama with the drug boss, but after you disarmed that intruder, we got busy and never did anything about it.'

He turns to Dao, half serious. 'And someone's got to keep an eye on you, too. God knows your instincts make you a bit of a liability. I know you both believe the world needs your brand of justice. What is it Hunter calls it - practical justice or something like it? All very well and good when it works, but dangerous too. And how do you differentiate between outright vigilante activity and your practical justice? And who is to say if one man's concept of practical justice *is* justice at all? Laws have been developed over centuries and adapted to fit modern society, agreed on by lawmakers who represent the majority of people - so I don't condone your attitude. The only reason I didn't say more to Bakker was the way she seemed to be looking for rope to hang you with, Hunter – and because I like you both a lot. But if you go too far, I won't let my feelings get in the way.'

'We do understand that Benson – we do, really! And thank you for not telling Bakker anything bad about Hunter. But you don't need to worry about me,' says Dao. 'Hunter already made me promise I won't get back into that block of flats illegally and look at more videos or go into the parking area under the building. And I don't want to anyway, I think what we've given Bakker is enough. And maybe her people already came to the same conclusions we did now that they've had more time to study the videos.'

That night I jerk awake from a nightmare about Afghanistan. It happens now and then, but much less often than it used to. Dao is on her back, so I know she is awake; she never sleeps like that. She scuffles over and rearranges my arm so she can snuggle in the way she likes to. 'Did you have a nightmare?'

'Yes, but it's OK. I'm here with you and it was just the same old memory dream.'

'The one when the bomb exploded and blew up the truck?'

'Yes – did I wake you up?'

'No, I was just thinking about how Grace went to the flat and got taken, instead of managing to help Mariko. But at least they had each other,' she says sadly. 'Linda said how lovely and calm Grace is – that must have been so nice for Mariko, even if it was just for a very short while.'

Going into town in the rush hour by bus is a new experience for me and very crowded. My idea is to make it as easy as possible for Dao to get back if I'm arrested, so I suggest a taxi, but Dao vetoes it.

'I want to go by bus – I like buses and I haven't been on one since I was a little girl. Looking at things from higher up is lovely. And I'll know which number bus to take when I go back, if I have to do it alone, and all that sort of thing.'

She is tense and determined and I give in; we go by bus. As we walk from the bus stop, only marginally late, I hand her my cell phone, and she looks at me in surprise. 'I know they'll take it from you if you get arrested, but you will need it when they let you go.'

'I know – but what if they have the right to get into it somehow and all my emails and stuff get downloaded. I'm not taking any risks with that hard-nosed bitch.'

At exactly quarter to ten we sit in a small room with Bakker and a detective, who introduces himself for the recording as Sergeant Apatu; he looks like your original Maori warrior. Bakker charges straight in and demands we tell her who let us into the communications room in the apartment block, and how we convinced that person that we had permission to be there. It's easy to tell from her tone that she believes we either tricked a tenant to let us into the building again, or that we did something else fraudulent. It is, as always, a pleasure to reply in a calm and measured way to someone whose anger is on open display.

'No, we didn't trick anyone, or tell any lies. And we didn't use someone's PIN for the keypad either,' I say. 'What made you think we were there without permission?'

An angry flush rises up her neck; she is about to lose her patience. 'So tell me how you got into that room, which is always locked!'

'Mr Silvano let us in – the building manager.'

If it's possible to choke on disappointment, Bakker would be struggling for breath now. 'And how did you get Silvano to let you in – did you pretend that Mr Anderson had authorised it?'

'No, we just called him and asked if we could go back and watch some more video, and he kindly met us at the building and let us in.'

Dao says in a helpful tone of voice, 'He was perfectly happy to let us in, you know. He didn't ask if Mr Anderson had said we could. I think he makes those kinds of decisions himself.'

'You are interfering with a police investigation, and I will not tolerate it!'

Dao hasn't finished being reasonable and helpful. 'We thought you might not have had time to draw the same conclusions we did from the recordings,' she says innocently. 'Had you really had time to work out all those connections?'

Bakker struggles with her conscience and finds a way to avoid an outright lie. 'Even if we hadn't pieced all of it together yet, we would have over time.'

'But we might have saved you some time?' Dao looks calm, but behind the mask she is angry. 'And by the way, I can also tell you that when Grace Harris resigned, she did so by a text message – which was sent from Mariko Goto's phone. And you know that the men, who hold Mariko captive, have her phone.'

Bakker's face is a study in rancour; I enjoy it while trying to maintain a straight face.

'And how do you know this?' Bakker sounds resentful. She needs a crash course in how to deal with people.

'Linda asked her manager where the text message came from, because she thought that Grace didn't have a cell phone. She is going to get in touch with you today about getting Grace's disappearance included in the investigation, but I thought you would want to know as soon as possible.'

To my surprise Bakker doesn't ask how we know Mariko's cell phone number; instead, we continue with detailed questions about how long we were at the apartment building, if we tried to copy any material, if Silvano came back to lock up, or if we went anywhere else in the building, and then she gets up from behind the table and tells me I'm under arrest.

"Why?' Dao gets to her feet, before Bakker gets any further, and now she doesn't look at all like an innocent teenager. 'What grounds have you for arresting him? Can you please tell me one single thing he did that contravenes the law? I don't think anything Hunter has done warrants an arrest, so I want to know what you base it on.'

Bakker is completely taken aback by Dao having suddenly transformed from a helpful young thing into a sophisticated and confronting adult with a gaze from her black eyes that could pierce armour plating. Apatu can't take his eyes off her.

'I'm arresting him because he has already interfered, even if it didn't break the law – he poses a potentially serious risk to our investigations. Just look at how he went to Miss Goto's apartment, got into the building by trickery and confronted the suspect - and possibly caused him to flee.'

'No, he didn't. I did that,' says Dao firmly. 'Hunter only got us into the building. It was *my* idea, I rang the doorbell, I talked to the man, and I recorded the video – as you well know.'

Bakker doesn't rise to the bait; she has no intention of arresting Dao as well.

'Mr Grant has a track record of disobeying instructions, taking the law into his own hands, and generally thinking he knows better than the police. He thinks he is above the law and can do whatever he wants - and I don't want him around to cause problems. Which is why I won't let him get bail. He'll stay in a cell until Monday when he will appear in court.'

Dao turns towards me and says quietly, 'I'll see you soon.' Then she walks calmly out of the room without saying goodbye to Bakker. As an exit it scores nine out of ten. I knew this was her plan, but I am deeply worried; for her, not for myself. Bakker stares in silence at the door Dao left open behind her, and Apatu's mouth twitches before he gets his face under control.

PART 3
DAO

13

Dao walked quietly down the corridor, through the door to a wider hallway, around the corner and out to the front foyer. Thankfully, the door, which could only be opened with a security card from the outside, opened from the inside and there was no need to interact with anyone. She stood in the shade under the tree on the corner of Cook Street, taking deep, slow breaths to calm herself. The traffic and the noise around her seemed vague and unsubstantial, as if she was in a bubble of silence. The little scene in the interview room had left her with a welter of emotions that sapped her mental energy and made her feel exhausted. She stood perfectly still, trying to regain the self-control that had nearly slipped away from her, when she walked through that door leaving Hunter behind. To reassure herself, she checked the shoulder bag she hardly ever carried: she had Hunter's phone, her keys and the remotes for the garage door and for the alarm. She got her own phone out of her pocket, called Charlie's number and left a voicemail message. 'Hi Charlie, it's Dao. Can you please call me back as soon as you are free? I need some help. Thanks.'

Walking down the street without Hunter made her feel very alone. He was always there, on the outside, nearest the edge of the sidewalk and his body felt like a safe wall beside her. Now it felt as if the air stream from the traffic could sweep her up and throw her to the ground; she moved closer to the walls of the buildings. She made her way to the bus stop she had identified on her phone as the closest one for going north and waited without noticing her surroundings; her mind a vacuum where random ideas floated aimlessly without making sense. She was on her last bus when Charlie returned her call. 'What's up, Dao? You need some help?'

'Hunter's been arrested. Can you please come to our place? When you have time. I can't talk about it just now, I'm on a bus.'

'On a bus? Never mind, I'll be there in a couple of hours – kia kaha, girl.'

Dao walked towards their house and tried to imagine what it would look like to someone who saw it for the first time, a three-storey town house in a row of six. It's quite impressive, she thought, you can tell it is big inside, and it looks sort of solid, like it's made of stone – it's my safe place. I can't let Nigel next-door find out that Hunter's been arrested. He'll get all neurotic again and start worrying about every noise in the night, like he did last time things were going on in our lives. He's such a fusspot, he'd probably come and check on me and keep calling to ask if I'm all right.

She deactivated the alarm, locked the front door behind her and realised she had never done this before, not on her own. Glancing down the long ground floor passage towards the courtyard she saw Scruff watching her through the glass door, wagging his tail in welcome. She let him in, sat down on the floor and cried.

By the time Charlie arrived, Dao had eaten a sandwich and considered what she needed to do. The muddled thoughts that had filled her head on the way back from the city had dispersed and she had decided what she wanted to do.

'Are you sure you don't want to come and stay at our house?' Charlie looked searchingly at Dao when she had been told the bare minimum. 'Kristen will be disappointed if you don't.'

'I thought I would do that,' said Dao seriously. 'I really did – but I can't. I must be here. I can't have Hunter in one place and me in another and the house empty – it feels horrible, like my life is breaking up. I'll just stay here with Scruff. I will keep the ground floor alarm on, and I'll be quite happy with Scruff to keep me company. If you have time to help me when you're not busy, I would love some help. I know exactly what I want to do.'

They made coffee and went to sit at the far end of the living room by the glass wall, where the sun was casting a wedge of bright light into the room.

'You can sit in Hunter's chair if you want to,' offered Dao and sat cross-legged in the corner of the sofa.

'No, I'll sit where I usually sit, thanks. I don't feel quite up to sitting in Hunter's chair. What is it you want to do?'

'I need to go to that place in Tamaki, soon. I need to get inside the fence and have a look through the windows.'

'What place is that? Hunter didn't mention it when he talked to me.'

Dao started telling Charlie about the White Investment company, which was owned by the Gray Investment company and all the ramifications, but after a couple of minutes she gave up and played the recording of their meeting with Simon again. She sat silent in her sofa corner and watched Charlie's face while she listened; now and then Charlie looked across at Dao with a frown. After a while Dao got up and went to her laptop; she printed the notes about the conclusions they had drawn from the CCTV clips and put the paper on the coffee table in front of Charlie.

When the recording ended Dao pointed at the paper, 'Please read that too.'

Charlie read it, put the paper down and looked hard at Dao. 'I'm damn sure Hunter wouldn't let you go there! Climbing a tall fence with a locked gate and going onto a property where someone lives in a flat at the back! Shit, girl - anything could happen. No way are we doing that!'

'OK,' said Dao meekly. 'Now, the second thing ...'

'Hang on a moment, Warrior Princess! That's not like you – are you planning to do something all on your own? I want to you to look me in the eye and tell me you are not going there.'

Dao looked steadily into Charlie's eyes and said, 'I can't promise. I must go – I've got a feeling about that place. Ever since I saw those guys take that box down in the lift on the security video, I've wondered where you would get rid of a box with a body inside. I mean, they could throw it in the sea perhaps or take it to a rubbish dump, but I wonder if the Tamaki place might be important. That legal letter said they were taking out a trespass order and we weren't to go on *any* properties owned by those companies, not just the block of flats. They might own more properties we don't know about, but Silvano mentioned the Tamaki one and that it's empty and I just have a feeling ...'

She stopped talking and Charlie knew there was no doubt that Dao would do exactly what she wanted to, whatever she said, and one way or another she must put a stop to it.

'And what would Hunter say, if he heard of this plan?'

'He would either come with me and we would do it together, or he would say I couldn't do it – and if he did, I wouldn't do it. I have promised him not to go back into the apartment block, but that was the only thing I promised, because he was really worried about that for some reason. This can't wait until they let him go, Charlie! He can't help with this - if he gets out on court bail and then does something illegal, he'd be in worse trouble than ever. Simon said they can lock him up in prison. It's much better that I do this on my own.'

Charlie shook her head, but she knew she would give in; unless she went with Dao and kept her safe, the only alternative would be to tie her up. She stalled for time. 'Have you told Simon and Benson that they arrested Hunter?'

'Oh yes - I called them while I waited for the bus. I had a long talk with Benson and he's coming over tomorrow, probably in the morning, and Simon will call me back tomorrow night, when he gets home from the wedding.'

'And Willow?'

'Not yet – she might start telling me how bad Hunter is and I couldn't bear it and I might say something horrid in return. I'll wait until Monday.' She smiled grimly and added. 'But I've got Hunter's phone, so I can see if she calls or sends a message. He gave it to me before we went in.'

'And?'

'Well, if she calls, I won't answer and if there's a message I'll reply, and she'll think it's Hunter.'

Willow and Matt were leaving for Hawaii on Monday, but if she told Charlie, she might want to inform them right away and then what would happen? Would they cancel their holiday and make a mess of her plans?

Charlie thought for a moment. 'Well, I suppose I have to take you to that damn place, or you'll go off on your own and then Hunter will kill me. What are you planning to do when we get there?'

'I would like to go there in daylight and have a really good look and then again after dark. The best thing would be if I could get a look at the guy who lives there or look in the windows – perhaps after dark, when it's easier to get in without anyone spotting me climbing the fence.'

'Shit, Dao - that won't work! If we're caught inside that fence, we'll never get out fast enough – not if the fence is as tall as you say. We'll have to re-think this and make a plan B. Like, we could go and look at the place this afternoon and decide how to go about it, check the chain and the padlock and see how we could get in. If we can open the gate, we'll have an escape route, and we might be able to do it.'

'OK, but then you would have to tell Kristen, and she'll say you can't do it because she worries you might get hurt, and then you can't help me anyway. I shouldn't have asked you - it's better I do it on my own.'

Dao's heart sank into the pit of her stomach, when she tried to imagine doing this on her own. She knew she must do it and it terrified her, but she couldn't drag Charlie into it; it wasn't her problem. But when she voiced this thought, Charlie exclaimed, 'Not my problem? Are you crazy? Hunter's my best mate and we went through hell together in Afghanistan - I flew the chopper that lifted him out after that IED nearly killed him. If I back out of helping you, my life won't be worth living – I'll have no self-respect. We'll go and have a look at the place and then I'll go home and get some gear and tell Kristen I'm staying here tonight and tomorrow. I'll just have to face the firestorm later on, when she finds out what we've done.'

Dao thought of the many times Kristen had taken her shopping, how lovely surprises would materialise whenever she visited Charlie and Kristen's house. The thought of getting Charlie into trouble, and Kristen being furious with both of them was awful, but the compulsion to get into the Tamaki site overrode all other considerations.

Charlie watched Dao's face; she could imagine the conflict in her mind. What was it that made Dao so determined? She must get to the bottom of it before they went any further.

'Now listen, warrior girl, you've got to tell me the truth – is there something you haven't told me about this factory site? Or anything else you're keeping to yourself? Because I just don't get it – this obsession to get into that factory, or at least onto the site, it just doesn't make sense. Why do you think it has something to do with those missing girls?'

Dao stared at her coffee mug and Charlie watched her troubled face and waited, but after a long silence she looked up and shook her head, admitting defeat.

'I can't explain it - I might have imagined it. Maybe it was just the combination of Silvano mentioning the site in Tamaki and then seeing those guys take the big carton down in the lift – perhaps my mind just built a story linking those things, trying to make sense of it. I don't know, Charlie – it sounds mad now when I think about it.'

'OK, let's call it a little road trip then. We'll go and have a look at that Tamaki factory and then I'll stay the night and Kristen can come and have dinner with us here.'

'Don't you have any jobs this weekend?'

'I flew two couples to Coromandel this morning, I'm free tomorrow and I have three jobs on Monday. People usually book me in advance - it's very unusual that I get a job thrown at me at short notice.'

14

The industrial area was quiet on a Saturday afternoon with roller doors shut, trucks and vans parked up for the weekend and no traffic. The sunshine and the wide, empty streets and the lack of anyone walking seemed surreal. It's like one of those films, thought Dao, everyone has mysteriously disappeared, and we are the only people left on Earth. Before they reached the corner, where they would turn into the street where the factory was, Dao exclaimed, 'Stop! Let's stop here - I think we should park here and walk.'

'Good idea – we'll put Scruff's lead on and look like we're just taking our dog for a walk.'

As they rounded the corner Dao said, 'Let's walk slowly so we can have a good look. See that place with the yellow and black sign saying Specialist Welding about five places down on the other side? That's the one.'

They let Scruff pause wherever he wanted and stood talking while they waited for him to be ready to move on. 'Perfect cover,' said Charlie. 'All this waiting while he sniffs and pees – lots of time to check the place out without looking suspicious. That padlock is just something to deter rascals from exploring around the back and the chain is a light one, a small bolt cutter would do the job in a second. But I can't see anything of real interest.'

Fifteen minutes later they were back at the car after walking around two blocks. 'Ready to leave?'

'Did you hear the hum?'

'What hum, where?'

'When Scruff peed on the lamp post just past the welding place gate. There was a hum – maybe something is on inside the factory. A machine or something.'

'Can't say I noticed, but you're a lot younger than I am – I bet your hearing is miles better. Could be some noise from the flat at the back or the place next door. Even streetlights hum sometimes.'

'It wasn't a streetlight – and they're not on anyway.' Dao hesitated. 'I think I have good directional hearing – Hunter often can't decide which direction noises come from, but I can.'

Charlie smiled grimly. 'I'm not surprised – his hearing is probably permanently damaged from that explosion. I'd better call Kristen and tell her what's going on.'

'I'll take Scruff for a fast run around a couple of blocks in the other direction,' said Dao. 'Then I won't have to walk him again tonight.'

When they got back to the car, panting and happy looking, one glance at Charlie's face made Dao pull up short. 'What's the matter? Is something wrong?'

'Kristen just reminded me – we've got her dad's birthday party tonight. There's no way I can't go, it's the first family occasion since her mum died a couple of months ago – I've got the be there.'

'It's OK,' said Dao. 'I've been thinking about it ever since we got here. I think it was all in my head - linking this place with what went on with those girls. You made me think about it before, when you asked me to explain – there *is* really no reason why this place should have anything to do with it. It was just my mind connecting two random things and making it seem logical. You and Kristen can come over tomorrow night instead and we'll have dinner together.'

By unspoken agreement they talked of nothing related to Hunter's arrest or their mission in Tamaki on the way back to the North Shore. It was nearly five o'clock when Charlie parked outside the house. 'Do you want me to come in with you?'

Dao smiled. 'I'm a big girl now, Charlie. You know this place is like a bank vault, when all the systems are activated. I'll see you tomorrow night!'

She got out of the car with Scruff and let herself into the house and Charlie waited until the front door closed behind her before she drove off. In her head she went over the conversation she had just had with Dao and the one in Tamaki, when they talked about the humming Dao had heard. But there had been nothing devious about the way Dao had said that she accepted that she had probably constructed a theory out of random details. She felt intense relief; Dao getting into trouble on her own was a dreadful thought.

Dao spent an hour thinking hard about the best way to go about things without involving anyone else, which was how she must do this. She must make sure that if things went wrong, she would be the only one in trouble, that all the blame would be hers alone and nobody apart from herself would get hurt. The thought that someone would come with her and then blame themselves, if something happened to her, was awful.

She curled up in Hunter's chair and tried to imagine discussing it with him, hearing his objections and suggestions. When she felt confident that she was prepared for whatever she could dream up in the way of difficulties and dangers, she turned her laptop on and looked up limousine companies and corporate car hire firms. She had never learnt to drive, and a taxi seemed less reliable and trustworthy than a hired car with a chauffeur.

Her bank balance and the balance on her credit card were very healthy and she thought how lucky it was that she never managed to spend even half of her monthly allowance. In her mind she could hear Hunter's voice, 'But you know you have access to my accounts, you're not limited to your personal money. Remember that we agreed to stick to the communist principle of the redistribution of wealth.' And then she imagined herself replying, 'But you wouldn't like me doing this, so I have to use my own money.'

She studied four limousine company websites and called the one that seemed to offer the most flexible arrangements. Five minutes later it was done; a car with a driver would pick her up at half past eight.

'He must stay with me all evening,' she said to the man at the limousine hire office. 'I might go to one or more places, and he must wait for me and then at the end, take me back to the address where he picked me up. And I would like a nice black car, please – not one of those long white ones.'

'Do you know how long you want the car for?'

'A few hours, I think. Do you have to know in advance?'

'We can leave it open-ended. Is it just for one person or are we picking up others at other addresses?'

'No, it's just me.'

15

Long before the hired car stopped outside, Dao was ready and waiting. She sat in the living room mentally checking her plan and going back over every eventuality, and how she would deal with it. At eight thirty she closed the front door behind her and armed the entire security system apart from the walled courtyard at the back, where Scruff was spending the evening. She was dressed in dark grey jeans, a black sweatshirt with pockets and black trainers. Her cell phone, keys and the alarm remote were in her pockets; she carried nothing.

The middle-aged driver looked surprised to find that his only passenger was a girl in casual clothes who looked like a teenager. He held the door to the back seat open for her, but she shook her head. 'Can I sit in the front, please?'

'Of course.'

I'm not what he expected, she thought, he probably he thinks I'm a lot younger than I am, like everyone does. I'll bring my story up casually, so he doesn't worry. I'm glad he's fit and useful looking.

'Where would you like to go first?'

'We are going to Tamaki. I'll tell you the way once we go

off the motorway. There's a place I promised my husband I would look at – and I don't drive.

It was the first time she had said 'my husband' and it felt funny, as if she was playing a role, but she had seen the slightly worried sideways glances he cast at her; she hoped that telling him she was married would make him look at her as older and more responsible.

'You won't see much in the dark,' was all he said. They drove over the Harbour bridge, through the city and out the other side without talking. Dao waited for the driver to start a conversation, but he said nothing. Perhaps it's limo driver etiquette, she thought, don't speak unless you're spoken to.

'When we get there, I am going to tell you where to park, and then I will walk around the corner, have a look at the place I'm interested in and then come back to the car.' She tried to sound as if this would be a perfectly normal thing do to, on her own and after dark on a Saturday night. The driver turned his head and their eyes met; he gave her a long hard look before he faced forward again.

Once the car had stopped and the engine was turned off, Dao swivelled on the seat to face him. 'What's your name?'

'Richard.'

'My name is Susan, as they might have told you. I'm going to tell you which building I want to look at, but I don't want you to either drive around there or walk to it. If I don't come back an hour from now, please call the police and tell them I am at the supposedly empty building that has Specialist Welding on the front.'

He hesitated before he spoke, never taking his eyes off her in the dim light. 'What are you going to do? This sounds very dicey – I'm not sure I should let you do this. Is it anything to do with drugs?'

'Of course not!' said Dao, outraged at the question. 'I would never have anything to do with drugs! I can't tell you the details, but I have to go and have a look. I might be back in ten minutes.'

'And you are really married? Why isn't your husband with you?'

She could see that in his mind things were stacking up against her; casual clothes, enough money to hire a limo, husband not by her side, doing something potentially dangerous – and he might end up being held responsible.

'Oh, please don't worry!' she said. 'Nothing will happen to me. My husband is away, and this has to be done now, it's very urgent. If I came in the daytime there might be a real estate agent or a property manager there with a client, and then it wouldn't work. I don't drive, so I can't get here on my own. Please don't try to stop me!'

He thought for a long moment, keeping his eyes on her face and finally he said, 'OK, but tell me how old you are, you look awfully young to be married.' Clearly the time for professional distance was long gone.

'I'm twenty-three,' she said and smiled at his open disbelief. 'Yes, I know – everyone thinks I'm fifteen or something. I'm a mathematician.'

Hopefully that last bit of information would add extra respectability to the situation. Surely, he wouldn't expect a mathematician to sneak around in the dark committing crimes.

'I've got two daughters a bit younger than you and I'd really hate for them to be doing this sort of thing.' He thought for another moment and added decisively. 'I'll come with you.'

'No, you can't! Absolutely not! Think of your job – I might get caught on a security camera and an alarm might go off – if I'm on my own I can cope with the fall-out, but for you it might be far worse, you could lose your job.'

She opened the door before he thought to ask what might happen that would make it necessary for him to call the police and walked quickly towards the corner a hundred meters ahead; there were no footsteps behind her. She got her phone out, turned the sound off and tucked it back in her pocket.

Once around the corner she crossed to be on the same side as the building she was interested in and slowed, her feet in trainers made no noise. The spring night was cool and still and there was no sound of traffic or voices.

Walking at an even pace close to the inner edge of the sidewalk she turned her head to study each property that she passed. There it was, three away from her goal; the place she had seen on Google Earth, with a drive down the side to an unfenced yard at the back. There were no cars outside, and all the windows were dark; she walked quickly down the side of the building and was out of sight from the street in a few seconds. At the back three trucks were parked in a tidy line, noses pointing out. Where the concrete yard ended was a simple barrier made of fenceposts with a metal pipe across the top.

She slipped under it and now she was in the narrow strip of vegetation between the buildings and the mangrove swamp, and it was as if the very air had changed. It's like stepping into a different reality, she thought and paused for a moment to look around and listen to the little night noises among the mangroves. One footstep from big buildings and trucks and smooth concrete, and now I'm surrounded by the smell of salt and mud, and in front of me is a swamp teeming with life I can't see. That smell probably means the tide is out and the mud is exposed. I like this place.

A very faint hum came from further along, carried on the still evening air. Like most of the other sites the back of the welding place was fenced with chain-link, not as tall as at the front, but too high for her to step over. She put her foot into a square of mesh, took hold of a fence post and climbed over. She was here; this was the place that had such a hold on her mind, that she had been unable to ignore it. She remained where she was, made sure there was no sound of anyone nearby and studied the building. Furthest away from her at the right-hand corner was a regular sized window and next to it a door, followed by another window the same size. The flat, she thought, and someone is home, the light is on in both windows and that noise I heard is an air conditioning unit - there it is on the wall above the first window. Between the flat and the left-hand corner long windows set higher showed muted light.

Silently she walked across the concrete yard to the left corner of the building, then along the wall under the high windows, around a rubbish bin and right up to the first window in the flat. She stopped there, back to the wall, and listened again before she moved her face very slowly past the window frame; a small living room cum kitchen with the barest minimum of furniture, a table with two chairs just inside the window, nobody in sight. To the right a door stood half open to a darker space. She ducked down, tiptoed past the door to the second window and repeated the cautious manoeuvre: an untidy bedroom with two single beds, a couple of bags and an open suitcase on the floor, clothes in untidy heaps. The room was empty. She retreated to the far corner to consider what to do next.

I need to work this out, she thought, I'll be able to slip around to the side of the building, if someone comes out. If someone comes down the drive at the other side, I'll run for the back fence and try to get over as fast as I can - I mustn't get trapped where I might only have the front yard to run to. I've got to get a look into those higher windows – that must be the actual factory space and there is a light on. That rubbish bin looks too wobbly to stand on and if it falls over it will make a noise. I know! My phone, maybe I'll be able to see something if I turn on the camera – those windows are above my height, but I can probably just reach them.

She got her phone out, shielded the screen with her arm to avoid showing light, and turned the camera on; now the screen only showed the dark environment she was in. Holding the phone in landscape mode she reached up to the first high window, slid the phone up to the glass and rested it on the metal frame at the bottom of the window. But now that it was flat against the window, she couldn't stand far enough back to see what the camera saw while she held the phone in place. She let her hand drop; apart from taking photos through the glass she could think of nothing useful. She set the camera to 'no flash' and reached up again.

Holding the phone close to her body she studied the first slightly blurry picture: a wall close to the window with the unmistakable logo of a shipping company filled the screen. There was a container in there with its short end against the left wall. She moved forward and reached up again, angled the phone out from the glass, so the image would show the space inside at a forty-five-degree angle; this time the picture was less clear but showed the corner of the container and an empty space beyond. In the furthest corner closest to the street sat a light-coloured van, behind it was the large roll-up door she had seen from the street that afternoon.

I want more pictures, she thought, but each one will increase the odds against me. It only needs someone inside to glance at the window and catch the movement of my hand with the phone, and I'll be in trouble, but I must do it, she told herself, I must! This might be my only chance to see the place with the light on.

Four times she reached up and held the phone in place against one window after another, pressed the button without looking at the pictures after each shot. The urge to be quick, to get out of there as fast as possible took hold of her and made it hard to breathe. Someone inside dropped something that made a metallic clang against the concrete floor and panic surged through her. Running on silent trainer soles she reached the fence and was only just over it, when the door to the flat opened, spilling a path of light across the yard.

Dao flung herself flat in the tall grass alongside the fence, face turned towards the mangroves, and lay perfectly still with her heart thudding. A moment later the door closed again, but fear held her rigid; the slightest movement could reveal where she was. Minutes passed before she slowly turned her head and scanned what she could see of the yard before she sat up. There was nobody there, but outside the closed door to the flat a small white bundle lay on the ground. She got to her feet and by looking just to the side of it she could make it out. Rubbish, she thought, he just tossed a bag out, instead of putting it in the bin.

She was nearly back to the site where she would slip under the barrier to go back to the street, when she had an idea: that bag might contain evidence of some kind. The thought of going back made her skin crawl with fear. To go back and risk being discovered seemed like an impossible task; far harder than it had been the first time around. She stood indecisive for only a moment; this was an opportunity to gain some solid evidence and if she hesitated too long her courage would fail. Seeing the container and the van inside proved that her theory was right, that this was where the men from flat 403 had gone when they left with Mariko. She turned and retraced her steps, tense and frightened, ready to flee at the first sign of danger.

16

When she got back to the car, Richard was standing beside it with his phone in his hand looking towards the corner. 'Thank God!' he said and got back into the car. Dao climbed into the back seat and put the rubbish bag on the floor, and he started the engine and moved off before she even had her seatbelt on.

'Thirty-seven minutes – I've been getting more nervous every second since you left.'

'Sorry, but I had to wait quite a while to make sure there was nobody there and walking along the edge of the mangroves in the dark was tricky, I had to be careful.'

'Mangroves? How far did you go?'

Dao got her phone out and opened the photo gallery while she replied. 'Oh, they're just behind all those buildings, there's a tidal swamp there and it's full of mangroves. I had to get to the building from behind because it's got a big fence and a gate in front. Can you please stop somewhere for a few minutes?'

He parked in a residential street ten minutes away, turned the interior light on and swung around. 'Are you all right?'

She managed a smile. 'I'm fine. I just want to check some photos I took.'

She studied them one by one, silent and concentrated. She needed more photos; she must go there again, even if it made her cringe with apprehension. The two last pictures were more promising than the others; a right-angle kitchen unit like a breakfast counter, was set against the far wall in front of the van. Two men sat on stools with their arms on the counter. On the far left of the image was the front end of the container she had seen first and beyond it another one, in the same position, its end up against the wall, and further back a long table with computer screens and some equipment that she could not identify.

'Can we please stay here for a while? I have to think.'

I must work out what I should do now: go back again or call the police? Would they raid a building on my evidence? If I call them and say 'there are a couple of guys inside a building that is supposed to be empty, and a van similar to the one we saw on the video from the apartment block' – would they come and have a look? Can they go and knock on the door and ask to see inside, just because someone says something strange might be going on there? If they came and then went away those men might kill Mariko right away – I'm sure she is in there. And if they need to get a warrant or something it would take time. And naturally they would call Bakker as the person in charge of the investigation, and she would probably arrest me too. And then what? If I tell Benson, he will be obliged to tell Bakker - no way can I let him help me do something illegal or dangerous. I can't tell Charlie – she would definitely help me, but I can't let her - if we get caught, she's in trouble with the law and then they might take her pilot's licence away.

The more she thought about it, the more obvious it became that she must go back alone, but first she must study the photos properly. I was right about the factory, she thought. Those two men, the containers inside, and the cables on the floor – I know I'm right. I can't go back tonight, I must have time to think, make sure I'm prepared for real trouble. And I must leave some sort of record of what I have seen and done, and what I plan to do – just in case the worst happens.

And then she finally felt that she had made a logical decision and said, 'Could you drive me again tomorrow night? Just the same as tonight, come and pick me up at the same time and take me back here?'

Without turning around to look at her, Richard said, 'Would you please come and sit in the front – we need to have a serious talk. Yes, I can drive you again tomorrow night, but I'll only do it if you explain what this is about. It smells dangerous to me, and I can't be party to letting you get into some terrible trouble – not unless I know what it is. What if something happened to you and nobody knew what you were up to? What would I do then?'

Dao stayed where she was for a moment, assessing the risk of telling him, the possibility that he would drive her home and refuse to pick her up tomorrow. The thought of hiring a car from a different company and having a different driver would add another layer of stress to the situation.

'OK, I will.'

She sat sideways in the front seat and began telling him an edited version of the background, but it didn't hang together; the things she left out meant that he continually side-tracked her by asking for explanations and the story got disjointed.

After a frustrating few minutes she gave up. 'I could play you a recording I have on my phone, it's from a meeting Hunter and I had with his lawyer. It's quite long, but it covers absolutely everything - if you listen to it, you'll understand the whole thing.'

'You told your lawyer? So, you're not doing something

illegal then? I thought you must be, to go to these lengths. And where is that husband of yours? What's the man thinking of, letting a little thing like you do this on your own?'

'He's been arrested - he's in a police cell until Monday. And please don't get worried about that, he's not a criminal! The recording explains everything, including why he got arrested. Just listen to it, and then you can decide if you're going to drive me tomorrow night. But you must promise not to tell *anyone* what you hear – you just can't! Not until this is over, it's very important!'

Thinking what a blessing it was to have the recording on her phone, she set it running for the third time, put the phone on the armrest between the front seats and returned to the back seat. With her trainers off she stretched out on the seat and was asleep within minutes and slept until Richard woke her up and handed her the phone.

'The battery is nearly flat, but I got to the end. I know who you are now - you must be the girl who was the witness in that big drug trial last year – the one this guy Hunter found in the bush in Northland. And your name isn't Susan, is it? And are you really married to Hunter whatever-his-name-is?'

Dao sat up and yawned. 'Oh, I am - we got married a couple of months ago. His name is Hunter Grant and Susan *is* my real name, but my mother always called me Dao, and Hunter does too. You can call me Dao if you like – perhaps you'd better now that you've heard the story. It's kind of like you're in on this now. Are you?'

He frowned. 'I might be. I surely know more than I should – I feel like I'm being dragged into something half illegal and totally dangerous.'

'But do you understand why I have to make sure I've got some real evidence, so I can get the police to go to that place?'

She sat up straighter and leaning forward between the front seats, she went through the list of all the reasons why she must go back before she told the police, so she could convince them to act. He kept asking questions and wanting her to explain the assumptions she had made about why the police would be slow to act or refuse to act, but in the end, he seemed to accept her logic.

'I think you're probably right,' he said reluctantly. 'They wouldn't go charging in just on your say-so. But getting enough evidence to convince them – I don't know how the heck you're going to do that. And what if there isn't anyone there apart from those two guys you saw tonight?'

'But what if Mariko *is* in one of those containers?' she asked him, urgent and intense. 'And maybe Grace wasn't in that box, maybe she's still alive too? How *could* I stop now? I just can't! I have to do this - I can't have it on my conscience that I did nothing.'

And then it struck her how unfair she was being and how much she was taking for granted; she was bullying and coercing this poor man to help her, when he probably just wanted to go home and go to bed.

'Oh no, please forget I said that! I'm sorry, I got carried away – it isn't fair to try to involve you. Of course, you don't have to do anything – this isn't your problem at all. Just take me home and forget all this.'

'And then what would you do?' He glared suspiciously at her over the back of his seat. 'Hire another car and another driver and go off again? Short of taking you home with me and locking you in our spare room, I can't stop you. If you are determined to go on with this, it might as well be me driving you rather than someone who doesn't know what you're up to - and who couldn't care less.'

17

Dao locked the door behind her, let Scruff in from the courtyard and lifted the intriguing plastic bag high in the air with one hand to keep it away from his inquisitive nose. She gave him an absent-minded pat as they went up the stairs together. Her head was full of conjecture and questions; she must make a completely new plan.

She set the ground-floor alarm and turned lights on, pulled the curtains over the glass wall and gave Scruff a snack in the kitchen. As she walked back and forth, her brain continued to come up with ideas, discarding some and filing others away. But before doing anything else she wanted to investigate the rubbish bag. She put on rubber gloves and started picking things out of the bag one by one. Halfway through she had only found perfectly ordinary pieces of household rubbish that went straight into the kitchen rubbish bin, but under a flattened cereal box lay a piece of clear moulded plastic, the first thing she could not immediately identify. She lifted it out by one corner and looked at it – the depression was cylinder-shaped and there was something printed on it in white. She turned on the rangehood light and held it up and could still not read it, but by holding a black potholder behind it the print stood out clearly: Gamma-hydroxybutyric acid. She put the piece of plastic in a zip-lock bag and continued checking the rubbish bag but found nothing else of interest. She stripped off the gloves and jotted down the words from the plastic mould on the kitchen shopping pad, while she still remembered.

With a mug of coffee and a bowl of ice cream beside her and Scruff asleep under the table Dao turned on her laptop and entered "Gamma-hydroxybutyric acid" in the search engine. The article she found described it as "also known as GHB, gamma-hydroxybutyric acid is a hypnotic depressant which can be swallowed or injected. It is sometimes referred to as a date-rape drug" and listed effects ranging from euphoria, disinhibition and increased libido to the most extreme effect: death. Of course, she knew she had heard that name. She sat for a moment considering the implications of this and nodded to herself; it made perfect sense in the context of flat 403 and what probably went on in the factory.

Next, she downloaded the photos from her phone, and though the images were easier to see on the bigger screen they were still not very sharp; in the second photo she could only just make out the van's number plate. Photos three and four showed that the doors on the container closest to the window were closed, but the other had a door half open. Cords snaked from the containers and connected to a multi-plug board under the table, and a thicker cord from there to a power socket on the wall.

Those containers are wired for lights, she said to herself, but why so many cables? Her mind conjured up images of what might be going on inside the containers; rape and brutality being filmed, maybe torture. And that other thing under the table – I still can't see it clearly enough. Maybe it's a piece of clothing?

She tried all the tricks she knew, one at a time; studied each resulting change, decided it hadn't worked well enough, undid the change and started over. If she made the images too bright, they lost definition, but by increasing the brightness by only a couple of percent and using the sharpening function, she got a crisper but not perfect image. The bundle under the table could be a large floppy bag in a crumpled heap. She enlarged the image and thought the dark streak disappearing in a curve behind it might be a shoulder strap. Mariko had carried a big bag with a pattern of large flowers in those last images of her entering the foyer and going up in the lift several weeks ago. The bag under the table was in shadow and looked blotchy, but it might be patterned.

Deep in thought Dao ate her melting ice cream, occasionally making a note on her pad. She studied the final two photos intently, enlarged them and scrutinised every detail. The two men at the improvised bar sat half turned towards each other. One was half facing her, but she doubted that she would recognise him in real life; his face was in shadow, and the blown-up image was grainy. The man with his back towards the camera was wearing a jacket of the same style as the one worn by the man who had brought the handcart up in the lift, but she couldn't see the sleeve where there might be a logo to match the one from the video. A broom and a mop leaned against the wall; beside them sat two buckets and a big white container. There were bottles, a couple of glasses, a bag of potato chips and a large pizza box on the bar counter and further back, beside the van, a wheelie-bin.

Dao saved the originals and the enhanced images in a folder on her hard drive, and after a moment's thought she copied them to a USB stick. Last of all she emailed the enhanced photos to herself, so they would also be accessible on her phone. Reading through her scribbled notes on the pad she pushed the bowl to one side, picked up the pen and made an exclamation mark beside "send txt to Benson and K&C and Simon". She would use the excuse of a sore throat and little sleep to keep visitors away. She didn't like telling lies, but on this occasion she must; she would never be able to lie convincingly to any of them face-to-face or even over the phone.

She was keenly aware that Hunter would be very upset if he knew what she had done tonight and if he could have foreseen it, he would have made her promise not to do it. And not only would the risks she had taken appal him, but now she was planning to do it again. She sighed and looked down the long room at his empty chair; thankful that he would only find out afterwards and not sit in a cell worrying about her.

To exercise her own judgement and make decisions about dangerous things and not ask anyone to stand by to help her; it was exciting and frightening at the same time. Since she escaped from captivity on the island, she had always had Hunter right beside her, or very nearly all the time. She missed him and wished she could discuss things with him, but she also felt empowered by the knowledge that she was capable of taking calculated risks, however terrified she was at what she was about to do.

She knew the Glock pistol Charlie had lent to Hunter would be either under the front seat of the car or in his bedside drawer, she would get it and work out how to use it. She wrote brief notes about things she must remember to tell people afterwards, the police, Simon and possibly a judge. She would list the reasons for doing this, why she thought the police would not act just on her word, and why she felt compelled to take action herself. She quailed at the thought of ending up on what she thought of as the bad side in a court case, but that was for later. The possibility that someone's life might depend on her outweighed other considerations.

Finally, she jotted down one last instruction to herself: to print out the document for Hunter when she had written it and to put the plastic bag with the GHB mould with it. She would list everything: what she had done tonight, what she was planning to do and the reasons that motivated her. Just in case, she thought, so he doesn't have to wonder - if I don't come back.

At quarter past two in the morning she went to bed, exhausted and full of apprehension, hoping she had thought of everything. She set the alarm and lay down on Hunter's side of the bed with Scruff beside her, feeling very lonely.

In the clear light of morning things seemed very different. Dao lay with her arm over Scruff and looked up at the blue sky through the skylight above the bed, thinking back over her frantic activity in the night and what she had thought she must do. Now, it seemed mad; the plans she had made in the night were a serious over-reaction. Of course, she had enough material to present to Bakker, no way could she refuse to believe what Dao said, when she saw the photos and heard that the factory belonged to White Investments.

I got carried away, she thought as she went downstairs. I didn't think I could just hand it over to the police, particularly to that woman, who doesn't want to listen to anything we say, but those photos prove I'm right beyond any doubt – it will over-ride her dislike of Hunter. The van and that bag, the containers and all that cabling would convince her. I can email the photos - of course she will believe me and do something straight away. Should I call 111 or the number for non-urgent calls?

Having made the decision, she felt light-hearted and relieved. She dialled 111 and in ten minutes it was over. The call-centre operator had listened patiently, asked questions and promised to forward her 'enquiry' to Bakker's staff. 'Someone will call you back,' he said. 'It might take a little while.'

She made coffee and fed Scruff and had a mock wrestling match with him to make him happy, but half an hour later nobody had called back. Don't get impatient, she told herself, they have to discuss it, maybe Bakker is at church, and they would have to talk to her first. There could be any number of explanations, but it was hard to wait, when her head was full of what she needed to say to them; the details, the various elements of proof she had, and how she had found out. She knew without a doubt that she must sound helpful and not let the smallest hint of criticism creep in, or she would antagonise Bakker, and this was not about scoring points.

An hour and twenty minutes later the call finally came. 'Is that Susan? OK, you called 111 a while ago. It's Sergeant Apatu here, we met yesterday morning. I need to ask you a few questions - I've spoken to Inspector Bakker, and she would like some more information.'

When she had answered his questions, she said she would send them the pictures, she mentioned the bag and the plastic mould and that the number plate on the van was legible.

'Thank you, that's great - I'll tell Inspector Bakker all that you have told me,' said Apatu, 'and then I'll call you back.'

'You will do something today, won't you?'

'I'll discuss everything you have told me with Inspector Bakker', as all he would say.

Another hour went by and when he called, she knew from the sound of his voice that nothing would happen immediately.

'Inspector Bakker asked me to thank you for the information. We'll have a look at the photos and discuss what you have told us. She will be in touch tomorrow morning.'

'Aren't you going to do anything *now*?' Dao was outraged; she knew her voice held a note of impatience, but she couldn't stop herself. 'Isn't somebody at least going to go and have a look – straight away?'

'Your information will be discussed at tomorrow morning's case review meeting at half past seven and we'll set out a course of action.' He sounded calm and collected, and she wondered if that was just his training, or if he really didn't understand the urgency.

'But the van!' she exclaimed, provoked to anger. 'And that bag, it looks like Mariko's bag - you must look at the photos. You've got to raid the place, now, before it's too late!'

She ended the call with a feeling of disbelief. When she woke up, she had been so certain that once she told them how all the details connected into a coherent and indisputable whole, they would act immediately. Now his response threw her into a state of self-doubt.

Am I being too naïve, she thought, as she sat dejected with her phone still clasped limply in her hand, or am I simply giving too much importance to things that could be explained as circumstance and coincidence? Or is it due to the stubborn antipathy of that horrible woman? And now I'm back to where I was last night, with that frantic feeling that I need to do something before it's too late - which I had decided was me over-reacting, because I had been so scared, and I was so tired, and Hunter wasn't here. She sent text messages to Simon, Benson and Charlie, saying that she had a sore throat and a bad headache, and she was going to turn her phone off and try to get some sleep. She curled up in Hunter's armchair, as if the chair itself could give her the feeling of protection and comfort he wasn't there to provide. Scruff sensed the turmoil in her mind and lay next to the chair, looking up at her every time she moved.

After an hour something in her head changed, like someone had flicked a switch and her naturally structured mind slid back into place, and she got up. 'OK, Scruff,' she said, 'we're probably on our own – nobody else seems to be in a hurry to do anything, and what if it's too late when they finally do something? How would they feel then – and more importantly, how would I feel then? Let's go for it and carry on with the plan, and if I get there and the cops *have* already raided the factory, then I'll just ask Richard to turn around and drive me home.'

While she had been sitting in Hunter's chair her phone had signalled incoming messages, and now she checked them. Charlie said to look after herself and offered to find someone to give her a lift to town the next day for Hunter's court appearance, and Simon said he would call as soon as he knew what time Hunter would come up in court.

She had missed a call from the limo hire company and quaking at the thought that Richard had told his boss what she had told him the previous night, she called them immediately. While she waited for them to answer, she constructed what she felt was a rational explanation for the events of the previous evening. She would explain it to them and say she had been overwrought, then she would cancel the booking and ask them to charge her credit card what she owed them. And then she would order a car from another company or a taxi. But reality was far less dramatic than what her imagination had constructed.

'Good morning Ms Grant,' said the nameless voice she had talked to yesterday, when she made the original booking. 'I'm calling about the booking you made with your driver last night. Is it correct that you would like him to drive you tonight again?'

'Yes, please. Can he do it?'

'It was supposed to be his day off, but he says he would like to drive you, so that's fine. And you want to be picked up at half past eight again?'

'Yes, please.'

18

Now that everything had once again become urgent and personal, time was precious. Dao ran down to get the Glock from under the driver's seat in the car, only to find that the pocket of her dark hoodie-jacket was too shallow for the pistol.

'I can't have it in the back pocket of my jeans, Scruff. I'll have to climb that fence and who knows, I might have to run really fast, and it would probably fall out. I think I'll carry it the way Hunter does - in the belt holster.'

But the holster didn't work; it hung too low, and it would get in the way. 'I'm too short,' she explained to Scruff. 'It would bump against my bottom all the time and I would never be able to get the gun out fast if I had to and if I have it closer to the front it sticks out past my hip – I haven't got enough body for a holster. We have to think of something else.'

To give herself a break from the frustrations with the pistol, she went to load the washing machine. And there, hanging from the hook on the back of the door, was the solution right in front of her eyes: the little cloth bag that she had been given when she bought the organic cotton T-shirts. She arranged the narrow strap diagonally across her chest, tied a knot to shorten it, put the gun in the bag and walked around, experimenting to get it perfect. She must be able to reach into the it and pull the gun out fast, but it mustn't hang so low that it bounced against her body or caught on things. 'And do you know what, Scruff? It's the perfect size for a pistol bag.'

She was making the bed when the doorbell went, and she ran down to the living area to check the tablet on the dining table. The camera at the front showed a white delivery van by the kerb and a man bending down to put a bunch of flowers on the doorstep. She waited until he had driven off before she picked them up and read the card before she even closed the front door: "Hope you feel better soon! I'll call you in the morning – golf club dinner tonight. Benson."

Oh God, she thought, this is awful – I have lied to Benson, and he sent me flowers! Now I feel terrible - I hope he'll forgive me when I tell him why I did it. Unless I end up in jail, and then he'll be so disappointed in me. And what if Charlie comes over, even though I told her not to? I'd better put my stuff for tonight upstairs, so she doesn't see it, if she comes.

She put the bag with the Glock and the magazine on the bed, threw her jacket over them and plugged in her phone to charge.

By mid-afternoon, Scruff had come in from the courtyard and was sleeping in the sun by the glass wall. Dao sat cross-legged in Hunter's armchair with a glass of juice and a sandwich on the table and the laptop on her knees, watching a YouTube video about safely handling Glock pistols. She remembered Hunter saying that he would never have the magazine in the pistol unless there was immediate danger, and she wanted to know that she remembered why.

"The moment the magazine is inserted, the first round is fed into the chamber and when you pull the trigger the gun fires. So, don't be careless!" said the serious American, speaking very fast. "The double trigger, or the trigger within the trigger as some call it, is not like a safety switch or safety button on other guns. If you pull the trigger far enough with a round in the chamber, this gun will fire."

I'll have the magazine in my jeans pocket and the gun in the bag, she thought, even if it means I can't use it instantly, but I don't feel confident enough to carry the gun loaded. What if I have to grab the gun fast and get hold of it the wrong way and shoot myself in the leg or something? I'll have to practice, figure out which hand should hold the gun and which hand I'll use to push the magazine in. It's got to be fast, and easy to do even in the dark. Once I've worked that out, I'll know which pocket to put the magazine in and which way to slant the strap.

She got the pistol and the magazine from the bedroom, emptied the magazine the way the video showed her, and took the round in the chamber out; now she could safely practise pushing the empty magazine in until she could do it blindfolded. Scruff woke up and wanted to take part in what looked like a game, and Dao laughed for the first time since Friday. 'Stop it, Scruff! This is serious – leave me alone or I'll drop something.

Twenty minutes later she could simultaneously pull out the gun and the magazine and push the magazine in without looking.

'I won't bother to practise aiming and using the sight,' she told Scruff. 'It's not as if I'm not going to try to hit anyone, I just want to be able to scare them – and perhaps fire if I have to, but I won't have time to aim. It's just to show them I'm serious and I'll try *not* to hit anyone.'

She picked up the gun and held it in both hands with her arms straight and tried to imagine firing it. How strong will the recoil be? When Charlie talked to Benson about the Glock, she said she chose this model because it's small and has a short recoil. That probably means it doesn't kick back very hard, but I have no basis for comparison. I'll just try to brace myself before I pull the trigger, so I don't drop it.

She took the magazine out, checked the chamber was still empty, loaded the ammunition back in the magazine and took everything upstairs again.

By late afternoon time was dragging. Dao wandered restlessly around the house and Scruff got bored following her and went to sleep under the table. She was apprehensive and impatient and tried to distract herself. If she had time to get too nervous, she might make bad decisions if things got dangerous.

Hunter's phone! The idea popped into her head, while she emptied the drier. She would give Hunter's phone to Richard while she was away from the car. It would mean he had her number and Charlie's and Benson's. She threw the bundle of dry washing on the dining table and ran upstairs to make sure the phone was charged.

Eating proper food was out of the question, so she ate half a block of chocolate she found in the fridge and some cashew nuts. When she had fed Scruff and put him out in the courtyard with a full water bowl, he went straight into his kennel and standing in the doorway she heard him moving around, arranging his blanket and towels the way he wanted them. It was such an ordinary and familiar sound, but it failed to comfort her. Behind every thought hovered the dark reality of how dangerous her plan was, and how easily she could find herself in a situation that she could neither control nor escape from.

Trying to have a nap was an exercise in frustration, as she mentally went through her preparations over and over, and relaxing was impossible. During the course of the day, her plan had expanded and piece by piece it got more complex and more detailed. Repeatedly working through it had identified additional elements of risk and forced her to consider what her options might be, what she could say or do if they discovered her, but there were no realistic options to explain why she was on that site.

She moved her supplies downstairs to the little table beside the front door and covered them with her jacket, still unable to banish the thought that Charlie might turn up. She was sitting on the stairs waiting, hoping time would pass quickly, when she suddenly remembered the note for Hunter.

'Oh no!' she said out loud and raced up to the living room. 'I must add a couple of things and print it – I will leave it on the table, so he'll see it when he gets home.'

She opened the document and read through the bullet point summary of her actions and findings from the previous night, which she had already sent to Bakker, added that the photos were on the USB stick and as an afterthought the name of the car hire company and the driver. Quickly, again in bullet point form, she listed the measures she was taking to keep safe, including the fact that she had Charlie's Glock pistol with her and had checked a YouTube video about how to use it. With minutes to spare she printed a copy, put it on the table with the USB stick and the zip-lock bag on top and turned her laptop off.

19

Dao got in as soon as the car stopped outside. 'Hi, Richard!' she said quickly. 'Please don't drive away yet. I want to talk to you first and I still have some stuff inside I want to bring.'

Richard's expression was one of resignation mixed with suspicion. 'Yes?'

'I want to swap cars – leave this one here and take our car. For you to drive, of course, as I can't. Is that OK with you?'

He was shaking his head, as if he couldn't believe what he was hearing. 'Take your car? Why?'

'In case it gets damaged – Hunter won't mind, but it would be awful if this lovely black car got smashed, and you would get into trouble.'

'Damaged? Why would it get damaged? I'm not getting into a car chase, or anything like it, whatever you say. I'll drive you there, wait for you and drive you back, but we're not having any so-called action – not while I'm on the job, we're not. And I've got some conditions.'

This was one of the contingencies she had planned for, the reason she had left her things inside. She had known how unlikely it was, that Richard would agree to what she asked, and then she would use plan B instead.

'I want a car parked across the gates at the place I'm going to – so nobody can drive out. They might try to ram that car, so I thought we'd take ours.'

'Now, listen to me, young lady!' said Richard. 'Whatever it is you're planning to do tonight sounds very dangerous to me. You said you wanted to find out if those women were there – I've been thinking about that. As far as I can see, you could only find that out if you went into the place – which would surely be the most dangerous thing you could do. If those guys are killers, they wouldn't hesitate to kill you too. I think we should sit here and talk through it and find some other solution. That's what I meant earlier when I said I had some conditions, I must know what you plan to do, and if it seems mad, I might say no. I think we should just call the cops right now and let them handle it. I know you have a lot of reasons why you think they wouldn't act fast, but we should at least try to convince them.'

Dao felt her stomach contract into a knot. She would have to do it without him, and she hadn't realised how much she had banked on him being there, waiting in the car, ready to take her and possibly someone else away. She steeled herself not to show her feelings, tried to make her voice even and calm.

'When I talked to that guy about the booking this morning, I said I wanted the car for the entire night, and I will pay for the whole night. But you can go back – even if you don't drive me anywhere, you'll still be paid.'

She opened the door, but before she put a foot on the ground Richard took hold of her arm. 'Not so fast! Look at me and tell me what you are going to do, if I don't take you – would you try to drive yourself or call a taxi or what?'

She swivelled around and met his eyes. 'Listen, Richard,' she said seriously. 'I know you are worried about what I'm up to, and that's very kind of you, but I am twenty-three years old and I make my own decisions about my safety. What I do, if you won't take me, is beside the point. I've thought of all possible ways of getting someone to do something fast, and I'm getting nowhere. I called the police this morning and I told them my conclusions and the links that led me there. I told them what I saw in the photos I took last night, and I emailed them. And that awful Bakker woman, who arrested Hunter because she hates him – she sent a message saying they will discuss it at a planning meeting first thing tomorrow morning. There is a tiny chance that they will do something today - and if they have, then I'll turn around and go straight home again. But I'm worried that Bakker will let her dislike of Hunter kind of corrupt her belief in the evidence I gave her – she will not consider it important because of where it came from, I'm sure of it.'

Richard was listening and she could tell he was really considering what she had told him, but what was he thinking?

'When we met with her, she showed such contempt for everything we had done – she wouldn't even admit that we had told them things they hadn't discovered yet. I need to find out if Mariko is alive, but I might be too late – and Grace too, of course, but I think they probably already killed her. Thank you for helping me last night, it was really good of you.'

She got quickly out of the car and headed for the front door, her focus now on calling a taxi and implementing plan B.

'Come back, Dao! I'll take you – get back in the car.' He was standing by the open driver's door, reluctant and grumpy, but he had made up his mind.

She smiled, grateful and relieved. 'Thank you! I know you don't really want to, but I feel much better going with you than with a taxi driver. I'll just get my stuff.'

As they drove away Dao debated how much she should tell him. I can't mention the Glock, she thought as they approached the motorway, but maybe it would be useful that he understands the additional evidence from the photos. At least he'll see that there's solid evidence that those men are the ones from the apartment - but on the other hand it might just make him less inclined to let me go on my own, and I can't let him come with me - it's not his problem and I don't want him on my conscience if it goes wrong. And two people are probably more likely to be discovered than one. But I will give him Hunter's phone when we stop - that will make him feel better. The poor man, he doesn't want to be part of this, he's just driving me because he's worried something will happen to me.

'We could park closer this time,' she said after a few minutes, 'so you can see the place I'm going to. There's a little parking area in front of the building across the street, and if you reverse in, you can look straight ahead at the welding place, so you'll know exactly where I am.'

'Cold comfort!' said Richard. 'Are you going to tell me what you are planning to do, if you can get in?'

'I can't – I don't even know myself. I'll use my phone to check through the windows and see who's there – well, I can see directly into the flat, so I'll check that first. It all depends. If I see that Mariko is alive, I'll call 111 and say I've found her and then come back and wait in the car with you.'

'OK, that doesn't sound too bad. And if you can't see Mariko – or worse, if you see her and she's dead?'

'If she is dead, I will do the same thing, come back to the car – I promise.'

She cast a quick glance at him and thought he looked slightly more relaxed. 'I've got Hunter's phone with me - I'll give it to you, so you can see where I am. We've both got that app that shows you exactly where the other person's phone is.'

As they approached the place where they had parked the previous night, Richard stopped. 'Are there any windows on the front of the building? If I'm going to reverse into a parking space directly across the road, my lights will sweep across the welding place – I think I'll turn my lights off before we turn the corner.'

'I hadn't thought of that,' said Dao gratefully. 'I can't remember any windows, but there might be. What a give-away that could have been – and someone looking out from the flat at the back might see light shining down the side of the building.'

With the headlights off they drove very slowly around the corner, until Dao said, 'Here! This is where you park, the next place on this side – the welding place is across the road, you can see the sign.'

When he had parked and turned the engine off, she got Hunter's phone out of the bag. 'I'll hold it down here, so the light isn't so obvious.' They bent forward to look at the phone in the shelter of the dashboard.

'The PIN to unlock the phone is 9241 – perhaps you should write it down. See this icon here on the first screen that comes up? That's the app that shows you where my phone is. I'll open it, so you can see what it looks like – see the blue dot? And then there's just ordinary stuff, Google Chrome and his Contacts folder and so on.'

She flicked the Contacts folder open. 'This name, Benson – that's a very good friend of ours, a police officer. And Charlie - just bit further down, that's Hunter's best mate from the army. They served in Afghanistan together – she's a helicopter pilot.'

She didn't say that Richard should call those people, if things went wrong, but she was sure he understood why she had pointed them out. He fished a pen out of the door pocket, wrote the PIN on the back of his left hand and took the phone. Dao was reaching for the door handle, when he said, 'Stop - wait! The interior light will come on. OK, it's safe now.'

She reached over and touched his hand. 'Thank you – I can't tell you how good it feels to have you waiting here!'

20

Dao walked away from the car and crossed the street to the building with the drive down the side, certain that Richard was watching her. The knowledge that if the worst happened, someone knew where she was, provided no comfort. She was well aware that by the time Richard decided she had been gone too long and called the police or came looking for her, it would be too late. At least the location app will prove where I was, she thought, and then Hunter can do a screenshot and have that little dot on the map forever, the dot that was me.

She ducked under the barrier and stood for a moment letting her eyes adapt to the environment; it was darker tonight and the halfmoon was concealed by light clouds. Somewhere out over the water a bird called twice, a lonely cry in the darkness. She walked slowly through the tall grass along the edge of the mangrove swamp, placing her feet carefully. A corridor of scents, she thought, I would recognise this place blindfolded by its smell of mangroves and salt and mud.

Before climbing over the fence, she paused and studied the building carefully. Tonight, the door to the flat was ajar, she could just make it out, but no light spilt from the crack.

The light was on in both rooms, but the only light in the high factory windows was vague and diffuse, not like last night. She climbed over the fence, crept quietly along the wall and stopped before she reached the first window of the flat to listen intently. There was no sound from inside. Cautiously she slid her face across the window frame: the kitchen was empty and the door to the space on the right was closed. She ducked down and ran on silent feet to the far side of the other window, half expecting someone to shout, to have seen her in the gap of the outer door. On this side she heard muffled voices, a conversation between at least two people, one voice much louder than the other. After a few of minutes, the conversation stopped. Either they stopped talking or they went back to the kitchen, she thought, or maybe into the factory. Slowly she moved her head just far enough over the edge of the window to look in. The bedroom was empty and on the beds were two duffel bags and an open suitcase. Beside the suitcase lay a jacket and a wallet.

Her breath caught in her throat. They were getting ready to leave and she might not have a lot of time; now she must find out where they were. She went back to the kitchen window, stopped to consider and hesitated. Looking in seemed like a risk too far. She could not take the chance, not now when she was so close to her goal and time was short. She put her phone against the bottom corner of the glass, took a photo and retreated to the far corner of the building to study it. The men were sitting at the table with an assortment of take-away containers in front of them. The man with his back to the window was reaching for a bottle of beer and the other was spooning rice onto his plate, looking down at his plate. If she had taken the photo a moment later, he might have looked up and seen the movement of the phone against the glass. Fear ran a cold finger down her spine, and she shivered briefly; so close, so very close! This was probably her chance to get into the factory before they left.

The kitchen and the bedroom are separated by a narrow

space, she thought. To go from one room to the other you cross that little passage, and right now the door to the kitchen is closed. I can go past the kitchen door and straight into the factory, provided there isn't a locked door at the end of the passage.

The thought of getting trapped there was terrifying, and for a moment her courage nearly failed; she would never get away with it, they would hear her or go back to the other room for something and see her, she couldn't do it. But the acute feeling of terror was held in check by the thought of what might happen if she did nothing. Would they take Mariko with them, if she was still alive and in one of those containers, or would they leave her there, or kill her before they went? Was time running out, was this the last opportunity to help her? She refused to consider the possibility that Mariko was already dead. Why would they have drugged her and walked her out of the apartment, if they were going to kill her? They had kept her alive all those weeks, while other girls came and went; there had to be a reason.

I must be prepared, she thought, I'll load the pistol before I go in, even though I didn't plan to, but I have to - just in case I need to use it fast. I will put it barrel first into the bag so I can get a grip on it quickly. She retreated to the far corner again, rammed the magazine in and returned the pistol to the bag, then forced her phone in sideways to keep the gun propped up.

Now it was all or nothing, she must act, or the chance would be gone. She walked back to the kitchen window, ducked down to pass under it and slowly pulled the door open, hoping it wouldn't creak. Inside was a narrow passage with the closed door to the kitchen on the left and the open bedroom door on the right spilling light into the passage. At the end of the passage the door to the factory space was wide open. She walked fast and silently through the passage and into the factory space.

To her left stood the two containers with their ends against the wall. Careful not to trip on the cables on the floor she went first to the container furthest away. The only light in the big high space was the ambient light from streetlamps coming in through the windows way up under the roof on the street side of the building and the indirect light from the bedroom into the little passage.

She peered into the open container, but she could make no sense of what she saw. After a moment's hesitation and a quick look over her shoulder, she stepped up and into the container, took a step sideways inside the closed half door and got her phone out. This time she must use the flash, or nothing would show in the photo. She briefly considered turning the phone flashlight on, but decided the risk was too great compared to the split-second flash. She opened the camera, reset it to use flash and took a picture, then stood frozen, listening for any sounds. She poked her head around the door; there was nobody there.

She wanted to look at the picture, but resisted the temptation: not here, not now. What had registered in her brain, when the flash lit the scene, took her completely by surprise. The inside of the container was a luxurious bedroom, fully furnished, shiny satin sheets and diaphanous wall hangings, carpet on the floor and some black things suspended from the walls.

She tiptoed to the other container and hesitated, tried to think of how best to take the next step. The doors were closed, but in her mind's eye she saw, as clearly as in a photo, the container she had come across in the Hunua ranges six months ago. Two doors, one slightly overlapping the other, two vertical rods on each door that rotated to lock into sockets at the top and the bottom when the lever-shaped handles were turned. She studied the container and checked the sockets at the top and bottom of the doors. On the righthand door only one rod was locked into its sockets; all she needed to do was push the big lever up, rotate it to disengage the rod and pull the door open. She had watched Hunter do it that day in the forest, she could picture the muscles in his arm bunching as he rotated the rod and the sound it had made, a rusty, harsh sound of metal grinding against metal. The men would hear it and come running, and the only way out was through the flat. To calm herself she retreated into the narrow space between the containers for a moment. Standing there, right back against the factory wall, she noticed that the containers were not right up against the outer wall; someone small could squeeze in sideways.

She knocked gently on the side of the container – nothing. She knocked again, the same little pattern of seven knocks and then a third time. And there it was, a response from inside – her sequence of knocks sent back to her. Her heart leapt in her chest, she put her mouth against the metal side and said, "Mariko, I'm coming", hoping the metal would transmit the sounds to the girl inside.

Pulling the lever out of its holder was easy and made no sound, but rotating the rod was harder and the harsh scraping sound bounced against her ear drums and made her flinch. Before she had time to pull the door open loud footsteps came charging towards her. She ran down the side of the container and just managed to squeeze in between the container's end and the wall before the first man reached her. He pushed his arm in as far as it would go, but the gap was too narrow for him to lean right in, his shoulder and ribcage could not fit. He shouted something in a foreign language and moments later the second man appeared on the other side, his arm was longer, and his hand just missed her arm. She was trapped between them.

She only thought of it afterwards, but in some strange way her fear diminished after the nervous apprehension she had been feeling up until then. Now she knew where the men were, and she must deal with the situation. Instead of a faceless potential threat, they were here and now, and she knew she had a very short window of opportunity before they devised a way to reach her; the only way was up. She must get up on top of the container – trying to use the pistol now would achieve nothing and there was a possibility that one of them was armed. Her hand slid over the cold surface of the container's steel wall, she moved her shoulder into one of the moulded depressions and twisted her body nearly sideways; with one shoulder at an angle, she just fit. The men were shouting at each other over her head and then one of them disappeared leaving the other like a dark shadow watching her from only a meter away. What has he gone to get, she wondered, a broom to shove me with or a gun?

Time was up and she must try what seemed like a nearly impossible solution, the only chance she had to save herself. She bent one foot half sideways against the wall behind her and used her hands, one flat against the wall and one against the container to raise herself a fraction off the floor, then lightning fast the other foot off the floor and nearly flat against the container. She felt the sole of her trainer grip, pushed hard with both feet and moved one hand up at a time, pressing hard against the sides, then the feet, one at a time. In her head she heard the climbing instructor's voice, 'Always three points of contact and exert tight pressure all the time, it's the only thing that keeps you there'. The man who remained at the container realised what she was doing and shouted again, and seconds later the other man reappeared. Dao was now nearly high enough to grip the top edge with her hands. Her hands and wrists were aching with the effort, but knowing she was nearly there kept her going. Both men tried to reach her, but she was too far up and still in the centre of the width. Getting up on the flat top of the container was awkward; letting go with the hand pressed against the wall and twisting was scary and she was worried about the pistol – the bag caught between her body and the edge of the container roof, desperate she yanked at it, got a leg up on the top and scrambled up.

She stayed where she was, crouching close to the wall,

frightened to stand up and expose more of herself. What next? Did they have a ladder, or would they leap up and grab the edge? She pulled the pistol out and waited, eyes scanning back and forth, heart beating fast. Seconds later something scraped against the concrete floor to the left; a pair of hands appeared on the edge, then a man was levering himself up on his forearms, trying to get one leg up. She rose to her feet, raised the gun with both hands, aimed it above his head and fired. Her hands jerked back, and the crack of the shot reverberated through the factory, bounced off hard surfaces and drove all thought from her mind for a moment. The man was no longer hanging on the edge of the container, and someone was shouting in a language she did not understand. She crept to the edge and looked down. A man lay unmoving on his back with his eyes closed and his arms flung out with an upturned chair beside him. The other man was on his knees beside him, and his was the voice she had heard. Had she actually hit him, even though she aimed so high? Should she try to get down now and run, or would that defeat the advantage she had up here?

She retreated to the centre of the roof and knelt, frightened by the thought that she might have killed the man, acutely aware of the danger both she and Mariko were in now. Her only advantage was the Glock, and she must use it. The men had been taken by surprise, but maybe she could contain them in one place for long enough to get out, and then work out what to do next.

She crept to the edge, knelt with her knees far apart to stabilise herself, and holding the pistol firmly with both hands she fired again. This time she aimed at the concrete floor just beyond the men, between the front ends of the containers and the result was spectacular. The sound of the bullet hitting the floor nearly deafened her, and a spray of concrete shards and dust erupted as it hit. She peered over the edge again. The man on the floor was lying just as before, with one leg bent and his arms flung out; his eyes were still shut. Where was the other one? She leaned out further and looked straight down at the top of his head; he was standing flat against the side of the container. Somewhere close by she heard the little pattern of taps on metal again.

I want to keep him there, she thought, he can't get between the containers and the wall. If I can keep him in the narrow passage between the containers, I might be able to get down on the opposite side and get away, but I must do it right now.

She stood up and holding the pistol with both hands fired a shot at the floor between the front ends of the containers again. Even as the noise bounced and echoed through the building she was moving to the other side. Looking down her breath caught in her throat; straight below her stood a girl, her face upturned. There was no time to do or say anything; Dao turned around, with the pistol still clutched in one hand she slid her body over the edge to drop to the floor and felt hands reach up to steady her as she fell.

'Run!' said Dao and turned, without looking to see if Mariko followed. At the door she paused, grabbed Mariko's arm and pushed her ahead, then swung around and fired a fourth time, aiming low, roughly in front of the containers. And then they were away, running through the little passage and out into the cool night.

'Quick - this way!' Dao sprinted across the yard, pushed the gun into her back jeans pocket and gestured for Mariko to climb over the fence before she scrambled over herself.

'Come on!' Dao took Mariko's hand and pulled her towards the edge of the swamp. They stumbled down the slope and into the dark knee-deep water under the mangroves.

'We must get further away,' she said breathlessly and dragged Mariko with her, out into the darkness among the trees.

The soft mud sucked at their feet and made progress difficult, the roots were unseen obstacles. Dao slowed to look behind them and could no longer see the buildings. They were in a dark and quiet world that seemed impossibly removed from where they had just been.

'Let's move very quietly,' whispered Dao. 'We'll stop now and then and listen - in case he comes after us.'

'Did you shoot one of those men?' Mariko face was very close, but Dao couldn't make out her features, just a pale face and dark hair.

'No, he fell off the container when I fired the first time – I think he hit his head on the floor, he was unconscious. How did you get out?'

'I heard you. First the little knocks and then your voice and then the creak when the door was unlocked, and I knew what that sound was. Then I heard the men shouting and you on the roof. When both men moved around to the same side, I pushed the door open and ran to the other side.'

'Let's move further out.' Dao took Mariko's hand again and they waded slowly among the concealing trees, feeling the way with their feet. A few minutes later they were in water up to the top of their thighs, and in front of them lay a stretch of open water with more mangroves on the other side.

'We could go to that side.' Mariko let go of Dao's hand and pointed. 'See that line of lights down to the right? There is a street not far away. We can probably get out there and find someone and ask for help.'

Walking was easier now that they were no longer amongst dense mangroves, but they had to push against the deeper water, and it was very cold. Suddenly Dao stepped into a hole and fell forward, but Mariko grabbed her jacket and pulled her up. Dao shook her head to clear water from her eyes and wiped her face with her wet sleeve. She felt for the gun in her back pocket and wondered vaguely if it would work when it was wet and lifted the bag strap over her head to hold it out of the water. The phone was obviously already wet, but it might still work.

'I can't swim and it's getting deeper.'

'I can't swim either,' said Mariko. 'Maybe we should walk along instead of across. We could keep to the outer edge of these trees, so we can't be seen from that side.'

'I don't know this area – but I think if we walk that way this inlet narrows,' Dao pointed into the darkness, 'and we should get to a place where there are houses, not factories, on the other side – and where there is hardly any open water in the middle. I remember it from looking at Google Earth.'

Inside her head Dao was debating with herself about the Glock. She must get rid of it, but how? Being found with the pistol was risking trouble and dropping it close to the edge of the swamp where it could be found was dangerous in case it could be traced back to Charlie, and she couldn't throw it here in the open or Mariko would see her do it.

'OK, let's go along the edge of the trees then and walk towards the narrow end. You can lead the way, you're taller than I am.'

She continued to hold the wet bag high, though she knew the phone might be useless after getting soaked, reluctant to do any further damage to it. It represented her only way of communicating with those who could help them, and she could only hope it worked. They made their way just along the edge of the mangroves, and then she tripped on something and fell forward, and the bag flew from her hand and disappeared in the darkness.

'Oh no, I lost the bag! It's got my phone in it. Can you see it? It might float before it sinks.' And even as she spoke, she realised that this was her chance, a perfect opportunity. While Mariko moved a few steps forward feeling for the bag with her hands in the nearly total darkness among the trees, Dao pulled the Glock from her back pocket, turned side-on and threw it in a big arc over Mariko's head, further out and way forward.

'What was that? Did you hear it?' Mariko stumbled back and bumped into Dao.

'I did,' she whispered. 'We'll stand still and listen.'

A few minutes passed and there were no more splashes. 'Let's move on, we should be able to cross to the other side soon, when we get to the narrow bit.' Dao felt for Mariko's hand and they continued, walking slowly and talking in whispers.

'Oh no,' she said after a while. 'I lost the gun too! It must have fallen out of my pocket when I tripped.' Then she laughed quietly and squeezed Mariko's hand. 'Never mind, we don't need the gun now, and getting wet had probably ruined it anyway, but it's sad that I lost my phone – Hunter, my husband, bought it for me. It was lucky I thought to leave the house keys and the alarm remote in Richard's car.'

'Who is Richard?'

'He's a limo driver. I can't drive myself, so I hired a car with a driver,' said Dao, her teeth chattering with cold. 'He's waiting in the car just across the street from where we were before - I expect he'll call the police now and they'll find us. Or we'll see a car and ask for a ride.' She coughed. 'This water tastes of mud!'

PART 4
HUNTER AND DAO

I lie wide awake on the too short, so-called bed waiting for morning. Spending a second night in a police cell has given me a new appreciation of home comforts. Simon will be in touch this morning and he will have spoken to Dao, who has been on my mind constantly. Not that she can't look after herself; there are few people who are more capable than Dao, but I would like to know she is OK. I don't have my phone and I don't wear a watch, so I have no idea what the time is, but I think its's close to dawn. I hear people in the corridor and then my door is unlocked, and a rather bulky police officer holds it wide open. 'Come with me, please.'

We walk in silence to the end of the corridor, turn left and proceed to the counter where they processed me before they locked me up. It is still dark outside and as I turn to him to ask where we are going and why, he pushes a sheet of paper towards me and hands me my keys and the alarm remote. 'You're free to go now. Can you please sign here that we have returned your possessions?'

As I sign the form, I hear Benson's voice talking to someone in the room behind the counter and then he comes through the doorway, looking as if he's been up all night.

'Good morning, Hunter. The charges against you have been dropped – come along!'

We go out into the chilly damp air of very early morning with just a trace of grey diluting the darkness of the sky. Outside, in a spot reserved for police cars sits a sleek, black car and a tall middle-aged guy with grey hair and a big nose stands beside it. He's wearing a black suit, white shirt and a dark tie and there's a logo embroidered on the breast pocket of his jacket.

'This is Richard Walters, Hunter. Please get in, we'll talk as we go.'

We all get into the car; Richard drives, Benson and I sit in the back, and Benson says, 'Richard has been Dao's driver the last two nights – she hired this limo.'

'What?' is the only thing that comes out of my mouth. The whole scene has an Alice in Wonderland quality to it. My mind seems to have seized and I haven't even asked why the charge against me has been withdrawn.

'I think it's better if you tell Hunter the story, Richard – seeing you are part of it,' says Benson and then he turns to me. 'I'll tell you my side later.'

Richard angles the rear vision mirror so he can see my face. 'It's a bit of a story, but I'll try to tell you in the order it happened.' He clears his throat. 'Dao ordered a car for Saturday night, pick-up at half past eight, no definite end time. She told me to take her to East Tamaki and asked me to stop in the industrial area. She said she was going to walk to a place in the next street, a place that had a sign saying something about welding - and if she wasn't back in an hour, I was to call the cops.'

'Christ! Please tell me you didn't let her do that!'

'I had to,' he says reasonably. 'I mean, I couldn't stop her, not unless I drove away and took her home again. Which I would have done, but she told me she's married – to you – and she's twenty-three and she said it wasn't to do with drugs, because I asked her. We did have quite a discussion about it, and she promised not to do anything silly, she just wanted to get right up to that building and have a look inside. She came back thirty-seven minutes later - I was getting nervous, ready to go and look for her, when she turned up.'

'Was she OK? Did she tell you what she had been doing?'

'She was OK, perhaps a bit worried – and she had some photos on her phone that she wanted to look at properly, so we parked in a quiet street a few minutes away and she sat there looking at the pictures for ages. Oh, and I didn't say – she had a white plastic rubbish bag with her – you know, a bin-liner, that she had picked up at that place. And then she said she wanted the car again the next night, that's yesterday, at the same time and she wanted me to drive her. Eventually she realised that she had to tell me more, because I wasn't happy about the whole thing, so she turned on a recording she had on her phone of you and her telling a lawyer all about this strange thing you're involved in – it took a while and meanwhile she had a snooze on the backseat. Incredible story!'

He negotiates a huge semi-trailer halfway across the road reversing into a supermarket delivery area and continues without expecting any response from me. He sounds as if he's told this story already this morning.

'So, I went to pick her up last night and she said, "let's take Hunter's car and leave this one here" and when I asked her why, she said she didn't want this nice shiny car damaged and I'd get into trouble if it got smashed up! I never heard anything like it! I knew she was planning something bad, and she said she wanted a vehicle parked across the gates to that place in Tamaki in case they tried to get away. I told her we were not taking your car and what we should do was tell the cops and let them deal with it.'

He turns his head and looks at me over his shoulder with a slight smile. 'And then I saw why she got so famous when that trial was on – my God, that girl is something else! She made a very firm statement saying she was an adult and any decisions about her safety would be made by her – but she thanked me for being concerned. And she said that earlier in the day she had changed her mind about doing anything herself and she *had* called the cops, but they said they would discuss it in a meeting on Monday morning, today that is. And now she was terrified that they would be too late to save that Japanese girl, because she said there were things in the photos that proved she was there, and she was worried those men might be planning to leave due to the police having found those flats they had been living in. Oh, and there's a van in there too and she recognised it from some CCTV video she had seen with you.'

By now I'm in a cold sweat and my heart is beating way too fast. Why am I in this car going to Tamaki before dawn with Benson? Something is wrong and I can't figure out what level of trouble Dao is in. If she was dead, Benson would have said straight away, if she was injured, we would be heading for a hospital.

'Benson, where the hell is Dao?'

'We don't know where she is,' he says calmly. 'Both men from the apartment were at the factory. One has now left, but he hasn't got the girls with him – we know that for a fact. The second man is lying dead inside the factory.'

'How do you know the guy who left hasn't taken the girls?'

Richard meets my eyes in the rear vision mirror. 'Because Dao was right about the whole thing, and last night she made me park right across the street from the welding place with no lights on, and then she cleverly gave me your phone, Hunter – Inspector Benson has it now. Before she went, she showed me how to unlock it and told me Benson and Charlie were in the Contacts folder and they were important – she explained who they were. And she showed me that I could check where she was on that app that she has on her phone too. You can see for yourself, if you look at the phone. After she'd been gone a while, I heard shots, three or four – I was just about to call 111 when a guy with a big bag slung over his shoulder came running from the back of the factory. He unhooked the padlock – it wasn't locked – and took off running fast. He didn't notice me, but I couldn't follow him until I knew Dao was OK, so I let him go and then I went in and found the dead guy – but there was nobody else there. I called the cops first on 111 and then Inspector Benson, and then I started looking for Dao, but I couldn't find her. I knew she had come in from the back of that place, from the mangrove swamp side so I went outside and called her name, but not too loud because I wasn't certain if there was someone else chasing her. And then I remembered the app on your phone. I could see that just minutes earlier, just after the shooting, I reckon, she had gone into the water and out quite a way – and then the track stopped.'

Benson hands me the phone, I open the tracking app and there it is, she was last in the middle of the tidal inlet behind the Tamaki factory. My heart misses a beat; she can't swim, and I have no idea of how deep that water is.

'She must have gone into the water to escape. I wonder if she and Mariko are both out there in the mangroves, but why does her track stop there? And who killed the guy in the factory? Christ, Benson, I've got to find her! What are your guys doing about it?'

'It's all under control,' says Benson in his usual calm way. 'Dao probably dropped her phone in the water. It's not that deep, the tide is out – I'd think she could walk across to the other side even at high tide, but without her phone she can't contact us. This all happened late last night. So, when Richard called me, I called Bakker to make sure the call centre had connected with her, not just sent a patrol car – she's got a big team out there now. As soon as it's light, they'll get volunteers in kayaks into that mangrove swamp, unless the chopper finds them first – I think both girls are out there because Mariko is not in the factory and Bakker thinks she has been held there, so odds are they're together. The dead guy wasn't shot, despite the sounds of gun fire Richard heard - he seems to have fallen, either off a chair or off the top of a container and hit his head on the concrete floor. There was an overturned chair beside him.'

None of this makes a lot of sense at the moment and my mind is churning with worry about Dao and questions that I don't ask because nobody has the answers.

Richard stops where crime scene tape blocks the street, Benson gets us past the man on guard and we walk towards the factory in the grey light of dawn. I only have a light sweatshirt on, and the chilly breeze coming off the water makes me shiver. The area in front of the factory is crowded with vehicles: two ambulances, a cluster of police cars and one of those white vans, whatever they are, that you see on TV when there's been a murder.

Benson walks us to the back of the building and holds out his hand to stop us. 'Wait here for a moment.' He pulls a pair of white shoe covers out of his pocket and disappears inside but comes back to the door nearly immediately. 'Put these on,' he says and hands us shoe covers. 'Bakker says you can come in.'

He registers the expression on my face and adds, 'And keep it toned down, will you, Hunter? I have gone out on a limb here and I don't want her to get all worked up again. I'm not part of this investigation, so it's all been done by goodwill and negotiation.'

I nod. 'I'll let you do the talking,'

Bakker is standing just inside the doorway talking quietly to a woman in a white overall. She gives us a nod and a curt 'good morning' and turns back to finish the conversation, which gives me a chance to look around. There is a whole team at work, but the place is eerily quiet with only the occasional scratchy sound of metal against concrete breaking the silence; big lights make it brighter than day. It's a big space, but it is pretty full; two containers on one side and some kind of makeshift bar at the opposite wall, a table full of what looks like computer gear and inside the big roller door a van of the same make as the one we saw in the CCTV videos.

Benson turns half sideways and says in an undertone. 'I think Dao was right – and so does Bakker, the Japanese girl was probably held here. Now keep your cool, my friend, or we'll be out of here in seconds. She has not taken it well that Dao proved her wrong.'

'Mr Grant,' says Bakker when she turns back to us. 'I'm sorry we haven't located Miss Johnson yet, but we are pretty certain Mariko was being held here. We have patrol cars out in the relevant areas – where they could have come ashore. Mr Walters had your phone and could see them moving through the mangroves.'

'Thank you,' I say politely. 'Do you know what happened here?'

'Well, no, not really.' She frowns as someone drops something heavy way behind her. 'It seems that there was some sort of confrontation - one or more persons were on top of the containers and shots were fired. One man fell hard, he's dead. Another man was seen leaving by Mr Walters, and we have cars out looking for him. He is on foot, so he might head for a bus stop or take a taxi – they've been alerted. Other than that, it's guesswork until Miss Johnson is located.'

'It's Mrs Grant, actually - we're married.'

'Oh, sorry,' says the unfortunate woman, and I can't resists replying, 'I'm not, I like it.'

Benson gives me a hard look; behind me Richard makes a noise like a suppressed chuckle. Bakker clamps her lips together and says nothing.

Benson comes to the rescue. 'Are those the bullet marks in the floor over there?' He points to some white markers on the concrete floor.

'Yes, three of them – one you can't see from here, it's just hidden by the corner of the first container. They were fired from the top of a container – there are three casings up there, and we found another one just inside the door - but we've only found three impact marks so far.'

Benson nods. 'OK, we won't get in your way any longer. You've got my phone number and Mr Grant's. We'll wait to hear from you.'

I thank her and we leave, and Benson shakes his head as soon as we are out of earshot. 'You couldn't bloody well resist, could you?' Then he chuckles. 'But it will make a great story – very funny.'

It's full daylight when we walk back to the car and the chilly breeze has died down. Richard, who seems to be permanent part of the team, says, 'Where should we go? I reckon we try across there first.' He points across the mangroves towards what looks like distant houses and Benson opens the door. 'Get in Hunter, let's go and find Dao and Mariko.'

Richard already has it worked out; he's been checking Google maps. He makes a smart U-turn and goes back the way we came. He gets something out of the door pocket and hands it to me over his shoulder: Dao's keys and her alarm system remote.

'Have a look at this,' he says five minutes later and pulls over to the side. Benson and I lean forward from the back seat to look at the dashboard screen and Richard uses a pen to point; I notice the PIN for my phone written on the back of his left hand.

'This is where we are now and there is the factory on the other side of this inlet. If you compare it to the app on your phone, you'll see that Dao's tracker stopped there.' He points again. 'So, I reckon they started out in a more or less straight line across to the other side.' He turns and looks at us over the back of his seat. 'I drove over there after the cops arrived. I told them about the app and how I knew Dao was in the water and said I wanted to see if I could find her. I went right down to the water's edge on the other side and called – I said, "it's Richard, come out Dao" and stuff like that, but no answer. So, I had another look while I waited for Benson to liberate you from that cell. And this is what I think now.'

He switches to Google Earth and points further along, to where the inlet narrows and penetrates further inland, where the mangroves fill the whole width with no open water in the middle.

I know what he means, he's a thinker, this guy. 'So, if the water where Dao dropped the phone was getting too deep for her, they might have backtracked and gone along instead of across. That makes sense – and she is very short.'

Nobody has used the word "drowned" but I'm sure it's in the back of everyone's mind. Richard switches back to Google maps and starts the car again. I open the Navigate app on my phone and Benson and I watch our blue dot moving across the map. Now that I know exactly where the welding factory is, I realise that Richard's reasoning is good. If the girls abandoned the 'across the water' trek and turned at right angles, following the edge of the mangroves, this is exactly where we might find them, heading for shallower water to get across. Benson leans over and I hand him the phone so he can see for himself. He studies it for a moment and nods. 'Either that or the opposite direction, but either way we'll find them.' I hope he is right.

Where we stop there is no line-up of commercial properties backing on to the edge of the inlet, but a wider open area between residential properties and the water, half wilderness, with shrubs and grass and a few scattered trees. We walk up a gentle rise and down the other side, across the scrubby grass to the mangroves and set out along the edge. Over to our right a helicopter is slowly working its way along the inlet, but in the other direction from where we are. After couple of minutes Benson says, as if he is not at all surprised, 'Ah - there they are. Good guess, Richard.'

They get up from the grass and walk towards us, wet and muddy and shoeless. When we meet, Dao says, 'I'm so cold, Hunter!' Her face is white, and she looks exhausted. Before I can reach out, she falls to her knees. Mariko crouches beside her and tries to help her up, and Benson takes his jacket off.

'You must be Mariko,' he says and wraps his jacket around her shoulders. She stands up, unsure of what to do and probably feeling shy with three strange men converging on her.

I lift Dao up like you do a child, one arm behind her back and one under her knees and turn to Mariko. 'I think you should put your arms into the sleeves of that jacket and get warmed up. I'm Hunter, Dao's husband and this is Richard, who drove Dao to the factory. He has helped us find you. And the guy who gave you his jacket is Benson – he is Dao's best friend and a police officer.'

Benson looks away into the distance, as if he hasn't heard, but I can tell he is pleased and embarrassed at the same time, but after two years of standing by Dao, worrying about her and loving her like a father, he deserves to hear it.

'Thank you, Hunter san,' she says and bows slightly, three times, thanking us individually; unfailingly polite in the beautiful Japanese tradition even in this situation. Everybody smiles and we start the walk back to the car.

Benson is on his phone, telling Bakker that we found the girls and that we are taking them straight to hospital to be checked over. She replies something that makes Benson shake his head as he listens. 'No, I think hospital is the place for them now. They are close to hypothermia – it looks as if they've been in the water until now, probably hiding until daylight. They've lost their shoes and who knows what kind of bacteria lurk in that swamp. I'll stay with them and keep in touch with you.'

Dao has said nothing since I picked her up. Her lips are blue and her entire body shivers against my chest; I am beginning to feel worried. Benson ends the call, glances at Dao and turns to Richard. 'Would you mind going ahead so you can get the heater going in the car? I hope you can drive us to hospital, seeing you're on the spot?'

'OK,' says Richard and jogs towards the car a couple of hundred meters ahead; an incongruous sight in his black suit and shiny black shoes running through the dew-wet grass. By the time we reach the car, the heater is going full blast and Richard is waiting, holding two foil rescue blankets.

'You're a man of many resources!' Benson grins. 'Is this standard limousine equipment?'

'We have great first aid kits – you never know what might happen,' says Richard and hands one foil blanket to me and unfolds one himself. With both girls wrapped up we bundle them into the backseat, one each side of me. Benson gets in the front and turns to Richard, 'Swing by the factory, but not right up to the tape, just to where I parked my car near the corner, then do another of your fast U-turns and head for the hospital - I'll follow you in my car.'

He gets his phone out and makes two calls, speaking very quietly. I smile to myself; Benson would never say it, but he is hoping to get the girls away without being noticed by Bakker. In the distance I see the helicopter turn and rise, heading away from Tamaki; it is lost to view as we turn a corner.

The only words I get from Dao, are a couple of short sentences spoken quietly against my chest. 'Hunter, listen,' she whispers. 'I'm going to lie to them. Don't contradict me, just listen and look as if you believe me.'

I look down at what I can see of her face, and she whispers

so quietly that I can hardly make out the words, 'It's important, I've worked it all out.'

'Of course,' I whisper back and tighten my arm around her, without the slightest idea what she is talking about. Mariko leans against me and I manage to get an arm around her too, hoping that the warmth from my body will be a comfort.

Benson tells Richard to drop us at the ambulance bay, but there is a lot of urgent activity there and we continue to the regular entrance to the emergency department.

'I won't come in,' says Richard, 'but let me know how they get on, won't you?'

I shake his hand. 'I will – and I'll call your office and organise everything, payment and so on. And thank you for all you've done, way beyond the call of duty - I'm very grateful!'

Benson, true to form, takes command of the situation. 'Police,' he says to the ED nurse, 'I called earlier. I would like these young women to be taken straight through and seen as soon as possible. We were supposed to go in via the ambulance bay, but it was a bit crowded there.'

The few people in the waiting area stare at the two girls wrapped in their silver foil blankets, with muddy legs, no shoes and wet hair. Nobody argues with Benson and within minutes the girls are in cubicles next to each other with the curtain between them pulled back. They sit on the edge of their respective beds, still in their foil blankets, pale and exhausted.

'Mariko, did Dao get a chance to explain how we found out about you? And that we got in touch with your father, and he came over here?'

'Oh, yes – she told me everything.' Mariko smiles tiredly across at Dao. 'We had a lot of time to talk.'

'I'll get in touch with John now and tell him you're safe. I don't know what the time is in Boston, but that doesn't matter. If he answers I'll let you talk to him.'

Benson sits on one of the two chairs talking quietly to the girls while I call John's number, but I get no answer, just voicemail. I leave a message saying that Mariko is safe and ask him to call back as soon as he can. Things swing into action the way they do when a team of professionals tackle an emergency situation. A kind of organised chaos surrounds the girls; two nurses and a doctor crowd in, pieces of equipment are pulled into place and a nurse says decisively, 'Would you two please wait outside for a few minutes.'

When we are allowed back in, both girls are tucked up with blankets up to their chins, blood pressure monitors attached and an IV line each; there are two piles of wet and muddy clothing on the floor. The doctor, who looks about nineteen, sees me looking at the drip and says comfortingly, 'Just saline.' Then he grins, 'Seems a bit mad when they've been in salty water for hours, but they might be dehydrated and getting fluids into them will help all round. Surprisingly they aren't clinically hypothermic, but they are quite cold.'

Dao manages a smile. 'We kept each other warm by hugging.'

'Very good idea,' says the doctor, and then he and one nurse leave for greater challenges elsewhere. 'We'll just keep them here for a couple of hours and then you can take them home,' he adds as they leave.

'Are you staying here for a few minutes?' Benson asks the remaining nurse, and when she says she will be here "for a while", he turns to me. 'Hunter, come with me for a couple of minutes.'

We retreat to a waiting area and sit on hard plastic chairs in a quiet corner, out of earshot of people waiting to be seen.

'Bakker is not pleased,' he says, and the corner of his mouth twitches, 'but I have appealed to her better nature.' He ignores my snort of derision. 'I have assured her that you can look after the girls' welfare and at the same time cooperate with the investigation. The only way I could achieve this, was by taking liberties with your life and property. Mariko can't go back to her apartment – they want nothing touched in either of those two apartments until at least Wednesday. I've promised that both girls will stay with you and not let themselves be interviewed or go on social media until they have been formally interviewed – the first interview will happen at your place this afternoon, barring any medical reasons or the girls being asleep.'

He pauses and waits for me to respond, but I just nod; it sounds fine to me.

'So, you take them home - Mariko can probably borrow some gear from Dao, and one of Bakker's off-siders - female - will get clothes for her, provided they are still in her wardrobe and not part of the general mess in the apartment. If that can't happen, you'll just have to go shopping. I think that's all.'

'Fine,' I say. 'Thank you for organising that! And what about your real duties – or did you have a day off anyway?'

'I called my boss at midnight last night, from the factory, and said I must have today off. Bakker was already there when I arrived, and when I realised the full extent of the drama, and with Dao missing, I thought I'd better infiltrate Bakker's team. Which as you might understand wasn't easy – she guards her territory like a tiger, and she is acutely sensitive about anyone muscling in or knowing more than she does.'

He looks hard at me then and adds, 'And no more of those sarcastic quips from you when you see her! You'd better act like a nice, helpful guy and try and keep on the right side of her.'

'I will – and I must thank her for withdrawing the charge and letting me out.'

Benson grins. 'And that wouldn't have happened until much later, if I hadn't prodded her - she knew she would have to do it eventually, but she was quite reluctant to let you go. Richard was the one who really made it happen - he was standing by my side during these negotiations, and he casually mentioned what a great TV drama it would make, this whole thing - with Dao hiring him and discovering that Mariko was in the factory and so on. That clinched the deal – Bakker got really worried he'd talk to media and get famous on her failure to act - which would be a killer blow to her ego.'

'Amazing guy,' I say and think of how awful the situation might have been, if Richard hadn't acted like Dao was his own daughter. 'I'll have to do something really nice for him – Dao will have some ideas maybe.'

When we return to the double cubicle, the place has been tidied up, the wet clothes are in a large plastic bag and the floor has been mopped. Both girls look a lot better, Dao's lips are no longer blue, and they are sitting up drinking tea and eating sandwiches.

'Food – in the emergency department? Really?' I say and the nurse laughs. 'Volunteers – they come in and do nice things. It helps a lot.'

'Did Richard just call you, or did he call Charlie as well?' Dao asks Benson. 'I don't want Charlie to worry about me.'

'No, he just called me and 111. We've given Hunter the background story and Bakker has agreed that you can both go home to your place and stay there for a while. She'll come and take a short formal statement from you this afternoon, if you are not asleep. So as soon as they unhook you from those bags of saline, I'll drive you back. God knows what you're going to wear on the way home.'

As it turns out, the nurse volunteers a solution; she says she will bend the rules, so I don't have to somehow get back to the North Shore, pick up clothes and then come back again.

'Stay in those gowns, just hold them together at the back.' She laughs. 'You don't want to give anyone a free view of your backsides. You can return them another day.'

Benson sees us into the house, drops the plastic bag of wet clothes on the floor inside the front door and leaves after getting a hug from Dao.

'I'll call later.' he says. 'And don't let Bakker change her mind and try to insist on interviewing the girls at the station – say they're traumatised and need to be in a safe environment or something. And they'll need a sleep anyway.'

23

Th first thing I must do is respond to Simon's messages. He has sent three increasingly impatient texts asking me to explain what is going on, so I text him to say that everyone is safe, but we're very busy and I will call and explain everything this evening. Next, I call Charlie and give her a brief outline and say I'll be in touch in a couple of days, that everyone here is exhausted and we can't see anyone until this chaos is sorted out. Poor Charlie feels that she should have been able to foresee what Dao was planning and somehow prevent it, but I hope I managed to calm her down. I doubt that anyone apart from Benson or myself could have stopped her.

An hour later some kind of order is restored; the girls have showered and washed their hair and dressed in clothes from Dao's wardrobe. There was a long low-voiced conversation in the spare bedroom upstairs while they were getting dressed and I would love to know what they were talking about. Dao's whispered warning in the car on the way to the hospital has made me very curious about what really happened at that place. When they come down to the living room, looking nearly like sisters with their hair up in ponytails, I comment on how much better they look now that they are clean and warm; they glance at each other and some kind of signal passes between them.

Scruff can't believe his luck when Dao promptly takes him into the kitchen and gives him breakfast and I don't mention that he already had breakfast while the girls were upstairs. Things feel nearly normal; the washing machine is on and I have ordered two pizzas to be delivered for lunch. I take advantage of Mariko going out on the balcony to look at the courtyard and ask Dao, if she wants to explain what went on in that factory and who fired the shots.

'Not now, just trust me,' she says quietly, as Mariko comes back through the living area. 'You'll hear it later – remember what I said in the car!'

We have just finished lunch and I am making coffee, when the doorbell goes. I go down and find Bakker and a younger man on the doorstep.

'I'm just making coffee,' I say, when we get back upstairs. 'Would you like some? And we ordered far too much pizza, so you can have some of that too.'

I can see from the expression that flits over Bakker face, that ideally, she would like to scorn this suggestion, but the offer of food proves too tempting. She and her companion, whose name sounds like Roof, sit down at the table and Dao comes to help me in the kitchen.

I hear Bakker asking Mariko how she is feeling, but her reply is inaudible. Dao re-heats what is left of the pizza and gets plates out, while I make two thermos jugs of coffee and load a tray with everything we need. Before we return to the living area, I give her a hug and she stands on tiptoes to kiss me and then she whispers, 'I'm so happy now.'

'This is nice,' says Roof and puts a piece of pizza on his plate. 'A break and some food - just what we need.'

'I must thank you for dropping the charge,' I say to Bakker. 'It would have been torture to sit in that cell knowing Dao was missing.'

She makes no direct reply, just says a casual 'that's OK'

and picks up a pizza triangle. 'I would like to take a statement from Dao first and then Mariko,' she says fifteen minutes and three pizza triangles later. 'I know you two must be exhausted, but it's important that we get as much information as possible right away. Would you like to talk to us alone, Dao? Perhaps there is another room we could use?'

Dao looks at her as if she is from another planet. 'No, of course not. Hunter is always my support person. And there's no need for Mariko go and sit in the bedroom, is there? She might as well hear what happened too – we didn't talk much while we were in the water.'

Both Mariko and I know this is not true and I glance in her direction, hoping she won't protest, but she just says quietly, 'We were very frightened of that man hearing us - in among those trees we couldn't see if anyone was close.' And I recall the look that passed between them before lunch.

Bakker is just about to start the interview with all of us sitting around the table like a rather oddly assorted family when Dao turns to me. 'I lost my phone in the water, Hunter. Can I borrow yours?'

I hand her my phone and she un-locks it, taps the screen a few times and puts it on the table. Bakker observes this in silence, and I can see from her expression that Sinclair must have told her about Dao's habit of recording things.

She asks Dao to tell it as it played out, starting with Saturday night, and only occasionally does she interrupt with a question. A lot of it I know already, from Richard and Benson, but it's interesting hearing Dao's side of it. When we get to the details of how she first approached the factory, she interrupts herself and asks if Bakker has looked at the photos she took.

'I have,' she says, and I think she's expecting Dao to ask why she didn't take some action yesterday, but Dao just continues the story. I suspect that asking about the photos was her way of reminding Bakker, that in Dao's opinion, she failed. She points out the significance of Mariko's bag under the table and the van, and how these facts made her certain Mariko was in one of the containers. Bakker listens impassively, Mariko's eyes stay on Dao's face throughout.

'And then you went there again last night,' says Bakker at the end. 'How did you get into the factory?'

With the possible exception of Mariko, who might have been told some of it during the night, nobody but Dao knows this part. We all lean slightly forward.

'I knew I had to do it,' says Dao, and I know from her voice that even re-living it now is stressful. 'I knew what I was planning to do was very dangerous and I was really scared of going in, terrified – in case I got trapped in there and what those guys might do to me, but I had to, because of those packed bags in their bedroom. They were getting ready to leave, and just then, when they were both in the kitchen having dinner might be the last opportunity to do something. The door from the kitchen to that little passage was closed, so I just tiptoed through and into the factory itself. It was quite dark in there, just the light from the streetlamps coming in through those high windows on the front wall and a bit of light from the passage – because the bedroom door was open. One container had a door open, so I looked inside it – it was furnished as a luxury bedroom, but you've seen it now, of course. I didn't dare turn on my phone torch, but I took a flash photo and got a split- second look.'

Dao's eyes are fixed on Bakker, she never so much as glances at anyone else and I wonder if this is what keeps Bakker from interrupting. Like a snake charmer, I think, never take your eyes off the danger.

'The other container was closed, but I tapped a little pattern of knocks on the wall, just quietly – I did it a couple of times, and then I heard Mariko doing it back to me, the same pattern – well, I thought it was Mariko. I saw that only one of those rods was locked into place to hold the door shut, and I had to open it and that was really scary – in case it made a terrible noise. I had nothing to defend myself with, not even something I could throw at them, nothing! You know that long table with the computer screens? I had a quick look to see if there was anything useful there, because my eyes had got used to the lack of light - and I saw a gun, so I took it.'

Bakker is instantly interested. 'What kind of gun?'

'Oh, I don't know,' says Dao innocently. 'I don't know anything about guns. Hunter has a shotgun that he takes to the cabin sometimes, but this was some kind of pistol, like people have on those American TV shows. Anyway,' she continues without pause, keeping it tight and leaving no loose ends, 'I tucked the gun in the back pocket of my jeans and lifted that big lever on the door and turned the rod – and it made a terrible screechy noise, so the men came running in - they heard it from the kitchen, of course.'

I can't quite see where this is going. Bakker had said the shots had been fired from the top of one of the containers: Was someone else armed and on top of the container? I keep a straight face and wait.

'Was someone up on one of the containers?' asks Bakker, as if she hears my thoughts, but she says nothing about knowing the shots were fired from there.

'Yes, I was,' says Dao. 'Those men came towards me and there was only one place to hide – I ran down the little passage between the containers and went into the gap between Mariko's container and the wall, it was just big enough. They nearly reached me, one from each side, but not quite – they couldn't squeeze their bodies in, just their arms - so I climbed up on top, because there was nowhere else to go.'

She sees Bakker's expression of near disbelief and there is a glint of a smile. 'I know how to do it – I go climbing at the Dominion Road indoor climbing place, and I had a lesson there once about how to climb what they call a chimney, they've got it set up so you can practise doing it. You know what I mean, you use your hands and feet – and sometimes your back against one side, it depends on how wide the chimney is and how long your legs are. The gap I was in is very narrow, I could just turn half sideways if I kept one shoulder kind of twisted. I managed to get one foot against the wall and the other against container. You know, to get the soles of my sneakers to grip.'

She stops talking and looks at me. 'Is there any more coffee?' Bakker sits silent, digesting what she has heard, and I pour Dao another cup of coffee. She drinks some of it, returns her focus to Bakker and continues.

'I put the gun in under my T-shirt first and then I tucked the T-shirt into my jeans while I had both feet on the floor – I couldn't hold it and climb at the same time and I was worried it would fall out of my pocket, it didn't fit that well. But when I got to the edge, I got into trouble, because the gun was in the way, I should have tucked in at the back, not the front - I was really hoping it wouldn't go off and shoot me.'

She considers this unpleasant possibility for a moment with a slight frown before she continues. 'Never mind, it didn't go off and I got up on the container roof. I kneeled and got the gun out, and then I realised one of the men had run around, so now they were both on the same side - in the space between the two containers, you know? They had a chair and one of them got on it to climb up. I thought he would probably kill me, so I aimed the gun just above him and held on tight with both hands and pressed the trigger, and the gun went off and I got such a fright I nearly lost my grip on it. I hadn't realised how loud it would be and it made my arms jerk, I nearly fell over. The man on the chair fell off and hit his head on the floor with a terrible crash and just lay there, unconscious. I couldn't see the other one, but I looked over the edge and he was standing with his back up against the side of the container - and that's when I heard a little tapping sound.'

She looks at Mariko and smiles. 'It was Mariko! She had pushed the door open while those men were both on the same side shouting at each other, and then she sneaked around to the other side - and she was tapping my little pattern to get my attention. So, I shot again, but I wasn't very good at aiming and I hit the floor quite a bit further out than I meant to, but it stopped that man from moving away from where he was. I slid backwards over the edge on Mariko's side and she caught me, and then we just ran like crazy.'

She stops talking, lifts her mug and drinks some more coffee. My mind is reacting on two levels; I know which part of this story is a lie, and the most likely reason for that lie, and at the same time I am marvelling at her courage, knowing how terrified she must have been.

Then she adds, 'Oh no, wait! I didn't say – I fired another shot from the doorway, just randomly at the floor, so that guy wouldn't come out from where he was standing - to give us a bit more time to get away.'

Bakker has a strange look on her face, the kind of expression people often have just before they move their head slowly from side to side, indicating how incredible something is. She is probably trying to reconcile this girl, who is built like a shrimp and looks fifteen, with what she has just heard. It's not the first time I've seen Dao having this effect on people, but this time I think my face wears the same expression.

'Where is the gun now?' asks Roof, who has sat mesmerised throughout, hardly blinking. 'We need to pick it up.'

'It's in the swamp. I didn't even realise I had lost it at first. I tucked it into my back pocket again when we climbed over the fence. I tripped on something and fell when we were in among the mangroves. Mariko pulled me up, but I lost the gun *and* my phone.' And as an afterthought she adds, 'And I think it's terrible that people dump rubbish sacks in that inlet.

There were two there – I nearly tripped on another one just a couple of steps further on.'

When it is Mariko's turn Bakker starts with how she was grabbed on the landing. She knows from Dao's video what one of the men look like, but she needs information about the second man and asks what they did and said. Mariko answers briefly and clearly; her English is excellent and there are no surprises. When the questions progress to the killing she witnessed, her confidence falters and she replies with few words, looking down at her hands. Dao reaches out and takes hold of one of Mariko's hands and the difficult moment passes. They discuss the tactics of the men, how they controlled what she communicated via her phone and the methods they used to intimidate their captives, and then Mariko suddenly stops. 'I'm sorry – I don't want to talk any more right now.'

To my surprise Bakker accepts it, says they will come back tomorrow, or 'maybe Mr Grant can bring you to the station' and leaves it at that. As they get up to leave, Dao picks up my phone from the table and turns it off. 'Would you like me to send the recording to you?'

Bakker smiles, possibly for the first time ever; her face doesn't adapt to it easily, but she says she would like to have it. 'Very useful, Dao – thank you.'

But Dao doesn't record this kind of thing to be helpful; she does it for herself. Once, after recording a long phone discussion we had with someone, she copied the audio file to her laptop and said, 'I think people say different things at different times – you know, they change what they say they can remember, or they say you told them something that you know you didn't, but it kind of suits their story. And their voices – sometimes it tells you when they are lying or leaving things out.'

From the age of ten, Dao survived for a decade alone with

a brutal and abusive man. Learning to read the subtle signals of reactions and intentions was for her a way of avoiding being punished, and she has honed those skills to perfection.

Bakker picks up the zip-lock bag with the plastic mould that Dao gave her when she arrived, thanks the girls for letting her talk to them when they are so tired, and I see her and Roof out.

24

Mariko, who looks as if she can only just keep her eyes open, goes up to the guest room to have a sleep and Dao says she will rest on the sofa.

'Come over here and sit beside me. I want to talk to you before I fall asleep and I'm so tired.'

I sit in the corner of the sofa, and she lies down with her head on my lap. 'Is it about the lie?' She nods. 'I took the Glock - I watched a long YouTube video of how to load the magazine and how to be safe, and then I practised. I took it with me last night in that little cloth bag I got my new T-shirts in.'

She sits up and leans against my chest. 'I'll fall asleep if I stay lying down, and I must tell you this. I had to take the gun, so I had something to threaten them with - I wasn't planning to shoot anyone. But once I had fired those shots, I knew I had to lie. There were holes in the floor, and I couldn't leave the gun there in case that man picked it up and came after us. I decided to pretend I found it there, because I was scared that Charlie might get into trouble for lending it to you, and then I would get into trouble for using it - because I don't have a licence. I thought the best thing would be to say I found it at the factory, and then I lost it. I'll have to buy a new Glock for Charlie now, but that's OK. But I'm worried that if they find it, there might be a number or something on it – would they be able to tell it was Charlie's?'

'No, I don't think so. Do you think they'll be able to find it?'

'Probably not – I took the chance when I tripped and lost the bag. My phone was in the bag, but the gun was still in my jeans pocket – I just shoved it in there before we climbed the fence. When I tripped among the mangroves and Mariko was feeling around in the water trying to find the bag and the phone it was the perfect chance to get rid of the gun. I just hurled it in a big arc into the mangroves way ahead of where we were. She didn't see me do it – it was so dark - and all we heard was a little splash far away.'

'Does Richard know you had the Glock?'

'God, no! I couldn't tell him – he would have been horrified and refused to drive me. I had it in the bag when I got in the car, and he never saw it.'

I kiss the top of her head. 'Well done, you clever little thing!'

She slides down, closes her eyes and mumbles, 'You promised not to call me a little thing, remember?' and falls instantly asleep.

I clear the table, get rid of the pizza boxes that always seem to smell more than the actual pizza, and transfer the washing to the dryer. It is late afternoon now and time to get organised.

Standing behind the sofa, where Dao sleeps peacefully, I pull the folded paper I found on the table from my pocket and read it again. It's a single sheet of A4 which documents in very few words what Dao did and planned to do, including in two places her reasoning behind her decisions and what she had done to be as safe as possible. I will keep this incredible testament to Dao's courage and focus, and at some time in the future I might show it to Benson and Charlie; they would both appreciate it.

I get my laptop and save the audio file of the interview from my phone to my hard drive and email it as an attachment to Bakker. After thinking for a minute, I send it to Simon and Benson with a short explanation and ask them both to be discreet and to say, if asked, that Dao told them the story. Richard would like to hear it, but not until this is over, if ever. Bakker would probably regard it as unacceptable that I sent it to Simon and Benson; letting Richard hear it would be asking for trouble.

'There is no charge,' says the guy at the limo hire company when I call. 'Your wife gave us her credit card details, but we have deleted them from our database and credited the payment for Saturday night back to her account. We had a discussion about it when the driver told us what had happened, and we've decided to waive the charges. Call it our contribution to the rescue of that poor girl.'

I thank him and send an email to the company; I thank them on our behalf and ask them to suggest something I can do for Richard and his family to acknowledge the support he provided for Dao and how he helped us find her.

Rather than call Linda at work I send her a long text message and she responds immediately: 'So happy Mariko is safe! I hope to meet her one day when this is over. I'm very sad about Grace, you sound as if you're sure they have killed her?'

There is no point in not being honest, so I reply and say that everything we know indicates that they killed her. Better that she is prepared for the worst, I think, rather than encourage her to keep hoping. Maybe I'm wrong, but it feels dishonest to say I hope that Grace is alive, now when I'm convinced that she is dead.

I sit in my armchair and look at Dao's sleeping face and try to make sense of how this evolved into a major personal drama for her. Several things contributed; we would never have become involved to the degree we did, if it hadn't been for Bakker's attitude at the start. Her intense dislike of me and her reluctance to take our information seriously, motivated us to go back and continue watching CCTV video, and when we showed her our findings, she arrested me. Dao's feeling of urgency set her on a dangerous path, but she would never have risked her life, if Bakker had acted yesterday when Dao called 111 and sent the photos she had taken at the factory.

We can't go on like this; twice now we have been approached by people, who for one reason or another feel the police are not proactive enough. Both occasions have involved cruelty and brutality towards women, and I'm not prepared to subject Dao to any further trauma. She needs a normal life without constantly being reminded of the dark side of humanity.

And while I sit there working through the sequence of cause and effect I suddenly realize that John Anderson hasn't replied to my message. It is now eight hours since I called, and I had expected something long before now. Has he contacted Bakker instead? Did she get in touch with him first, and is he already on his way here? I text Bakker and ask what he said, when she told him Mariko has been found. She replies half an hour later. 'Tried to call him twice, left message that Mariko is safe and with you, no reply so far. Will call station and ask them to email him, very busy here. Have found a phone that might be Mariko's.'

I am in the kitchen talking to Simon, who has had time to listen to the interview recording and is very impressed with Dao's handling of the situation in the factory.

'Intrepid,' he says decisively. 'A fine old word and perfect for describing Dao. You told me once that your friend Charlie sometimes calls her a girl warrior, and she is. Thank God she found that gun or things could have ended very differently.'

Simon and I have been friends since primary school and he is totally trustworthy, so I give myself the pleasure of telling him the truth. 'She didn't find it in the factory. She took the Glock pistol, that Charlie had lent me, and then she threw it into that damn swamp to get rid of it in case someone got into trouble over it.'

His shout of laughter nearly deafens me, and I laugh too, and then I remember the warrior asleep on the sofa. I walk over to have a look, but she is out like a light with her arm over Scruff, who has decided that today is an exception to the no-dogs-on-the-furniture rule and is asleep beside her.

'Lucky you taught her to shoot, then.'

'I didn't – but she watched a YouTube video before she went out.'

'Jesus – that girl!' Once over the hilarity, Simon gets down to business. 'I wrote a formal response to the Cayman Islands law firm that sent the "cease and desist" letter. I don't think anything will come of it. But you must admit it seems suspicious, that whoever owns White Investments wanted you out of picture and sent that letter. I think they must have known about the activity in the apartment block and at the factory.'

'I know, the way they got rid of a perfectly good tenant - and those containers and all the gear on that table, that wasn't set up in five minutes. Not to mention the open container furnished like a Hollywood star's bedroom. I'm sure we have the same suspicion about this?'

'There's probably only one conclusion to be drawn, if you look at it step by step. Street kids and runaways picked up and taken to an apartment, a holding bay, if you like. And then transferred to the factory for something - live-streaming porn or something worse that I'd rather not think about. Send me an email about what you want in your new will. Now you're married you might want to mention specific amounts for Plum and Willow rather than proportions of your total assets.'

'OK, I'll think about it and email you.'

'And by the way, and don't tell me if you don't want to, but how much do you think you're worth in total?

I tell him and there is silence for a moment. 'Holy shit!'

25

'Thank you for coming in, it saves us a lot of time,' says Bakker the next morning. She sounds quite friendly; she's making great progress with her courtesy lessons.

Mariko says she wants Dao and me in the interview room, and Bakker doesn't object. 'Now then,' she says when we are seated on one side of the table opposite her and Apatu. 'What we want is as much detail as you can give us about all those young women who spent time with you in the flat, and the boys, of course. Do you want to tell us straight from memory or would it be a help if you see your textbook notes?'

'I would like to see the notes, please. It will make it easier. I think it was after the second or third girl I started writing things in the physics book, so the information is accurate - I wrote it when each one had just been taken away.'

Bakker puts transcripts of the relevant textbook pages on the table and Mariko studies them in silence for a couple of minutes. 'I wouldn't remember the order or how long each one stayed without this list – or what they told me about themselves.'

'One thing to start with,' Bakker says and looks genuinely interested. 'The book was found in Grace Harris' office, in a desk drawer. She resigned from her job and the book was

189

found by her workmate Linda - the girl who got in touch with Mr Grant. How did Grace get it in the first place? Did you see Grace again and throw it out the window?'

'Yes, the window only opened a little bit, I could only get my hand out. I think I wrote about how one day I saw a woman standing on the other side of the street, with something white in her hand, and I thought it might be the origami shape I had thrown out just before. She just stood there looking up at the building for a long time. I used to spend a lot of time standing at the window looking at the street. I saw her again that last morning - I recognised her even from so high up, short dark hair and a pale coat with a hood. She was standing just like she had before, looking up at the building as if she was trying to figure something out. So, I decided to give her the book with all the writing in case I never saw her again. I waved the white T-shirt out of the window, and she spotted it and waved at me. So, I tied the book up in the T-shirt and threw it out. She ran across the street straight away, right through all the traffic, to pick it up. And then she went back to the other side, and she held it up, so I could see it. It made me feel so good.'

She looks around at us all, not sure who knows what. 'Can I tell you about Grace, please, before we talk about the others?'

'Of course.'

Mariko looks down for a moment before she starts. 'They took Grace – she got into the building somehow after she finished work that day and she rang the doorbell, she knew the number of the flat from the notes she had picked up, and they just grabbed hold of her and shoved her in with me and locked the door. Then they forced her to say where she worked, and we didn't understand why they asked – we discussed it and we couldn't make sense of it. But they must have looked up her workplace on the internet and somehow, they got the phone number to her manager. They didn't get her to type that message saying she was resigning, they did it on my phone and then they told her what they had done. The message will still be there on my phone.'

Mariko is close to tears now and makes an effort to continue. 'When they told us, I knew they would kill her – and I think she knew too. She told me all about her friend Linda, and how they had unfolded the origami notes and read them together and taken photos of them. And about going to the police. She told me that after I threw the book out that morning, she read some of it with a magnifying glass she had, and she left it in her desk drawer to show Linda all the writing the next day. She said she left the book at work because she didn't want to risk having it with her – she had decided to try to get into the building on her way home and she knew she might get into trouble, so she didn't take it with her. But she said, "I was sure that if something happened to me, Linda would find the book, she's very smart and she'll get someone to come and rescue you" – she was a very kind woman.'

'Did you see them kill her?'

'No, they held her down and gave her an injection and soon after she fell on the floor - and they dragged her out and locked the door again.'

'And you never saw her again?'

'No,' says Mariko, and wipes her wet eyes with her fingers. 'I feel as if I killed her – she only came because of the book I threw out for her. But I didn't mean for her to take any risks, I just wanted her to take the book to the police.'

'What Grace decided to do was her decision and nothing you need to blame yourself for,' says Bakker kindly. 'You had only one way to save yourself and you did it very cleverly. Let's have a break now and then we can talk about the other young women. But we don't have to go through them all today.'

Dao and Mariko go for a walk in the corridor, talking quietly with their heads close together; I'm sure Dao is comforting Mariko. Bakker calls a minion who delivers coffee and biscuits, and fifteen minutes later we start again.

I have to admit that whatever I feel about Bakker in general, she gives us a masterclass in how to draw additional information out of a witness. Talking back and forth about each girl and asking Mariko to describe them, what they talked about and what the girls asked her, elicits more and more detail. I listen with amazement to how much Mariko can contribute, when she is guided through it by an expert, far more than she wrote in the book. Feeling that she is of real help seems to cheer her up a bit and I hope it compensates a little for the guilt she feels about Grace.

When Bakker ends the session, Mariko hesitates and asks if she looked in the container where they locked her up. It's obvious that Bakker understands Mariko's hesitation; something significant is being communicated between the two of them.

'Yes, we've taken lots of photographs and got fingerprints and we are doing all kinds of other tests. We'll get your prints before you go, for comparison, and a DNA sample if you are OK with that. If you stay and get that done now, I'll have a police officer take you to your apartment afterwards. I imagine you want to pick up some more clothes and personal belongings. And at the same time, you can point out things that don't belong to you, that those men left behind. We'll get a patrol car to drive you back to Mr Grant's place afterwards.'

My phone pings with an email message as we head back to the North Shore and Dao checks it. 'It's from John Anderson. Listen to this: Very relieved to hear that Mariko is safe, thank you for looking after her. Give her my love. I can't come over right now, will email asap.'

'I suppose he's busy – maybe he has a court case or something.'

Within minutes a call from Bakker's off-sider comes through to tell us that she got a reply from John; we compare notes, and he has said much the same as in his message to me.

'Did you notice Bakker's face when Mariko asked if she'd seen inside the container?' asks Dao.

'I did, and I guess it's important. Do you think Mariko will tell you?'

'I don't know – she's not said anything about it so far. I'm not going to ask.'

In the afternoon Mariko arrives back with a suitcase and a large canvas bag. 'It took so long!' she says. 'First we did the fingerprint thing, and they took the DNA sample and then we went to my flat.' She makes a disgusted face. 'The flat is a complete mess – it's full of that black dust they use to see fingerprints, and the police have been through everything. Those men never cleaned up - they left lots of dirty dishes and filthy sheets and some of their dirty clothes were on the floor in the bathroom – yuk! Thank God they didn't touch my clothes! The police gave me the name of a cleaning company and they will clean everything up.'

I carry her suitcase up to the bedroom and Dao comes with us. 'I've moved stuff out of the wardrobe so you can hang things up, and there's an empty drawer in that chest.'

'Thank you! I'll do it later. I really need a drink of water – I couldn't bear to use anything in my flat that those men had used.'

'What do you think I should do?' asks Mariko, when we sit down with a lunch that is a couple of hours late. 'I got my phone back, but I can't make up my mind. Should I text and email everyone and tell them what happened, in case some of my messages sounded a bit strange? I mean the ones I replied to while I was locked in. Or should I just mention it to my friends in Japan? They must have thought I was mad when I suddenly started replying in English.'

'You know how I told you about what happened to me?' says Dao seriously. 'When Hunter saved me, and we talked to the police there was very little in the papers about me personally. But once I'd been a witness in that court case, things went crazy. My picture was in the paper and on the news for days, and people tried to get in touch with me - they wanted selfies and one guy stood outside the house for days, like a stalker. It was awful! If you tell your friends here in New Zealand what happened, you will be famous in the same way – and you've only just been set free. I think you should leave things alone until that guy comes up in court – if they ever catch him.'

'I think you're right,' Mariko says. 'I won't say anything to my friends here. I'll go back to lectures as if nothing happened – those men made me tell the university I had to go back to Japan for family reasons, so I'll pretend I just came back. I don't want a lot of fuss. Those men left my laptop at the flat, so I've got all my university stuff, but the tablet is gone, of course. When they grabbed me outside the lift, I stood on it and it broke.'

'Bad luck,' I say, 'but I suppose the laptop is more important – at least for your studies.'

'That whole thing was so strange and sudden,' says Mariko. 'Because they didn't see me through the little window in the door to the stairs, they opened the door and they were as surprised as I was, because I was kneeling just by the lift. I had taken lots of things out of my bag to find my keys and I was down on the floor. And then when they grabbed me and I tried to get away, I put my foot on the tablet, I heard it break.'

'I had a text from John,' I say. 'And Bakker got one too. I'll show you. But now you have your phone back you can tell him you're OK yourself.'

'Oh, I forgot to say, another thing that I asked Inspector

Bakker about,' says Mariko. 'I wanted to know if the police did anything when Grace handed in those notes? I mean did they go to the flat or anything. And they did - but one of those men was so clever, he laughed and said it was their teenage cousin playing silly games and he would tell her off and make sure she did not do it next time she came for a visit. He said she was crazy about folding origami and he hadn't realized she was writing pretend help messages inside them.'

We look at each other in silence and I am sure we all think the same thing, that if the police had not been successfully fobbed off Grace would still be alive today.

'I'm still tired,' says Dao. 'I need a nap. Do you need a rest, Mariko?'

'If you're both going to have a sleep, I'll go out and do some errands,' I say. 'I'll set the ground-floor alarm. I'll be back in a couple of hours.'

When I return, Dao is reading in the sofa corner and Mariko is upstairs organising her belongings.

'Good timing,' says Dao. 'We just woke up a few minutes ago.'

'I got a new cell phone for you. Same make but a newer model and I got a tablet for Mariko – don't know what brand hers was, but we can change it if she doesn't like it.'

Dao gives me a hug and sprints up the stairs so fast that Scruff is left confused. Wasn't she here a second ago? Where did she go? Before he makes up his mind, Dao returns with Mariko in tow.

She puts her hands together and bows, 'Thank you, Hunter san!' I love Japanese manners; they make the rest of us look like barbarians. 'I will pay you back.'

'It's a reward,' I say, 'a present for being so clever with those origami shapes. I don't think we'd be standing here now, if you hadn't folded them and caught Grace's attention.'

We sit down to get the devices charging and set up, and then Mariko goes back upstairs.

'I thought she was going to hug you!' says Dao. 'Lucky she didn't!'

To my surprise Bakker calls again right at the end of the afternoon. 'I'm sending you a couple of photos by email,' she says. 'Please get Dao to have a look. I'll put my cell phone number in the email so she can call me back – as soon as you can. And can I speak to Mariko, please.'

Hearing one side of the conversation tells me little; Mariko listens more than she speaks, says 'no' and 'only that one time when they talked about money' and 'I don't think so' and then she ends the call.

The email arrives a few minutes later. "Please ask Dao if she remembers seeing something similar to photo #1 on the table in the factory. Would have been where I have drawn a circle on photo #2."

Photo #1 is a dark grey rectangular object with a cable coming from one end. There is a ruler beside it which shows it is 14 cm long. Photo #2 is the table in the factory: two computers, two keyboards, and a mixture of junk and technical gadgets that I don't recognise. The circle is drawn halfway between the two computers, where two cords lie unplugged.

'But I have no idea what was there,' says Dao. 'Of course, Bakker thinks I found the gun on the table, but I didn't even look at it. Can you please call her back and tell her I didn't see it?'

'I'll call her, but she'll want to talk to you.'

Dao makes a hideous face. 'OK.' She talks to Bakker for a couple of minutes and then hands the phone to me. 'She wants to talk to you again.'

'Hunter,' says Bakker, who suddenly seems to be on first name terms with us. 'Would you please ask Mariko to look at those photos too? It's a crucial piece of the puzzle.'

'What is it?'

'The tech guys tell me it's probably an external hard drive – for backup. They say the way the cables are lying unattached on the table, one from each computer, would be because both computers could be plugged into it – one at a time. We've got the rough size of it from the dust free area where it was – that table is filthy. Everything that they filmed in those containers is probably backed up on that hard drive, so it's very important that we find it.'

'Isn't it saved on the computers too?'

'No, apparently not – I've just been told the details an hour ago, but it seems whatever they saved on that hard drive was live-streamed as well – via some kind of satellite link. And to have everything stored on a device that could be picked up and taken away very easily was probably a security thing – easy to remove fast, not like carrying a laptop or a computer away in a hurry. They might have hidden it somewhere, that's one option. I think maybe the guy who disappeared took it with him. We just need to know.'

'Is there a washing machine carton at the factory? Perhaps outside? I've been thinking about that video clip from the apartment block - the guy taking it down to the parking garage.'

'No, we've looked for it at the factory, but no sign of it. We are searching the apartment block now.'

'Try the mangroves,' I say on an impulse. 'Perhaps they just tossed the carton in the water.'

'And if Mariko remembers anything about that third man, get her to call me asap.'

'What third man?'

'We've seen the two guys from flat 403 with someone we can't identify – only once, they are on the lift camera, they went down in the lift together and it's obvious they know each other. So, we re-checked all the video - he's very easy to recognise. He has come and gone via the parking garage lots of times over the last few weeks, but he never used the lift apart from that one time – he always went up the stairs. But because there aren't any cameras on the landings, we can't say for sure that he went to 403 each time – he might be a tenant. He arrives on foot, gets into the underground car park with a card, same as residents.'

'If he doesn't live there, I suppose the guys in 403 could have given him one of their cards,' I say, not sure if she is really open to discussion or suggestions.

'We're doing a big door knocking exercise right now, trying to talk to every resident, showing them a picture of him. I don't really expect it to lead to anything, but you never know. Let me know if Mariko comes up with anything else.'

I can't believe she's talking to me like this, volunteering information, but probably she wants to engage my interest and make sure I bring it up with Mariko.

I'm not sure what I had expected Mariko to be like. What she wrote about herself in the textbook was concise and unemotional, more a potted history than a personal document. What she wrote about her mother insisting they spoke English regularly explains her ease and fluency with the language, but that isn't what makes her so confident, her personality is extraordinary. Somehow, I imagined she would be a bit shy and maybe hesitant, unsure of how to deal with new people and a strange household. Instead, she is self-possessed, calm and comfortable in her own skin. Now she surprises me again with how proactive and on to it she is.

'I called the cleaning company,' she says after dinner. 'I've given them a list of things to do, well, everything really – empty the fridge, put everything in the kitchen through the dishwasher and strip the bed. They specialise in cleaning up crime scenes and they're used to doing it properly. But I need the name of the man who let you watch video – the one who manages the building. I need new keys – no, I need a new lock and new keys. Apparently, he organises things like that.'

'Silvano,' says Dao. 'He's very nice.'

'Can I stay here until my flat is clean, please?'

'You can stay as long as you like,' I say. 'You might want to have some company for a bit longer before you move back.'

26

I'm at the desk in our bedroom, while Dao studies and Mariko is on her way to the university to meet with her dean about how to catch up on her studies. Today I must get some work done and a few hours of solid effort will take care of it. But when I log on, the first thing that pops up is an email from John.

Hunter

I am sorry to leave you in loco parentis, but I find myself in a difficult situation which limits my movements. I am no longer in the US and cannot travel anywhere. I have made some arrangements for Mariko, and I would be grateful if you can help her find an attorney to do anything that needs doing at your end. The flat she has been living in is now hers, copies of the paperwork are attached, nothing more needs to be done about that. The trust fund that has paid her expenses so far will last until she completes her degree (trust deed attached).

I have informed a colleague (copy of letter of instruction to him is attached), that Mariko is my daughter and appointed him sole trustee of the trust fund. Please print the documents and give them to Mariko and give copies to her lawyer.

Many thanks, John

PS This email address is being discontinued, as is my work address and cell phone number.

Gobsmacked is the only word for it. I sit there, reading and re-reading his letter while speculations and consequences spin through my head. I wonder about New Zealand law and possible implications regarding Mariko's apartment. I want to discuss this with someone sensible, so I call Benson.

'Hunter,' he says. 'How are things?'

'Are you busy or can you spare ten minutes? You can call me back if you like.'

'No, just tell me. You sound stressed. Is Dao OK?'

'Holy cow!' he says, when I have read out John's letter. 'What has he done? Sounds like he's expecting to be charged with something very serious. I suppose you have a theory?'

'It's got to be that he is involved on some level in what went on here. The way he left the US, it sounds permanent – cutting off all links like phone and email. I think he must have had an escape planned and ready to go – funds in some country with no extradition agreement with the US, maybe a new identity. What do you think?'

'Sounds like it. It's not something I have any experience of, but I imagine it takes time to get things like that set up.'

'Would you like to stop by on your way home tonight? I need to sit down with Mariko and discuss this – there will be questions and speculation from her and Dao. And you're the voice of authority on all things illegal - I would appreciate your help.'

'Hang on a moment, will you?'

I hear someone talking to him in the background, he says something I can't hear, somebody laughs and then comes back to me. 'OK, I can probably be there about half past six.'

Willow would be a perfect lawyer for Mariko from a personal angle; she is kind and understanding and Mariko would soon regard her as a friend. But it was only a couple of weeks ago that she told me how much she has on her plate and how she struggles to spend enough time with the twins, so I forward John's email to Simon. He already knows the background, which is an advantage, and if Mariko doesn't want to deal with him, I know he will keep his mouth shut about what I have told him.

I get busy with a new quote for a prospective client in Mexico. He doesn't say what he does, but it's either drugs or dangerous politics – or possibly both. He wants bodyguards who are trained to drive a heavy vehicle, like a three-ton armoured Mercedes. He says he will provide appropriate weapons and deal with the visa situation, so he has friends in the right places or plenty of money for bribes. It is a simple enough situation and I draft a basic proposal; two men with protection experience, at least one of them with evasive driving training. No need for a personal army, like the crazy job we set up six months ago, when a client in Africa wanted what amounted to a small assault unit made up of men with combat experience. We still have eight of our men out there, earning big money and doing the job they are trained for.

Dao has just brought me a cup of coffee and returned downstairs when Simon calls. 'This gets more interesting every day,' he says. 'I will help Mariko deal with this – it isn't every day I get to feel I'm involved in international crime. There might be potential ramifications that would be better dealt with early on, to protect her assets. Just text me if you want me to come over – I haven't been to your place for a while. Have you still got some of that fabulous red from Craggy Range?'

I decide not to tell Dao that Benson is coming; her spontaneous reaction when he or Charlie arrives is the kind of five-star welcome most people never get, and I know he loves it. For the rest of the day my thoughts keep reverting to John Anderson and his apparent flight from the US. I try to recall exactly what he said when he told us he acted for the owners of the apartment block, but as far as I can remember it was pretty vague, and the only significant moment was when he reacted to Dao's talking about the Cayman Islands company.

When Dao goes down to play with Scruff in the courtyard after lunch, I take the opportunity to print the documents John sent. Twenty-four pages in total – I feel no compunction about reading them, he has already told me what they contain. They seem to cover all possible eventualities, and the care he is taking to make sure Mariko is financially secure makes me feel better towards him, though I reserve judgement on his general ethics until I know more about why he has gone into hiding. There is a raft of questions I would like answers to. Has he left his wife behind, and his other children? Did he know what went on in those containers? And is he wealthy because he is, or was, a successful lawyer - or did criminal activities provide all the money he seems to have amassed? I staple the documents together and put them aside; I won't tell Dao about this until Mariko comes back.

When she does arrive, she is full of news about her day and wants to tell us all about it; this is an upbeat side of her we haven't seen before. She has met with her dean and a couple of lecturers and sorted out how to catch up on her studies after missing lectures and lab sessions, and she has had lunch with some friends. Last of all she mentions that Bakker has texted her and asked her to come in to be interviewed again.

'They're trying to work out who those girls were - they're comparing what I told them with their register of people reported missing,' she says. 'They found some of the girls from the apartment on video from the garage and the lifts and they want me to come in and see if I can name them. I think they are hoping to contact their families to see if they have returned home - or perhaps just tell them something bad probably happened to them. I would hate to have her job!'

'I had an email from John,' I say after a while. 'He

probably thought you might not have your computer or your phone, so he sent it to me.' I hand her the printed email message, and she reads it twice, then sits looking down at the paper in her hand for a long time, before she looks up at me. 'Do you understand this?'

'I think I do – but I could be wrong.'

Dao is looking at me and then at Mariko, trying to work out what is going on; the tension in Mariko's voice is obvious. I pick up the pile of stapled documents and hand them to her. 'These are the documents he attached to the email.'

There is a long silence. Mariko looks at the papers in her hand and makes no move to read them, just sits silently thinking before she puts them down on the coffee table. 'Have you told Dao?'

'No – it's for you to decide if you want to tell her.'

She hands Dao the email message and she reads it, shakes her head and frowns. 'I don't know what you think, Hunter, but I think he's taken off – and he's not going back.'

'Yes, probably.'

'And you don't know where he is now?' asks Mariko.

'I have no idea – but I'd guess he's in some country that the US authorities can't extradite him from. I think it must mean that he knows a lot more than he let on when he was here, and whatever has been going on is not confined to New Zealand, it involves the authorities in the US too and maybe other countries - and he thinks or knows that he will be implicated. I honestly don't know what to think about his role – was he part of something illegal knowingly, is he a criminal? Or did he just act for the company that own the buildings and now he has discovered they are criminals and he's running scared?'

But of course, I don't think that. No way would he abandon his whole life and go into hiding abroad if it was just a client connection. He must have had a much closer involvement than that to take such a drastic step, and to effectively disappear he must have made a lot of preparations far in advance.

'I can't *believe* it!' Mariko bursts out, dismayed at the thought her father is probably a criminal. 'First, I had no father for most of my life, then I found him, but he didn't want to get to know me. And then he did get to know me, and he was really kind – and generous, and I was so happy. He didn't pretend he loved me or anything, but he liked me, he said so. He is probably not a man with a lot of emotions, I don't think. And he made it so easy for me to come here to study. He gave me a choice of USA or somewhere else where they speak English and I picked New Zealand. And now he has disappeared, and he might be a criminal! I don't know what I feel about him now.'

'He's still your father, whatever he was involved in,' says Dao. 'And he's obviously concerned about you – look what he has set up for you. He wants you to be safe and happy. And he came rushing over here as soon as he found out what had happened to you.'

Personally, I think that the urgency was probably a combination of two things: he knew what apartment 403 was used for and was terrified about something happening to Mariko, but he was also concerned about the fall-out for himself. But there is no point in ruining Mariko's opinion of her father any further.

'You're going to need a lawyer. Do you have one?' I ask, to divert her for a moment, and she shakes her head. 'No – John did everything, got me a student visa, organised the flat and my bank account.' She gives me a wry smile, 'Once our neighbour's nephew had agreed to take over the flat, all I had to do was decide what I wanted to study and pack my clothes.'

'My friend Simon is my lawyer and Dao's too - and he already knows a lot about this from when we went to ask his advice when Bakker first threatened to arrest me, and I've talked to him since. Would you like to meet him? And if you decide you trust him, I'm sure he would help you with whatever you need to do next.'

'Thank you, Hunter san, you are very kind.'

I text Simon and ask him to come over after work and say we'll give him dinner.

27

When Benson arrives, Dao runs down to let him in and while they have a long conversation in the downstairs hall, I say quietly to Mariko, 'I told Benson about the letter – not the details. He might know something and he's always helpful.'

'Dao trusts him, so I trust him too,' she says calmly.

I pour Benson a beer and a glass of wine for myself; Dao and Mariko both want a glass of Dao's favourite Lemon, Lime and Bitters, and by the time that is done, Simon arrives. He and Benson have never met but have both heard me talk about the other.

'Nice to meet you finally, Benson!' says Simon, when I introduce them. 'I've heard a lot about you from Hunter and Dao. I believe you belong to Dao's fan club?'

'Founding member,' says Benson, not batting an eyelid. 'Nice to meet you too.'

I recap what we know, and Simon turns to Mariko, 'Would you mind if I read the documents your father sent?'

She hands them to him without comment and he reads them, while Dao tells Benson about the interview with Bakker. 'She has improved a bit, you know. She doesn't seem to hate Hunter now – it's not as if she suddenly loves him, but she treats him nearly like a normal person.'

'I'm glad to hear that. I have found out why she was to antagonistic to start with - it's linked to that thing I tried to remember when we talked about this earlier, Hunter. I'll tell you the details another time.'

'Hmm,' says Simon and puts the papers back on the coffee table. 'I'll have to look into trust laws in the US first, but it looks OK to me, Mariko. The only thing you might want to consider is to ask that chap, who is now the sole trustee, if he would agree to invest the capital in New Zealand government bonds or something rock solid in Japan, rather than US shares. You don't want to lose it all, if there's another global financial crisis. Not that anything is totally safe, but there are degrees of risk to consider.'

'Are the papers for the apartment real – I mean, do I really own the apartment?'

'It certainly looks as if you do. I'll check it tomorrow and call you, but it looks fine.'

We have dinner out of the freezer, where we always have plenty of backup dinners: our staple salmon pasta-bake from our favourite deli and then homemade ice cream, courtesy of Tama and Tyler, who gave us their experimental ice cream recipes when we bought an ice cream maker like theirs.

'Great ice cream,' says Benson and looks at the bright pink in his bowl. 'I can't imagine what it is, but it's good!'

Dao laughs, 'You're not going to believe it – beetroot and sweet basil and a bit of honey! And cream, of course. Tama invented it.'

'Aha, the famous Tama,' says Benson. 'I hear he's doing OK. Back on the job and promoted.'

We exchange a smile; we were worried his career would suffer, despite the fact that he identified a murderer when it was discovered how much confidential information he had given to me and subsequently to the police.

'Nobody deserves it more,' I say, and Dao adds seriously, 'If it hadn't been for him, nobody would ever have found out what had happened to Hope – he is so clever and now he's a friend.'

And then, suddenly, Mariko pushes her ice cream bowl to one side and turns to Benson with a look of nearly desperate determination on her face. 'Did Bakker tell you about the container I was in?'

He shakes his head. 'No, but there's no reason for her to tell me things. The investigation is nothing to do with me - it was only that phone call from Dao's driver that got me involved at all, and I'm out of the loop now. What was inside the container?'

She hesitates, looks briefly at each one of us, as if she is assessing if we can handle what she is about to say. 'It looked like the inside of a fridge. Everything was lined with smooth panels, like white plastic - the walls and the ceiling. The floor was some kind of grey rubber tiles and there were spotlights in the corners and above the bed, if you can call it that - and a hole in the floor.'

She is looking steadily at us, waiting for a reaction. I know what I think, but I'm not going to say it. 'Wasn't it a real bed?'

'There was nothing in there apart from a raised – platform, I suppose you could call it – a box shape, also covered in that white plastic panel stuff. I slept on the floor.'

Her expression is one of tight control; she looks around the table at our faces, but nobody seems to know what to say. Dao is looking puzzled and I desperately don't want Mariko to say what is probably on the tip of her tongue. And then she says it. 'There were hooks on the sides of the box thing – I think they probably tied people down, maybe they tortured or killed some of those girls there. And then they washed the blood off, and all the water ran out through the hole. There's probably a drain under the container.'

Benson looks inscrutable, as he nearly always does, and

Simon says 'shit!' very quietly. I glance at Dao; her face is calm, but that means nothing. That blank look is a form of self-protection she developed during her years in captivity.

Someone has to say something. 'Was there anything else in there?' I ask. 'Something that made you think that's what they used it for?'

'Only some hooks in the walls and in the ceiling. Before they brought me there from the flat, they gave me something - some drug that made me feel drunk so I couldn't protest or even walk properly, and when we got to the factory, they opened the container and pushed me in. It smelt funny in there, the smell kind of woke me up a bit.' She nods to herself. 'It was bleach – a very strong smell of bleach.'

Dao makes a nearly inaudible groan, gets up and runs upstairs and Benson looks at me with raised eyebrows; I nod and get up to follow her. Out of the corner of my eye I see Simon look a question at Benson. I leave them to it; Benson will take care of it.

Dao is sitting on the edge of the bed; her hands are clenched into tight fists, her expression agonised. I close the door and crouch in front of her and take her hands.

'It's horrible, I know. I'll stop them talking about it – Mariko can tell Bakker about the bleach tomorrow.' I uncurl her fingers and rub her palms with my thumbs.

'No, it's not that – it's the rubbish sacks!' she says urgently, and her voice is full of revulsion. 'Those rubbish sacks I tripped on - in the water! I stood on someone's dead body!'

I sit down beside her and pull her on to my lap, she leans into me and after a couple of minutes, she speaks into my neck. 'Thanks, I'm OK now. Let's go back down – I must tell Benson.'

'Are you sure?'

'You know what?' she says over her shoulder, as she opens the door. 'When you hold me, I feel stronger, like I'm taking some of your strength - it feels lovely.'

'You've got plenty of your own, but you're welcome to mine when you need it.'

Downstairs they all look at Dao, concerned about her reaction, but she's totally focused on Benson. 'We've got to call Bakker now – right away. If Mariko is right, I think I know where the bodies are.'

There is stunned silence for a moment and then Benson says gently, 'Yes?' and Dao nods decisively. 'When Mariko and I were wading through the mangroves, I tripped and fell right in. That's when I lost my phone. We kind of felt around with our hands and feet, to see if we could find it. And I realised I had tripped on a rubbish sack, and there was another one further on, I felt them with my feet – I had lost my shoes, I felt the shiny plastic. With hard … things inside.'

She stops to draw breath and for a moment nobody speaks; they just sit there looking at her, and then Benson gets his phone out. 'I'll call Bakker now.'

He goes down and sits at the bottom of the stairs to the ground floor and talks to her for a long time. Conversation around the table is subdued and when Benson comes back up, his face grim. 'Bakker agrees with you about the container, Mariko. The hole in the floor is connected to a drain, and they found traces of blood when they sprayed luminol – there's been blood everywhere, on the floor and on the walls, and in the joins between the panels and inside the drain. They've already organised a team to go out to search the swamp first thing tomorrow.'

'Aha, that's what the bleach smell was about. But does luminol work if they cleaned with bleach?' asks Simon. 'I thought criminals used it to conceal blood stains.'

Benson smiles wryly. 'We used to think that's how it worked, but we know better now – a university in the US did some research on it a few years ago. Chlorine bleach does conceal the traces of blood for about eight hours, and then you can detect the blood again, as good as ever when you spray with luminol. So, if the place smells of bleach, you just wait until you can see the blood again when you spray it. But if they use peroxide-based bleach you can't get DNA from it. The best way to get rid of all traces of blood, is to wash repeatedly with cold water.'

I suddenly realise I haven't told them about the third man; Mariko knows of course, but she and I haven't discussed it.

'Listen,' I say. 'Another thing that Bakker told me – much to my surprise – is that there's a third man involved. He comes and goes via the underground car park at the apartments, on foot and he has a swipe card for the gate. He's only used the lift once, when he was with the two guys from flat 403. Bakker said it was obvious that they know each other. But apart from being on the lift camera once, he's always used the stairs from the car parking level.'

Benson turns to Mariko. 'That might have been the man who was in the flat when you heard them speaking English. When they discussed how to transfer money without being traced. Did you ever hear them speak English to anyone again?'

'No, but I didn't usually hear them talking at all. I don't know if there was always one man in the same flat as I was – if I didn't hear anything, it didn't mean one of them wasn't there. I never dared try to attract attention even when it had been quiet for hours, so I always assumed one of them was there – I knew what they might do to me. Very occasionally I heard them talking through the bathroom wall, when they were both in my flat.'

'I wonder what he did, that third one?' Simon reaches for the wine bottle. 'A local perhaps. Could be a tech guy who set up the recording stuff in the factory?'

'Are you driving?' asks Benson casually, watching Simon fill his glass. 'If you drink that glass of wine, I'll take your car keys off you. I'll overlook just so much, but this is where it stops.'

'Oops,' says Simon. 'I got carried away with this gorgeous red. You're quite right, sorry!'

It's not that I enjoy Simon being marginally embarrassed, but it needed to happen. He has been doing this for years; drinking too much and then getting into his car to drive home. It is a miracle he hasn't been caught or caused an accident. I catch Benson's eye and smile. 'Always on the job – you saved me saying it this time.'

He nods. 'It's one thing I never let up on. Doesn't matter who it is or where – I saw too much tragedy on the roads when I was a young cop, marked me for life.'

I turn back to Mariko. 'And you don't remember anything else about what they said that day? Something that might help Bakker find out who he is. She said he is very easy to recognize and they're knocking on every single door in the whole building - showing people a picture of him. But I forgot to ask what makes him so recognizable.'

Mariko is distracted, thinking about something else. I wait for her to answer, but she doesn't say anything, and the conversation reverts to general topics. Just as Benson announces that he must leave, he has to be up very early in the morning, Mariko exclaims, 'He had an American accent.'

Benson is immediately alert. 'Are you sure?'

'Yes, I've just kind of played it back, inside my head, you know – what I heard that time they argued about getting money from John – ransom I suppose it was. He did have an American accent, or maybe Canadian. I can't really tell the difference.'

Benson gets his phone out and calls Bakker again. 'Hope she hasn't gone to bed.'

But she is awake and very interested. Benson passes his phone to Mariko and she tells Bakker what she just told us; the conversation takes several minutes because Bakker is asking a lot of questions.

'Let me ask you something,' Mariko says politely, with a slight emphasis on 'you' and I hear the 'for a change' strongly implied at the end. 'Hunter told me you said the man is easy to recognize – in what way?'

Bakker replies at length, and Mariko's gaze is unfocused as she listens. 'And when was that?' She nods at whatever Bakker tells her, says goodbye and passes the phone back to Benson.

'He is very tall, a little taller than Hunter probably, not skinny, he wears t-shirts even when it's cold and his head is shaved. She says his nose has been broken and he looks as if he works out – big muscles in his arms. The last video of him was the same day the men moved me to the factory – very early in the morning.'

When we finally get to bed, Dao wriggles close. 'I was really scared, Hunter – in the factory, I mean. And on the way there, when I was thinking of what I might have to do - you know, go in and maybe get trapped in there and what they might do to me … I know I'm safe now, but it's like the fear won't quite let go, it's still with me for no reason.'

I hold her close, and she melts into me as if she is trying to get under my skin. 'This stops now,' I say. 'We are never getting involved in anything like this again. It's too damaging. I don't care if we have to move or change our name – but I promise you, this is stopping. All we have to do is say "no" if somebody asks us for help again.'

She sighs and whispers, 'Good.'

At two in the morning, I am woken by Dao crying quietly with her back turned. I reach out and pull her close. She sobs into my chest and her tears run down my ribs; it takes several minutes to calm her and when she finally speaks, her voice is muffled by crying.

'I had a horrible dream that I was walking in that swamp and there were dead bodies in rubbish sacks on the bottom – everywhere - and my feet kept touching them and standing on them and …'

There is nothing I can say. I wrap her in my arms until she settles down. Her breathing slows and she falls asleep, but I lie awake for a long time, thinking of all that has happened to her in her short life. Nothing will damage her again if I can possibly prevent it. There is only so much anyone can take, even intrepid Dao. We need to have a normal life.

We hear it on the news the next morning when we are making breakfast: A foreign national, wanted in connection with a human trafficking ring, has been arrested at Auckland airport. The report is brief and mentions no specifics. Dao goes up to tell Mariko, who is getting dressed and I hear them discussing it. They sound quite relaxed about it, and not for the first time I wonder why they never worried that he would try to locate them, to silence them, something that has been in the back of mind since they escaped. If he is the one who killed the girl in the flat, and Mariko the only one who could testify against him, then she would have been his primary target.

But Mariko, that self-possessed young woman, continues to seem surprisingly normal. She takes herself off to yet another interview with Bakker and stays in town to meet with Simon, who must have called her on her cell phone after she left our place. She texts late in the afternoon and says she will be home a bit late, and she will take a taxi, because she has some big parcels.

Dao, who for the first half of the day never ventured further than an arm's length from me, is in the courtyard, once again trying to teach Scruff to count. I lean over the glass barrier of the balcony and tell her about Mariko's message, and she looks up and smiles. 'Linen,' she says cryptically and turns back to Scruff.

Later she comes up for a drink of water and perches on the arm of my chair, leans her head against mine. 'It gets very hot in the courtyard – it's so sheltered. Do you think dogs can get heatstroke?'

'I don't know, but we can do a search on the Internet. We could put up a shade sail for him.'

'Yes, let's do that! And I will buy him a paddling pool, so he can cool off. And when we need to change the water, we just tip it out and it waters the grass.'

'How is Scruff getting on with his counting?'

'I'm not sure maths is his thing,' says Dao seriously. 'He usually likes learning – he's a natural student, but I don't think he's interested in numbers.'

'Never mind, he has learnt lots since you've been teaching him. I never taught him anything apart from walking to heel. And by the way, what did you mean when you said "linen"?'

'She's buying new sheets and things – she can't stand the thought of sleeping on the ones those men used, even after they've been washed. She told the cleaning company to take them away.'

She gets up, but changes her mind, sits down on the arm of my chair again and moves my arm, so it is around her back. 'I want to tell you something – it's about the day they arrested you. You know how I'd said that morning that I would just get up and leave if they arrested you, because I knew I would cry if I had to watch them do things to you?'

'I know, it was a good plan – and your exit and the way you left the door open behind you, that was great. Apatu particularly enjoyed it.'

'I didn't know I would feel so lonely – no, not just lonely, I felt unprotected when I walked to the bus stop. You're always there beside me, or practically always, and it was horrible, like someone had taken part of me away. And then when I got home and I let Scruff in, he looked past me to see where you were – I couldn't help it, I just sat down on the floor by the courtyard door and cried and cried.'

I can't say anything or I might cry myself. I pull her onto my lap, and we sit there for a long time, close together.

A couple of days pass without much excitement and everyone settles down a bit. We ask Mariko to stay a bit longer and she says she will; however well she is coping I think she likes having company. She goes to lectures by bus and often stays a bit longer in town to be with her friends.

Things change when Sergeant Apatu calls early one morning to apologize for not offering Mariko and Dao help from Victim Support. 'There's no excuse,' he says and sounds as if he means it. 'It's always offered to anyone affected - I don't know what happened. There are counsellors and therapists available to deal with any after-effects.'

'They seem OK so far, thanks, but I'll ask them and call you back,' I say and think that anything could be brewing under the surface, ready to erupt. I have a pretty good idea about what goes on in Dao's mind and I think I can help her deal with it, but you never know. I go down to the courtyard where Dao is trying to entice Scruff to get into his new paddling pool.

Mariko is standing in the shade of the wall laughing and taking pictures with her phone. 'You might as well give up, Dao,' she says and darts to one side to avoid getting splashed. 'You're getting wetter than he is. He thinks it's a big water bowl for him to drink from and he can't understand why you're standing in it.'

When I talk to them about Apatu's call, they look at each other and then at me and shake their heads. 'I've got you - I don't need anyone else,' says Dao. 'And I have Mariko and Benson – I don't want to talk to some stranger who doesn't know me!'

'What about you, Mariko?' However well-adjusted she might seem on the surface I am concerned about her. I think she is very good at hiding her feelings, so who knows what she might need?

'No, thank you, Hunter san. I think I'm all right – Dao and I talk about it quite a lot. And I talk to you. I don't think I need anything else.' And then she smiles. 'And being with my friends in town is great, nobody knows anything about it – it's kind of like it never happened when I'm with them. It was good advice you gave me, not to tell anyone yet. But I've got to get ready to go to class now – I'll see you later.'

I return Apatu's call to tell him this and there is a lot of noise going on in the background and he shouts, 'Hang on, can't hear you – I'll go outside.'

Someone speaks to him as he walks past, I hear him say, 'OK, I'm talking to him right now.'

'Sorry,' he says a moment later. 'We have noisy machinery in there and the whole place is reverberating. What did the girls say? Should I ask victim support to send someone over to have a chat?'

'They say they have each other, and they talk to me – they are obviously disturbed by all they've been through, but I think we can cope.'

'Well, call me if you change your mind – these things often pop up later and cause all kinds of trouble.'

Which I know, of course, from personal experience. 'Thanks. What's all the noise inside about?' I don't expect him to answer; it's none of my business, but you can always ask.

Instead of answering he says, 'I'm supposed to have a chat with you about what we have found here. Have you got a moment?'

'Of course.'

Behind me Mariko calls out 'Bye!' and runs down the stairs on her way out.

'Well,' he pauses, as if he is unsure of where to start. 'First up, this – the swamp is being grid searched and so far, we have found the bodies of two girls and a young boy. It will be on the news tonight, but we are not releasing any details of how they died. You might want to assure Mariko, if she asks, that we won't ask her to identify which of the victims she can link to specific details in her notes. What went on in that slaughterhouse is extreme – I've never seen anything like it – harrowing. We'll get Mariko to ID the airport guy, of course – tell us if he's the one who killed that first girl in the flat, but we're pretty sure he is.'

I can only be grateful that Dao and Mariko didn't see any of those bodies; to hear a staunch-looking warrior like Apatu describe the sight as harrowing tells me all I need to know.

'We've also discovered that the whole site was covered by CCTV – there are cameras in three places. One at the back, mounted at an angle behind a downpipe on the rear corner of the building - very hard to notice. And then two at the front, one in a hole in the front of that container that's sitting out there, and one on a streetlamp pole.'

'I wondered about that container. Is that all it was for – to mount a camera?'

'No, it's like a hub for their technical and communications gear, connected by some kind of fancy cable to the factory – out through a hole in one wall and then into the container. Not that we understand why they didn't have that gear inside the building – the current theory is that it's so it can be removed in one lift, so to speak, without dismantling anything. I'm not a tech person, but the High-tech Crimes people say there's equipment for live-streaming what they filmed inside the factory via some sophisticated gear. And also something called a video management system that stores the footage from the outside cameras – which also got streamed somewhere else. And some other gear that I've forgotten what it's called, something to do with satellites. Not sure if my terminology is correct, but that's the gist of it. I'll wait until they write a report and then I'll get a grip on it.'

'And?' I can tell there's more to come; he's not telling me

this just because he thinks I'm interested; somehow this has to do with us.

'The thing is that the guys are having a good look at everything, and they found some very good video of Dao – and you. And vehicles.'

Now I get it. Dao and I went there on the way to have dinner with Simon, so that's my car recorded. Charlie took Dao there while I was in the cell, so probably her car is on record. And then Dao went into the back yard from the swamp side and got recorded at the back. The second time she went, Richard parked across the street and Dao got out of that car and walked along to the site she used to access the strip along the swamp, so she was captured at least twice just heading in.

'Night vision?'

'Yeah, everything, the best you can buy - very high definition, infrared, even some kind of automatic zoom function triggered in certain situations.'

'What situations?'

'I don't know. The guys say there's very sharp high-definition close-ups of Dao's face as she approaches the building from the back. And daylight images of her and a woman walking a dog. And good shots of you driving past with your window down and Dao in the passenger seat, stopping and looking directly at the building.'

There's a warning implied in what he's revealing. He doesn't say "number plate clearly visible" but I can hear it. I want to find out what is behind it. 'Tell me, does Bakker think they might come after Dao or me? And if she believes that, why?'

He clears his throat. 'The guy we caught at the airport - he didn't have the external backup device that's missing from the table in the factory. Well, we're pretty certain that's what had been attached to those cables – that was the storage, so to speak and at the same time the video went to the live-streaming set-up in the outside container. It's possible he gave the backup hard drive to someone, but so far we only know one of their contacts – that third guy who came and went to the apartment. Maybe one of them hid the hard drive somewhere, so they could sell it back to whoever runs this operation - you know, like ransom. If that hard drive contains all they ever filmed, it's worth big money – as blackmail and for on-selling.'

I can hear what he's not saying, so I say it for him. 'It could also mean that someone thinks Dao or Mariko took it. Have you located that third guy?'

'No, not yet.'

'And you never told me what all the noise inside is about.' I might as well get all the information I can, seeing he is not holding back.

'We've got big forklifts in to move the containers out onto the forecourt to load on a truck, but it's tricky manoeuvring them out of the building and the echo effect in there is terrible. The truck is waiting out the front as we speak – they can't load inside because with the container onboard it would be too tall to get out under that roller door. But to go back to those videos – the boss thinks the possibility of trouble is remote, so don't worry too much about it.'

29

History repeats itself they say. It's only six or seven months ago that I felt the deep relief that comes of knowing something intensely dangerous is over, that life is back to normal. On that occasion fate stepped in and quickly proved me wrong and I never imagined it would happen again. I don't care what Bakker thinks; we have the same facts at our disposal and what she believes is only her opinion, not worth any more than mine.

I am not really interested in trying to assess how likely it is that someone, for example the third guy, has found out who we are and where we live. If there is the slightest chance of danger, I will take measures to protect us. My only problem is what to tell Dao and Mariko. If I paint too dark a picture, they might never feel safe again, and then I'm the one who has caused damage. If I don't tell them, they won't be alert to risk. I sit there for a long time with the phone in my hand and try to balance pros and cons, but I need more information. I go upstairs and sit at the desk in the bedroom and call Apatu again, because I don't want Dao to overhear this call.

'Hi, it's Hunter again – just a question for your guys who are going through the CCTV footage from the factory – maybe they could call me back or send a message. I want to know what the backyard camera filmed when Dao and Mariko escaped. I want to know if there are clear images that show that neither of them could have carried the hard drive.'

He sounds surprised, 'Really? But OK, I'll ask someone to call you back. I can't promise when – everyone's pretty busy.'

I hope the call will come soon, so I can question them in detail about the footage from that backyard camera and I don't want the girls to hear me; I'm going to be very specific. Mariko is at lectures today and not expected back until the end of the day. When I went upstairs Dao was at the dining table watching something on her laptop with headphones on. I run downstairs and circle behind her to see what she's watching; a lecture delivered by a man with glasses standing in front of a green 'blackboard' full of unintelligible mathematics. She is taking notes as she listens and it has a long way to run, so she will be there for a while yet. I retreat upstairs and wait for the call.

'Hi, Hunter,' says a woman's voice, 'about the video of the girls escaping out the back of this place? I've got it in front of me now. Do you want me to tell you frame by frame what I see, or should I just send it to you?'

This is unexpected, I didn't even consider asking if I could see it. 'I'd like to have it if that's OK with you.'

'Saves me a lot of time,' she says cheerfully, 'and I can't see any harm in it.'

I give her my email address and hope she gets a chance to send it before someone tells her she can't. I still half expect Bakker to start treating me like public enemy number one again one day, so if she hears one of the tech people is sending me CCTV footage, she might decide I can't have it. She did seem to regard me as a normal human being the last couple of times I talked to her, but I am not banking on it being permanent.

Five minutes later I have the video clip, which shows Dao and Mariko running diagonally across the yard behind the factory, filmed from the far corner of the building. They erupt out of the door and race side by side towards the far end of the concrete yard. Dao reaches the fence first, stops to tuck the pistol into her back pocket, gestures for Mariko to climb over and follows her. They run hand in hand through the grass towards the mangroves, down the incline and disappear into the darkness among the trees.

I go over it again and again, stop on certain images and enlarge them, study every detail. There is no way Mariko could have concealed anything, not even a 12 cm long case, not even a slim one. When she twists at the top of the fence, holds on to the tall fence post and jumps down on the other side, you see her, back and front. She is wearing leggings and a close-fitting, long-sleeved top - she is not carrying anything. Dao is a different matter; she has pockets and the little soft bag that hangs just in front of her left hip with her phone in it.

I turn the recording off and run through the possible consequences in my head. Someone who has not had access to the CCTV footage might suspect one of the girls took the hard drive. And if they have seen the footage, they might think Dao had it in the bag. If they track us via the number plate on my car and come after us, then I must get Mariko out of the house and to some place not directly traceable. It seems unlikely that those men knew what or where she studies and the third man no longer has access to her cell phone, so he can't find out that way. But every time she leaves or comes back to our house poses an element of risk; for her and for us. Charlie and Kristen might be a possibility; they have a spare room and would provide company, but I'm not sure Mariko would agree to go and stay there; she doesn't know them. Perhaps she has a university friend she can camp with, if we come up with a good excuse for why she can't live in her own flat for a while? Stage one will be to sit down and discuss it with her tonight.

To make sure Dao is safe, I will simply reinstate the

measures I set up two years ago: the ground floor alarm always armed, external cameras on constant recording, the Remington shotgun always handy, and Dao never on a lower level in the house than where I am. The aim is to make sure that nobody can get to Dao unless they get past me first. We can have shopping delivered and neither of us need to leave the house. I think through various defence options and end up reconsidering if I should show Dao the video. She would see for herself that someone who saw the CCTV footage would see that Mariko can't have concealed the hard drive, but that she herself could have carried it. And then she will be more inclined to accept that I want to put us in siege mode, and that Mariko must be moved out of harm's way.

She is on the phone talking to Charlie when I go back downstairs. 'But I *want* to buy you another one,' she says and sounds as if she has said this several times already. 'It's *not* a question of whether you need it now that you're not a bodyguard any longer. It's because I lost your gun – well, let's be honest, I *stole* your gun and then I threw it away! Can you please go to the gun shop, or whatever those places are called, and buy another one? And then I'll pay you for it. I'm sure it was really expensive, so I want to do the right thing. If I could buy it myself, I would – but I don't have a firearms licence.'

This debate could go on for some time; I retreat to the kitchen and inspect the fridge and the pantry. I make a comprehensive list, probably extreme, and leave it on the kitchen bench before I get the Remington from the locked cabinet in the garage. When I get back to the living area, Dao is waiting.

'Charlie is being so stubborn, and she says she doesn't know why she ever bought the second Glock anyway, so there's no point replacing it, because she doesn't need two. She takes one when she flies foreign political people to luxury lodges.'

Dao is clearly frustrated at this obstacle to her wish to do the right thing. 'And she says that in the last three years she's only taken the second Glock out of her gun safe three times - when she lent it to you. Can you go and get one just the same, so I can give it to her please? I really don't care if she wants it or not. I've got to do the right thing. Or I suppose I could find out what they cost and give her the money.'

My first instinct is to say she should listen to Charlie and count herself lucky she doesn't have to spend all that money, but a second thought gives me pause. Right now, I would quite like to have a pistol in the house; it would be a handy addition to the Remington.

'I'll talk to her a bit later and sort it out. Don't worry about it just now. I want to show you something.'

We sit down and watch the CCTV clip from the factory and as I expected she is fascinated. 'Oh no! I didn't know they had cameras. Lucky those men weren't keeping an eye on them, or I could have walked straight into a trap!'

'Why did you have the bag hanging across to the left?' I think I know, but as always, I'm interested in hearing how she works things out.

'Well, I couldn't use the holster, it just didn't work on me - I experimented for ages. The guy on the safety video on YouTube said that the minute you put the magazine in there's a bullet in the chamber — and I didn't want to shoot myself by mistake, so I wanted to have the two parts separately, but I had to be able to assemble them really fast. Having the bag like that was perfect.' She stands up to demonstrate. 'It was easy to reach across with my right hand without the bag wobbling around and I could kind of anchor it against my hip with my left hand, like this - so I could pull the gun out without it snagging, and then straight away when the gun was free of the bag, I pulled the magazine out of my front left jeans pocket with my left hand. I had it in the pocket top down, so when I pulled it out, I was holding the bottom of it — and I just shoved it straight into the gun and I was ready!'

'You are such a smart little thing! I'm very proud of you.'

She doesn't tell me off for calling her a little thing, instead she grins. 'And if I mentioned the bag Bakker might have wondered why I had it. So, I just made up the story about how I tucked the gun up inside my top and tucked the top into the jeans to keep it there after I found it. If she was going to believe I found the gun on the table, it all had to fit.'

'I think you would have got away with it anyway, even if you had mentioned the bag, but it's always good to cover all the bases. You are such a planner Dao - you continually surprise me.'

'That's good! But it's not good that you have corrupted me – I'm lying all the time now, I think I'm getting used to it. My mother would be so upset.'

She listens while I explain why I got this particular video clip and what the implications are.

'So, we wouldn't even go out in the car with me hiding in the far back under the cover, like we had to do before? We would just stay here – all the time?'

'Yeah, and we'll have shopping delivered. When we had to live like this before, we went out for dinner and to buy pizza - and that's when bad things happened. This time we'll just stay here and be totally safe, and not take any risks at all.'

'You're right, it would be safer. It's lucky you do your work from home! But maybe you can back the car out now and then, so Scruff and I can play squash in the garage – no, I suppose that would be too dangerous too, what a shame. I suppose he can chase me up and down the stairs, he likes that.'

A year ago, Dao invented a two-dimensional form of squash that she and Scruff play in the empty garage, usually when I'm cleaning the car outside. She uses an up-side-down broom as a stick and hits a tennis ball hard across the floor, so it bounces off the walls, and Scruff runs like a demon to catch it; great exercise for Scruff and a perfect opportunity for someone to get inside, when I'm backing the car out and the big garage door is open. And Dao is right, there is no way I'm going to comply with this wish, far too risky.

'What was that lecture about – the one you watched just now? It looked very complicated, but then your maths always looks complicated to me,' I say to divert her thoughts. I ask this sort of thing now and then; I never understand the answers, but I like hearing the explanations anyway.

'It was so interesting! It was about a thing I came across in a book about number theory – it's called Goldbach's Conjecture. Goldbach lived a long time ago, in the seventeen-hundreds and he believed that every even integer greater than two can be expressed as the sum of two primes. Nobody has ever been able to prove it, lots of people have worked on it. And listen to this - he wrote a letter to Euler about it! Isn't it interesting that they corresponded? Remember how I told you about Euler's polyhedron formula?'

I do remember, and I never looked up what polyhedron means, so I still don't know; I promise myself that I will do it today.

Over lunch I tell Dao that I've been thinking about Mariko and how to keep her distanced from us, so she's safe, and the problem of finding somewhere for her to stay for a while, so she has company.

'I don't know who we could ask, unless she has some friend who has a spare bedroom. What do you think?'

'We can't ask Willow and Matt because they're in Hawaii – or is it *on* Hawaii?' says Dao. 'No, I think it is *in*. Anyway, they aren't home. What about Charlie and Kristen?'

'We could suggest it, but she's never met them – I don't know how comfortable she'd be with that.'

'Let's just ask her,' says Dao. 'We just have to make sure she doesn't think it's because we don't want her here.'

30

I set up an account with the supermarket to have groceries delivered and place a gigantic order. David, my partner in London, sends a message to say the African politician, who already has eight of our men, now wants an additional four.

'This chap is either planning something or he is expecting an assassination attempt', he writes. 'This morning I dealt with a job that was so simplistic the client might as well have hired his teenage nephew to do the job, and then we get this complex demand for personnel with very specific experience and thousands of conditions, and it becomes a full-day headache. Can you have a look at the database and see who you can find that might fit the bill – we've got so many of our best men out already we're just about to run out.'

I smile at his comment about the nephew and have just decided to go downstairs, when Bakker calls, and as soon as she says 'hi' I know she is either angry or stressed. My sense of self-preservation ramps up a notch.

'Has Mariko been able to get hold of her father yet?'

'No, he seems to have absconded – I thought you knew.'

'He hasn't been in touch since he replied to the first message I sent – the one we both got where he said he couldn't come immediately. Mariko told me she thinks he's "away abroad somewhere"' but she seemed uncertain, said she has no details – do you know anything about this?'

I make a snap decision to give her the information that Mariko might not have told her, for two reasons. The primary one is that Bakker will realise there must be a connection between what went on in flat 403 and John, that there is serious involvement, though she might know this already. The second reason is that she might stop regarding me as a hindrance and realise we are working towards the same goal.

'I don't know anything for sure, just what he implied when he sent me a long email message about what he has organised for Mariko. She might not have wanted to tell you, because it seems quite suspicious - John has provided future financial security for her and she now owns her apartment, and he has appointed a colleague to see to it that her university fees are paid and so on. He attached all the legal paperwork and Mariko has seen a local lawyer about it – everything is as it should be. But he said in the message that his phone number and email address would be stopped and that he is somewhere outside the US, and he can't or won't travel. We have heard nothing since. Personally, I think that he must be directly involved in this whole nasty business.'

'I agree – we've found out a couple of things that make it seem likely. I knew he acted for the company that owns the apartment block, he told us about that when he was here, but that can't be the reason. Didn't he tell you anything that might be useful to know when you met with him?'

'No, nothing. We had dinner with him the night he left. I should have told you earlier what he did that night, it made Dao furious – she never trusted him from the start, but even she was surprised at the deviousness of it. At the time we couldn't work out why he did it, but now it starts to make sense.'

She listens as I tell her about waiting in John's hotel suite and finding out he had recorded us, and she is stunned. 'What a bloody thing! But you're right – it does make sense.

We're starting a separate investigation into his whereabouts – or more correctly, his involvement.'

'Dao has the name of the US law firm he works for, if you want to call them.'

'We did that already – they refuse to comment, say they can't give out confidential personal information unless we charge him or some nonsense. But I notice that they've taken him off the list of partners on their website now. That's another thing that makes me suspicious.'

'I think he knew what those guys in were doing in that flat,' I suggest, treading carefully, 'either because he was part of the business, or he just knew what was going on and was well paid to keep silent. And that's why he came over here so fast when we told him his daughter had been taken and mentioned flat 403.'

'Yeah – if he knew the danger that she might be in, he would come over straight away. I bet the guys in flat 403 didn't realise that her father was connected to what they were doing, they probably never heard his name. We've speculated about this – talk about a tangled web.'

So, she has worked through that link already. Good, I didn't get her worked up because I knew something she didn't. I stick my neck out and supply the rest of the argument.

'And when you raided the factory and arrested that guy at the airport, John panicked – he worried about what you would find out and where that would lead. But he must have been prepared for flight and had a place to go to all lined up, money in another country etcetera – you can't leave your entire life behind on the spur of a moment.'

She doesn't reply for a moment, and I wait, then she asks abruptly, 'Do you know what the Darknet is?'

'I've heard of it, of course, but I don't know how it works – only that it is like an alternative version of the Internet where the really objectionable and illegal material is traded.'

I consider for a moment; this conversation is very

interesting, but if I ask too much, she might clam up again. On the other hand, she called me to ask questions, maybe I can risk a couple myself.

'Apatu said something about material being live-streamed, and I think you did too, earlier on. Can your people track where it went?'

'They're working on it – there's probably some dreadful equivalent of a social media site on the Darknet that people subscribe to for all kinds of perverted reasons and where this stuff was accessed. But the link to where it went has been deleted.' She sighs and sounds discouraged. 'It seems that the streaming equipment in the tech hub, as we call the container with all the gear, was closed down remotely the morning after Dao found Mariko. And it's impossible to tell where that was done from – could be anywhere in the world. The guys from the high-tech crimes unit cooperate with agencies all over the globe and they're trying to get to the bottom of it.'

I forward John's email to her without the attachments, so she has the evidence that he has fled in his own words.

I sit there thinking about this rather strange woman and then I realise Benson never told me what he found out, so I text him: 'You didn't tell me about Bakker. Never know how to act when she calls. It's like dealing with Jekyll and Hyde.'

He calls half an hour later, he sounds harried: 'Just a quick call – I'll probably be here half the night and then I'll forget to tell you again. She got into trouble for publicly ripping into the brother of a girl who was raped and murdered – I've seen the pictures and he looked a bit like you, and he was ex-army too. He wanted revenge on the suspect before any charges had been laid, so he organised a vigilante group, or perhaps it was a lynch mob – they were planning to pay him a surprise visit. Bakker went way too far in what she said about the brother to the media, got very personal - and he filed a formal complaint, and she was censured and had to apologise. Confidential, so don't share it. Sorry, got to run.'

And he's gone before I have time to say, 'thank you'. It

explains her antipathy; to her I am just another example of the same kind of vigilante extremist. I can't deny there's a small grain of truth in it, but I would never go after someone, if I didn't know with one hundred percent certainty that they were guilty and that they were about to get away scot free. I can only hope she can see there is a difference, but I wouldn't bank on it. First impressions last a long time and colour things even in the face of evidence to the contrary. I decide to take my mind off it by making a risotto, which is a new skill and quite pleasant in a slow way.

We start the discussion with Mariko after dinner, when she has just cleared the table and Dao had fed Scruff, so the scene is domestic and comfortable. I sit down with a glass of wine and tell her about the situation that Dao and I were in a couple of years ago: that Dao was the only eyewitness who could testify against the man who held her captive for ten years, and not just about that, but also about the drug distribution that was run from his place on the coast.

'We were literally under siege for some time,' I tell Mariko, who is unlikely to have heard about our past. 'We got a very comprehensive security system and we lived in daily expectation of an attack. And it did happen - and if we hadn't had our mega security system and hadn't been prepared, we would possibly both be dead.'

'What Hunter means by prepared,' says Dao, 'is that we had the ground floor alarm on all the time, the outside cameras too – and Hunter kept his shotgun near him on whatever level of the house we were on. We never went to the door without checking the cameras and he had Charlie's Glock pistol too, loaded. When we went out in the car, I had to get into the far back with the luggage cover over me before he even opened the garage door. It was very complicated and quite frightening.'

Mariko asks casually, 'Was that when you went to Simon's

office and had the pistol with you and he nearly died of fright?'

Dao and I look at each other; what have we missed? Did someone mention this the other night when Simon was here?

'He told me a bit about you, when I went to see him about the papers my father sent. He said that once you sat in that very same chair and you had a loaded gun with you.' She laughs and shakes her head. 'He said he's never had anything to do with guns – he was very funny telling me.' And before we can reply, she continues, 'Did you really find Dao in the forest?'

'It was Scruff who found her – she was lying in a damp hollow, frozen, practically unconscious. She had escaped from the drug dealer.'

'I think it would have been more romantic if you had found her yourself, Hunter, but I suppose it's nearly as good – and you *did* save her life.'

Simon must have told her this, so she knows a lot more than I expected; at least she understands the background to what I am saying about safety.

'And now we are in a similar situation. Not you, because we can remove you from the equation – you are only exposed to danger if you stay here. There is a possibility that the guy we call the third man thinks that Dao took the hard drive from the factory. It turns out there was extensive CCTV cover at the factory site, and it was streamed to some other location – we don't know who has had access to it. In the video clip you can see that Dao had pockets and that little bag, so she could have carried it, and it shows very clearly that you don't have it, so you should be OK - but living here involves you in danger and I can't accept that.'

'But you are at risk too!'

'Yes, and we'll just go back to what I described earlier and act as if we're under siege, even if it turns out later that we weren't. But we must find a place for you to stay so you can continue to go to lectures and see your friends – and you need company, I think, so your flat probably isn't a good idea yet. Perhaps there's a friend from the university who has a spare room - or our friends Charlie and Kristen would be happy to have you come and stay.'

'I'll ask Simon,' she says, as cool as a cucumber. 'He's got a lovely big spare room, he won't mind.' Then she grins and adds, 'He would like it.'

This statement is followed by total silence from Dao and me; neither of us can think what to say and it takes a while to process it. Meanwhile Mariko sits watching us with the slightest suspicion of a smile.

'I think you have to fill us in,' I say finally, once again taken aback by how self-possessed she is. It's no wonder she managed to be so clever and inventive while she was held in that apartment. 'You must have seen more of him than I was aware of. If you don't mind? It's not my business, but it would be useful to know.'

Dao looks inscrutable, but I suspect she's trying not to laugh.

'Oh, I don't mind telling you,' says Mariko casually. 'I was going to anyway, it's not a secret. When I went to see him about all those legal papers, I asked if he would be my lawyer for anything else as well that I might need help with, and he said no. Which seemed a bit rude, when he had already said he would be happy to help me, so I asked why not. And he said it was because he would like to get to know me better and take me out, like on a date, provided I wanted to get to know him, of course – and lawyers aren't allowed to do that! Did you know they are not supposed to date their clients?'

Dao shakes her head and I say I knew, but I hadn't registered the fact that Simon was interested.

'I didn't either,' says Mariko and smiles. 'I was really surprised, but he is interested, very interested. We're just friends so far – he's a bit old, of course. Oh sorry, Hunter, he's your age – I shouldn't have said that!'

Dao finds her voice. 'It's exactly the same age gap as

between Hunter and me. Perfect really – who wants a boy? I would rather have a man.'

Mariko bursts out laughing, and Dao joins in and I look on in silent amazement.

'Simon is not the slightest bit like Hunter!' says Mariko finally. 'They couldn't be more different. But I like him and I'm not going to marry a Japanese man – they expect far too much of their wives, I think. I'm going to do something interesting in physics and have a great career – I won't have time for food that takes hours to prepare and all those wife things. And I like Simon a lot, he's very funny and he needs someone to make sure that he doesn't drink too much. Perfect!'

'Does he love you?' Dao abandons polite discretion and gives her curiosity free rein.

Mariko frowns, as if she is considering this for the first time. 'I *think* he does. He will never love me in that crazy, totally-forever way that Hunter loves you, but I don't think that happens very often. But he will love me enough, I think. And I do like him – a lot. He is funny and clever, and we talk about everything.'

I try to not twitch at having my emotional life dissected so coolly. Dao casts a sideways glance loaded with secret amusement in my direction, and says sweetly, 'And I love Hunter in that crazy, totally-forever kind of way too – perfect!'

And then, thank God, Dao breaks the spell and jumps up. 'Oh no! Richard! I forgot to call Richard!'

She leaves Mariko and me sitting there staring after her, as she grabs her phone from the dining table and disappears upstairs. Scruff gets up and trots up the stairs after her.

'Richard – the driver?' Mariko looks at me and I nod; must be, it's the only Richard we know. I know I should have consulted her or at least informed her of what I did, but it's too late now. I wonder if we are all in some mild state of PTSD; things seem to get laid aside and then suddenly rediscovered – like Richard. I start to wonder about Charlie and how much we have told her. The story and the background have been retold so many times now, either in part or in full, that it's hard to remember who knows what. The only person I know for sure has no idea at all of what has been going on is Willow.

Mariko makes herself green tea in a teapot she brought from her flat, as such a thing has never existed in my house before, and I have another glass of wine. A while later Dao comes down and hugs me from behind. 'Richard told me. Perfect - thank you!'

Mariko looks at Dao. 'Perfect?'

'Hunter talked to the guy who runs the limo hire company and asked what he could do for Richard – you know, like a reward for all he did. And he told him Richard is saving to take his family to California.' She heads for the kitchen and returns with a mug so she can share Mariko's tea. I can see that this isn't satisfactory as far as Mariko is concerned, her forehead creases, and she turns to me for an explanation.

'The manager said Richard's sister lives there and they haven't seen each other for years. Paying for their air fares seemed like a nice idea.'

'I feel bad about him,' Mariko says. 'I should have thanked him more properly too. It's been a bit strange lately - some days too much is going on with the police and things, and in between things seem normal. And time seems to move at different speeds, sometimes there isn't enough time to think about anything properly, and then there's hours of time moving very slowly. I've never felt this way before – it's very strange.'

'Post-traumatic stress syndrome,' I say. 'It plays nasty little games with your mind. Have you had flash backs of being held in that bedroom or being in the container? Or of seeing that girl being killed?'

She shakes her head. 'I thought I might have nightmares, but I haven't. The only thing that happens quite a lot is that my imagination tries to show me what might have gone on in that container. And that's very horrible and very hard to stop.'

'You could talk to a counsellor – Victim Support will organise it.'

'No, thank you, Hunter san,' she says coolly. 'Simon invented a thing he calls distraction therapy, and it works quite well.'

Dao stares at her. 'What is it? How does it work?'

'I have to mentally list every single action since I woke up, every little thing, in the right order - and before I get very far, I have to go back and start again, because I realise that I forgot one thing – like cleaning my teeth – or I got things in the wrong order. And then suddenly everything feels all right again, and my imagination has stopped showing me horrible ideas. Simon does it when he can't go to sleep.'

Obviously one of those things that men never talk to each other about, but women find out in five minutes.

In bed that evening I ask Dao how much she told Charlie, when they argued about replacing the Glock.

'More or less everything – but just from my point of view. Not things that only happened to Mariko, like how they drugged her to take her to the factory or what she saw inside that container or some other things she told me when we were hiding in the mangroves - that's private and for her to tell people if she wants to. And Charlie already knew all the rest from when we showed her all those notes and things that we scanned, of course. What are we going to do about the Glock?'

'We'll buy a later model than the one you used. I had a look online – the new small model is even more compact, which Charlie will like. I will hold on to it until after this period of danger is over, and then you can give it to her. Did you tell Benson you took it with you to the factory?'

'Of course not! He would be so cross - I can never tell him. I've not told anybody apart from you and Charlie.'

I think to myself that I might tell Benson at some future date; show him that note she left on the table. He will love the story about Dao watching YouTube to learn what she describes as "all about it", but while the investigation is still ongoing, he must not find out. And then I think of Simon and hope he keeps his mouth shut and doesn't tell Mariko. When I told him, I had no inkling this instant relationship would develop. I make a mental note to call him in the morning and remind him to keep it strictly to himself– without telling him I know about his crush on Mariko, of course. I look forward to hearing how he will inform me of that; he was never good at that sort of thing, worse than me by a mile.

In the early hours of the morning Dao cries out in her sleep and I pull her closer and talk to her, so she wakes up slowly. 'It's just a dream – you're safe now. It's all right. Do you want to tell me about it? Was it rubbish sacks again?'

'Worse,' she sobs. 'Much worse - I was in the mangroves and the dead bodies were coming after me and they looked horrible and I turned around to see how close they were and then I tripped, and they were going to get me.'

Gradually she calms down. 'Can you tell me a story?'

'OK – which one do you want?' Periods of sleepless nights are nothing new in this house; over the last couple of years the frequency has diminished to nearly nothing, but now we are in for another nightmare-riddled time. Telling Dao stories works well; my storytelling seems to be so boring, that she generally falls asleep before I reach the end. Perfect! as the girls say so often. My stories come in three flavours; childhood stories about Willow and me, army stories of a non-traumatic kind and stories about crazy jobs David and I have dealt with.

'Tell me about how Charlie got into trouble that time in Afghanistan.'

'When she flew the guys out to shoot goats?'

'No, not that one. I want the one that you say that one day you'll tell Kristen about it, and Charlie says, 'If you do that, I'll kill you, Hunter' and you laugh.'

'God no! Never - it's very rude and very bad. I will never tell you that one!'

'But I like very bad – please!'

'No, I'm not telling you – she would never speak to me again.'

'OK then, I just thought you might. When I wanted her to go into the factory with me, she said, 'no way - Hunter would kill me' - you always say things like that about each other.'

'It's just a habit – she wouldn't actually do it, and keeping secrets is what good friends do, they keep each other's secrets and don't let bad things happen to the other person. You're good at keeping secrets yourself – very good. You and I have some secrets, things we've seen and done – and we'd never tell anyone else, would we?'

31

Mariko beats me to it. I call Simon from our bedroom with the door shut, while she and Dao make breakfast, to warn him about not telling the Glock story, but Mariko has already called him and got her move organised, so he thinks that's why I called.

'No, it wasn't – let's park that one for now. I just wanted to make sure that Mariko doesn't find out that Dao took the Glock to that factory.'

'Of course not, I wouldn't tell anyone! What do you take me for? It would get everyone into trouble – Dao and you and Charlie. I'm certainly not telling Mariko stuff like that. Anything you tell me as my client goes nowhere – and I've decided that practically everything you tell me these days comes under the heading of client confidentiality - your life is so full of dangerous things.'

That makes me smile; I think back to that famous day when I sat in his visitor's chair, and he discovered I had the Glock in the holster. He couldn't have looked more horrified if I'd put a snake on his desk.

'And you're OK with her staying at your place? Did she tell you the background?'

'Yes, to both those things. She's just great, isn't she? I've never met anyone so cool in my life – apart from Dao, of course. And how she's holding up under all this trauma and stress – it's incredible. She's like some manga character. I'll drive her over from her late lab session this afternoon so she can pick up her belongings.'

When Mariko leaves to catch her bus, I suggest to Dao that she and Scruff stay in the house while I go alone to buy the new Glock. 'I think we'll start being careful right away.'

'OK - I'll set the ground floor alarm when you've gone. I've set the cameras to record continuously already.' And then she laughs and points at the Remington leaning into the corner by the stairs. 'Mariko noticed the shotgun – she said she's never seen one before. I had to tell her not to touch it.'

I relate my conversation with Simon, but Dao already knows. 'She called him last night. He is bringing her over after her lab and I said they could have dinner here, but he's taking her out somewhere. Probably that place where we had dinner with him, it seems to be his favourite.'

'Do you know what manga means? Simon said it just now.'

'It's that style of cartoons and films the Japanese do – you know we watched one on Netflix a while ago. They have a special look, really different. I like it!'

I will get an alert on my phone if the alarm goes off and I feel an urge to rush, but this might be my last chance to get a couple of things done for a while, so I tell myself to calm down. I get home and find Dao asleep on our bed with a book open beside her and Scruff on the floor keeping her company. When I put my little bag of hardware supplies on the desk, she opens her eyes, blinks twice and sits up; all in a space of a second. 'What's in the bag?'

'Some bolts - I thought they might be useful.'

'For the bedroom door?'

I hand her one of the bolts and she turns it over in her hands. 'But all these screws! They will ruin the doors.'

'We'll take them off later and fill the screw holes. I thought we could have them on this door and on our bathroom door, and one on the toilet door behind the kitchen and then one on the bathroom door on the ground floor. If something happens, wherever one of us is, we'll have a place to lock ourselves in. The locks on the bathroom doors are useless.'

'OK, that's a good idea.'

We are both thinking of the time the armed intruder broke in downstairs on the courtyard side before I replaced the windows down there with mesh-reinforced glass. We were on the living room level and he came charging up the stairs so fast that all I had time to do was shout 'hide' to Dao and grab the Remington.

'But if we'd had those when that man broke in,' says Dao, 'then I would have run into the loo and locked myself in and I wouldn't have been hiding in the kitchen and I would have been no help at all.'

'True – but this time we'll be safer.'

On that occasion nearly two years ago, I reached the Remington, which was sitting where it is now, one second before the guy got to the top of the stairs. I surprised him and it worked well, and Dao was indeed useful. She tiptoed out of the kitchen, behind the back of the man I had at gunpoint, took his sawn-off shotgun when I made him put it down and silently put it out of his reach.

When I mention this, she reminds me that she also got the cable ties from the kitchen drawer, so I could tie him up.

'True - you're a very brave and useful little thing, but this time we'll both go for a room with a bolt on the door.'

'And we really won't go out at all? What about the courtyard? I've got to pick up the dog poo and put clean water in Scruff's bowl.'

'Yes, but I'll be there too.'

She casts one of those slanting Dao glances at me, and I laugh. 'OK, you're right – I'll be there too, *and* I'll have the

Glock. I can't hang around outside with the Remington – Nigel would have heart failure.'

'I forgot that's why you went out! Let's have a look at it.'

The new Glock pistol is neat and compact. Dao takes it out of the box, passes it from one hand to the other and smiles. 'Charlie will love it! It is smaller, I can feel it's smaller in my hand – and a bit lighter, I think. I hope it fits the holster that she got for the old one.'

We try it and it fits well, so I leave all the parts on the table and get the toolkit out. Dao is watching me screw the first bolt into place when she suddenly thinks of something. 'What if Bakker wants to see us and we say we can't go into town?'

'I'll tell her why, of course. She can't force us – and I think it's unlikely she will want to talk to us again. That long conversation I had on the phone with her yesterday was about John, that's why she called – all the rest was mostly her telling me things. Very surprising.'

'It's your famous charm,' says Dao and laughs at my expression. 'It's happened before, people tell you things – mostly without you even asking, it's very clever.'

'I don't think that applies to Bakker – she just let her guard down and couldn't resist discussing all the new information.'

The idea that Bakker would be susceptible to charm is too far-fetched to contemplate; not my dubious brand of it anyway.

Simon brings Mariko back from town and sits down for a chat while Dao helps with the packing upstairs. He glances at the stairs and says quietly, 'How worried are you? Do you really think something might happen?'

I show him the video clip from the factory and explain the rationale; that the CCTV got streamed somewhere else, and someone might think Dao had that hard drive in the bag and that they could work out how to find us. 'I'm not taking any risks this time, Simon. We can't be lucky all the time.'

'I wouldn't call it lucky. Last time it wasn't luck that saved you when that guy broke in. You were prepared – that's what saved you.'

When he hears that we are going to live as if we are in a fortress, he sits quietly for a moment, thinking it over. 'OK, it's extreme, but I suppose over the top precaution is better than not enough. And if you need anything you can't have delivered, just call me and I'll get it.'

'No, not even that – we'll not open the front door again until this is over.'

They leave with two bags and the big parcels of linen and both of them hug Dao. Mariko thanks us in the beautiful Japanese manner before she walks out the door and then we are alone in the house again.

'Will you let them come and visit – while we are locked up here?'

'I told Simon we're having no visitors at all. If someone is watching the house and they see someone arrive, they could wait until the visitor leaves and pounce – I'd rather not leave us open to any surprises. Every time the front door is opened, even briefly, it presents an opportunity for someone to take us by surprise, so the front door stays shut.'

'What about the supermarket orders?'

'I've instructed them to leave the delivery on the doorstep. We'll get the alert from the camera that someone is approaching the front door, we can see them leave - and then you lock yourself into a safe space and I open the door and bring the stuff in. If someone's going to rush me, at least you will be safe. That's the last time we open that door.

She considers this and to my surprise she starts laughing. 'I just thought of it – those safe spaces are our boltholes – get it? Bolts, safe space to hide – bolthole! Perfect!'

Charlie calls to see how we are, and when I tell her about the Glock, she protests. 'You didn't need to do that! I told Dao it wasn't necessary, but it's very kind of you.'

'You'll like this one, and I bet you end up using it instead of the one you still have. It's both smaller and lighter, Dao says she can feel the difference.'

'Well, she should damn well know!' says Charlie. 'You know, I never expected her to go back to that place in Tamaki. And to take the bloody thing with her – and use it! She had never fired a weapon in her life. That's what comes of being a warrior princess. Maybe I should have taken it away when I dropped her off - I knew it would probably be under the seat in your car, but she convinced me completely, so I never dreamed she was still on a mission.'

'And if she had gone without it, things would probably be very different now,' I say. 'She was on a mission - and gun or no gun, she was going. But this is the last time. It has left a horrible mark on her mind and it's going to take time to get over it. Well, you and I know that you never 'get over' these things, but you learn to handle the memories. Anyway, we are never letting anyone persuade us to help them again. I've told her I'm happy to do whatever it takes to stop people finding us and asking for help. We can move to Hokitika or go and live in Australia or we could change our name and become Mr and Mrs Smith.'

'What did she say when you told her all this?'

'I said it when she had a nightmare, just told her briefly, to comfort her and she just said 'good'. But when we had a proper talk about it later, she said she never wants to live anywhere else ever – and she means it. She said this place is her happy place and she wants us to stay here.'

I don't tell her the words Dao actually used: 'We can't leave this house – every room has a memory, it's full of us.'

Then I realise that Charlie doesn't know about the risk that is facing us right now, so I tell her that whole story, and she exclaims, suddenly furious, 'Shit! Not again! You're right, all this crazy stuff has got to stop – you'd better mean it. And keep that new Glock for a while.'

'I was coming to that – I'd like to keep it until this is over.' I tell her about the bolts on the doors and the supermarket delivery service and how we are having no visitors.

'It sounds over-engineered to me, but you're the protection expert, so I'll take your word for it. Any chance you could send me the video clip you got from the cops? I'd love to have a look at it.'

Every now and then some random comment brings back vivid memories of things I experienced in Afghanistan, like that brief comment I made to Charlie about how you never get over it. It suddenly snapped me back; images of carnage that fills me with impotent rage against the universe, mindless brutality against innocent people, meted out by fanatics fuelled by religious intolerance – it's not something you can forget. You can put it aside temporarily, but it leaves a crease in your soul that time can't smooth over.

As soon as Willow and Matt and the twins are back, which must be any day now, I must explain the whole thing to them too, so they understand that we cannot have visitors; it is not a conversation I'm looking forward to.

When I mention this to Dao, she says. 'Oh, please don't try to tell her, not in a conversation – she'll just say how reckless we are and how we should have left it to the cops and then you might argue. Why don't you do it by email? You could send her the recording we made when we told Simon in the restaurant – I have it on my laptop. Good thing I saved it, seeing the phone's gone. Anyway, send her that and all the scanned stuff first, so she knows the background. And explain why we are going to live like this. Send her the photos Bakker sent, of the table in the factory, and the video clip that shows me with the bag, and then tell her about the third man and how he – or someone else, perhaps, could find us from the number plate. Much better than spending hours telling the whole story again.'

'Perfect!' I say and Dao laughs. 'I know you're teasing, but it's such a good word – perfect, actually. And think how pleased Willow will be that she was right – she always said one day you would go too far and get arrested.'

32

Before I get around to warning Benson not to visit, he rings the doorbell just before dinner. Dao checks the security camera and goes flying down to open the door for him. On the way up she tells him about how we are going to lock ourselves in, as she calls it, and then she sees my face and claps a hand to her mouth. 'Oh, no! I did it, I just opened the door without thinking. I should have taken the Remington with me.'

'Poor Benson, he would have had a heart attack. And if you ever touch that gun, you'll be in serious trouble.'

He looks from Dao to me and back again, a crease between his eyebrows.

'I'm not really telling Dao off - look at that wicked smile. Come and sit down and Dao can give you a cold beer to compensate. She thinks she's Rambo ever since she found that pistol in the factory.'

This last bit is a reminder to Dao that at least for now Benson must not find out she had Charlie's pistol with her.

Dao laughs. 'Hunter never tells me off, Benson, don't worry! If he did, I'd call you and you could come and arrest him.'

'I've been very close to it a couple of times, Dao, very close! – but then I reckoned you need to have him around, so I didn't. But just say the word and I'll bring the handcuffs.'

Hearing her fooling around with Benson is very encouraging; they have a great relationship and I know he would move heaven and earth to help her, if she was in trouble.

'OK, show me that video,' says Benson, snapping back into police mode. 'I want to see why someone might think Dao took that back-up gizmo.'

I pass my laptop over and he watches the clip without comment. 'Tell me exactly what you're going to do – how is Fortress Hunter going to keep you safe?'

We go through the whole thing again, and Benson asks questions and wants more explanations, until he is finally satisfied. 'It sounds pretty waterproof – provided Dao doesn't forget the rules again.'

'I won't, I promise - I was just so pleased you had come to see us!' And that makes him smile.

'Do you agree? About the bag?'

'I do – if I was trying to work out who might have that hard drive, I'd think first of the guy who ran out the gate with his big bag, the one Richard saw leaving – that would be my number one suspect. Or Dao – provided I had access to the CCTV recordings and saw her with the little bag. And you can see there is something flat and oblong inside it – which we know is a phone, of course. We know the canvas bag guy didn't have it in his luggage when they caught him at the airport. He could, of course, have hidden it between the time he left the factory and when he tried to leave the country – he must have been holed up somewhere during that time. But how would the third man know that he didn't have it with him at the airport? He could only know that if he had contacts in the police.'

We discuss it back and forth for a few minutes, but I can tell Benson is turning something over in his mind. Dao invites him to stay for dinner and I go and add the other half of the smoked chicken to what I already got out. The experimental supermarket delivery arrived as ordered, a large number of brown paper carrier bags lined up on the doorstep; the freezer and fridge are full, the pantry is bursting.

I hear Dao and Benson laughing at something and when I return to the living room Dao says, 'I've been telling Benson about Mariko and how she's gone to stay in Simon's spare room. And what she said about keeping Simon from drinking too much. And do you know what he said?'

'No, tell me!'

'He said he thinks Simon had better obey her or he will be in serious trouble.' Dao thinks this is hilarious, but I tend to agree with Benson. Mariko is a force to be reckoned with and the way she calmly considers her relationship with Simon and her future shows how pragmatic and focused she is.

After dinner Benson asks me to tell him everything Bakker has said the last few times I talked to her. 'You said you had quite a long conversation with her recently. Dao tells me your famous charm has won her over – for some reason she's discussed their findings with you. I would like to know what she told you. I want to get a grip on the bigger picture, because there must be more to this than what I've heard so far.'

It takes a while. I go back over it in my mind and collate the various bits she revealed at different times and try to connect them into one string of information and Benson listens patiently. Scruff turns up with his tug-of-war toy and Dao gets down on the floor with him to play as they sometimes do. It usually results in some kind of chaos, like mock wresting under the coffee table, so I push the table to one side. Benson lifts his beer bottle in the last moment. He looks amused but makes no comment, he has never seen this side of Dao before.

When I finish the story, he says decisively, 'If you don't mind, I'd like to either ask some questions of Bakker myself, or else tell you what I think you should ask her. You need all the facts and I have a feeling there are things she hasn't told you – not deliberately perhaps, but you can only protect yourself if you have the full picture.' He stares at the beer bottle in his hand and nods to himself. 'There's got to be more to it!'

'I think you should call her, Benson. It's hard to predict how she'll react if I call and say I discussed it with you. Perhaps even if you call her, and then she realises we have met and talked about it, she'll feel undermined, and I'll be *persona non grata* for ever.'

'Hmm,' he says, and then he nods. 'You're right. She knows we are friends, but I'll say I've been thinking of things, and she'll think it's just professional interest. Probably best we don't let her get the idea we've been colluding.'

He takes his bottle of beer and retires to sit at the bottom of the stairs again and I sort out the kitchen mess until I hear him coming back up about ten minutes later. We go back to the armchairs and find Dao curled up asleep on the floor with her arm over Scruff; I pick up the rug that hangs over the back of the sofa and cover them with it.

'She keeps doing this – we've been awake a lot in the night lately.'

'Incredible to think how she coped with the situation in the factory,' says Benson. 'She looks like a child. Will she wake up if we talk?'

'No, I don't think so – she might sleep for a couple of hours.'

I tell him what Dao's dreams have been like and he shakes his head. 'That's the last damn thing she needs, now that she was just beginning to come right. It's a wonder she smiles as much as she does.'

'What did Bakker say?' I ask. 'Did you get hold of her?'

'She was quite amenable to being questioned – but I managed to tread lightly and not cause offence. They've checked through miles of CCTV recordings from the factory that were stored on the video management system in the tech hub as they call it. That third man came and went there too, always when at least one of the other two was there. They've got an alert out for his car, but the number plate is fake. They've loaded the fake number into the system that reads plates straight from the patrol cars and at some petrol stations, but nothing yet. He might have more than one set of fake plates, of course. There has been no sign of the washing machine carton, but they could have taken Grace's body out of it at the apartment car park and put her in the back of the van. Maybe the carton was put out for recycling, there or elsewhere.'

'So, we have no idea if her body is in the mangroves or hidden somewhere else? What about the recordings from the camera at the back of the factory? There must be footage of them carrying rubbish sacks down to the inlet?'

'I asked that, but no luck there. There's a lens cap hanging from a string where the camera is mounted and every now and then one of the men reached up and put it over the lens, always at night. They were very risk averse.'

'Anything else new?' I feel frustration growing; there seems to be little of substance coming to light.

Benson smiles. 'Don't be impatient – this is typical of some cases we get. Things move slowly, by tiny increments. If you have a suspect that you think did it, then it's about proving or disproving it. But if you really don't know for sure what the hell went on, there's often a stage when it's like wading through porridge – you advance at a snail's pace, and it seems like you're making no progress. But eventually little pieces of information surface and when you have enough of them, things start falling into place. I think Bakker is doing a good, thorough job - nobody ever doubted her ability. The high-tech crimes unit that deals with that kind of stuff are on to it, too. They've made progress, and they are in touch with other units in other countries, of course. It seems that what went on in that place was pretty awful.'

Before I can reply, he continues. 'And Bakker told me something else, which I'm sure will interest you, but maybe keep it to yourself for now. The US authorities have been in touch and they seem fairly certain that Anderson was totally involved – he was the respectable legal middleman, who bought properties and allocated leases and all that stuff, simplified the infrastructure of that evil empire and made it look legit. And they paid the law firm for his time, but they probably also paid him big money not to talk.'

'Money deposited into an account in his name in the Caymans, perhaps? Do you think they will ever find out?'

'Probably not – he left the US on a flight to Jamaica, under his own name and there the trace peters out. So, he was well prepared, everything in place – fake passport, money and all that's necessary to disappear. Probably knew from the start that one day it might all turn to shit, and he would have to disappear fast.'

He glances at Dao. 'If she's having nightmares, I sure as hell don't want her to hear what else Bakker told me.'

He gets up and moves towards the kitchen. 'Come over here and I'll tell you – I don't want to talk about this next to her, even when she's asleep.'

We stand in the kitchen leaning against the bench, Benson clears his throat and keeps his voice low. 'There's an international market for perverts with big money, people who'll pay up to a million for a performed-to-order killing. They mostly involve some combination of sex and torture, specified by the customer. It's live-streamed to some site on the darknet, where the customer has the sole log-on and can watch as it takes place at a pre-determined time.'

He shakes his head in disgust. 'It's the ultimate perversion. Apparently, the videos are accessible for a limited time to only the person who placed the order – and only he can download them and save them or go back and watch them repeatedly. Then they become available for others to watch, but not to download - anyone who pays a very big fee.'

'God, that's sick! When Mariko described the interior of the container that they put her in, it was obvious that horrible things had been going on. They wouldn't have a specially equipped container just to murder someone they wanted to get rid of. I've heard of so-called snuff videos, but people ordering it so they can watch it live – it's inhuman. Those poor kids.'

'I know – it's the worst part of policing, the dreadful things that people do to each other. How those guys in the special unit cope, I don't know. Bakker said they might never find out the full reach of this business. Someone set it up, found premises and equipment, hired cruel men, hired people to manage the technical side – expensive and risky. And it's got to be un-trackable, of course. Probably they organised the business, so each layer of participants only knows those they need to have direct contact with - like spy networks in the movies. Each group only knows their cell, so to speak. And the workers, if we can call them that, don't ever know the people at the top, of course, the ones who rake in the big money.'

He frowns and shakes his head in disgust. 'And these days that evil entity they call the Darknet complicates things. Bakker said it seems likely this was just one branch of the business and there will be others in other countries. Apparently, there's quite a long list of countries where this sort of thing is suspected of going on or has gone on and been discovered. It could be that John Anderson did not know all of it, but he was obviously involved to a degree that made it necessary for him to disappear. Bakker's team got access to the US police interview with his wife – she is devastated, had no idea. And the authorities over there are going to delve into his finances et cetera, check on the details of his life. His former partners in the law firm seem to have had no suspicions, but who knows what will come out by and by – the firm is being investigated too.'

'What about the man they arrested at the airport?'

'Saying absolutely nothing, so far. Literally nothing, just sits there – not a word out of him.'

'Why do you think they bothered to buy buildings?'

'Could be that it's a way of laundering money perhaps? Or is Bitcoin these days? But it's not at all certain that the property investment company set up the killing business – maybe that company is genuinely just for investments and John Anderson acted for them in that regard, totally legitimately. Perhaps his link to the murder business was a separate enterprise, perhaps he ran it himself or acted for those who set it up? He had access to convenient information about the properties the investment company owns, and he might have been able to use that knowledge for his own ends – nobody knows at the moment. I'm quite glad it isn't my case. The only thing that Bakker seems certain of is that the third man is probably the one who performed the ordered killings. Unless they smuggled in someone else inside the van, he is the only one that came to the factory apart from the two from the flat and the kids they brought in the van, and he must have had a specific role – rapist and/or killer. Most of the fingerprints in that tech hub as they call it belonged to the dead man. So he was a skilled guy and perhaps the one who sits in a cell and won't talk is just his mate who came along to be a grassroots worker. It seems probable that they were from Bulgaria, but the passports aren't in their real names, so nothing is certain.'

I feel demoralised by the inhuman evil of these people. 'It makes me feel sick! At least in war the aggressor is usually motivated by some kind of ideology, religious or otherwise – but this? Cruelty and brutality inflicted for money. I think we might need another drink - or will I have to take your car keys off you, if you have another beer?'

I fetch the cheese plate from the coffee table and have a look at Dao, who hasn't stirred. Scruff opens one eye to check who it is and closes it again. We sit down at the dining table with fresh drinks and leave Dao to sleep in peace. Benson cuts a piece of Gryere and casts a measuring glance at me, and I wonder what's coming now.

'Listen Hunter – I've never asked you about this before and maybe I should have, but Dao said John Anderson was pretty scathing about your job – implied you deal with the scum of the earth for big money. What do you actually do?'

'I suppose you could say it's a bit like being an employment agency – it's just that the people we place in jobs have very specific skills, and the employers who contact us need people with those skills,' I say and study his face, not quite sure why he's really asking. 'John Anderson assumed we deal with mercenaries, that we provide soldiers for hire to rebel armies or terrorists, but that's not what we do. There are many countries where people are at serious risk just doing what they do. The sort of place where being in politics or standing in an election against a dictator type leader, or being the owner of news media, can put you at risk of assassination. Sometimes clients lie, of course – they tell us a good reason for why they need a butler who can handle a semi-automatic and driver who is trained in unarmed combat, and we know they're lying. And it's not our business to sort out who's genuinely at risk and who is not.'

'I got the impression a couple of years ago, when you had first rescued Dao, that you were employed by a London company that did deal mainly with mercenaries.'

'I was, but about a year and a half ago David, that's my London partner, and I set up our own firm. Just us two - and a lot of the personnel we had placed over the years followed us. The ones who want to be in what's called ethical jobs but still armed to the teeth so to speak. The ones who thrive on danger, addicted to adrenaline.'

I drink some of my wine and watch Benson's face over the

rim of the glass, but there's no particular reaction and I'm still not sure why this has come up.

'Some of the clients I get to meet in person are ruthless and scary – mostly that applies to politicians in countries where the law exists but isn't observed. And they are sometimes surrounded by people you would never want to meet on a dark night. Politicians in dicey countries are often just ordinary people like you and me - and we have never set up protection for a dictator, that's one of the things we agreed on right at the start. The men we employ are all ex-armed forces and they basically come under one of two headings – those who can't find a civilian job that pays well and who have limited skills for civilian life, who don't feel they fit in, and those who still yearn for danger and the feel of a weapon in their hands. And the money is very good, both for the men and for us.'

He has listened without much reaction, but now he smiles, surprised. 'Really? You actually meet these clients personally? Where does that happen, and why?'

'David fields the incoming requests and sends a lot my way. Once a contract has been negotiated, he or I – or sometimes both together go through our database of personnel and find the right men for the job. It's usually I who visit clients if that's needed – it's kind of my speciality, I suppose you can say.'

'Why would a visit be necessary? I would have thought the clients would come to you. Is it so you can assess why they really need protection?'

'God, no - I don't really care if they need it or not. If they're willing to pay big money, they're welcome, even if it's only based on a nightmare they had. But I must get a grip on *what* they need – which is often nothing like what they think they need. People just don't understand how many variables there are to take into account - the layout of buildings, sniper vantage points, and the security measures already in place, the routes they use to commute, the vehicle they drive, how they communicate, where the driver lets them out – the list goes on. Google Earth is a great tool for an overview, but things like alternative points of egress and exit can't be assessed just from images and descriptions and neither can sniper angles.'

He is really interested now; perhaps he always thought I just sold the services of our personnel to the highest bidder and judged me by it. 'What's the worst job you've done? The most complicated.'

'Just a few months ago, we got a request from a client in an African country I won't name - an opposition politician, who wanted what amounted to an assault unit made up of men with combat experience. The guy told us he had an arms bunker at his residence, so he was expecting serious trouble. What made it complex was that he had trained as an officer at Sandhurst in the UK - and he thought he knew it all. God, that man was a nightmare to deal with! The specifications were endless – we could have sold him the services of too many men with too many high-level, expensive skills. It took a while to set up and we've still got eight of our men out there, no sorry – we'll soon have twelve men there, he just asked for another four. All those guys are earning big money, very happy with their roles.'

'Amazing! I never expected to find someone like you in New Zealand, but I suppose you can do it from anywhere, if you have access to the personnel – and the contacts and the reputation, of course. I understand you a lot better these days.'

He leaves shortly after this, but before he goes, he returns to the living room and stands for a moment looking down at Dao. At the front door he pauses. 'This can't go on, Hunter! It's putting Dao's health at risk, quite apart from the physical danger.'

That penetrating gaze of his never leaves my face. 'I can't allow it, so make sure it stops! And make sure you keep her safe while this goes on, won't you? You know how to do it.'

He opens the front door, turns and looks straight into my eyes. 'I mean it - whatever the hell it takes.'

I never thought I would ever hear Benson say anything like it, practically giving me permission to take matters into my own hands. I lock the door and go back upstairs.

33

The skylight above our bed is a square of pale blue without a single cloud. Beside me Dao sleeps after a slightly disturbed night and I'm doing one of my favourite things; watching Dao sleep. There are two reasons for this. She looks so cute when she sleeps and if I'm lucky I'll see her wake up, which is often an amazing performance. This morning, without any preliminary twitches she opens her eyes, sits up and says accusingly, 'Yesterday you called me a little thing twice!'

And when I laugh at this unexpected attack, she laughs too. 'But it's true – you did!'

'Sorry, I didn't mean to.'

After breakfast I put a note on the dining table, where Dao usually sits when she's studying:

'Dear Little Thing, I'm not the kind of man who uses words like 'darling' or 'honey' – they don't come naturally to me. Would it be OK if I say Little Thing with capital letters, like a name?'

I need to explain our situation to Tama, who sometimes calls in when he and Tyler visit the uncle who lives on the North Shore. I want to make sure he doesn't make an impromptu visit and we have to turn him away. When I call him there is no answer, and I leave a message saying that I need to tell him something that will take at least ten minutes, and can he please call when it is convenient. He calls in his lunch hour and listens in total silence, not a single question, until my well-rehearsed tale is told.

'For Christ's sake, Hunter - you have to stop this!' he says fiercely. 'It's ridiculous – it's the second time in less than a year you've got yourself involved in something dangerous. One day you'll get yourself killed – or worse, you'll get Dao killed.'

'I know, I know - we are stopping, we've discussed it and I've promised Dao we will never help anyone again. And Benson has practically made me take an oath that I will never do it again. Don't worry – it's not that I want to do these damn things!'

I don't tell him what Benson said when he left last night. I can still hardly believe it myself. Tama asks to speak to Dao and whatever he says makes her laugh. 'No, of course he won't. Yes, I'm quite sure – he made a double promise the way my dad taught me. Nobody and nothing can break a double promise - and it lasts forever, even after you die.'

She hands my phone back and I notice a new line of writing on the note I left on the table:

'How will I know you're using capitals when you talk?'

In the afternoon Linda calls, devastated and I put the call on speaker so Dao can hear what she has to say.

'Inspector Bakker just called me – they found Grace this morning. They've asked me to do the formal identification at five. Could you please come with me? I've never seen anybody dead before. Oh God, I don't want to see her dead.'

'I'm very sorry, Linda, but we can't. We're in a bit of a situation and we won't leave the house until it's over.'

I tell her just the basic facts, that someone who was involved in the abductions of those girls, the same people who killed Grace, might think that Dao knows something important and how they can find out where we live.

'Oh no, that's awful! And you don't even know how long it's going to be?'

'No idea – but we're OK here until the cops sort it out,' says Dao. 'Hunter has turned the house into a fortress, and we've got everything we need. But we're having no visitors at all, just to keep things as safe as we can and definitely not going out.'

Linda says she'll ask the admin manager to go with her to identify Grace, and it's only then I realise something.

'Hey, listen – I've just thought of it, did we tell you that Grace Harris wasn't her real name? She changed it and we know what it was before. I know we planned to tell Bakker, but I don't think we did – I think the arrest got in the way and distracted us. There will be relatives to be informed and maybe someone else who can identify her.'

I go to turn the kettle on before I make the call to Bakker and pick up the note from the table on the way to the kitchen. I write one last sentence on it: *'You will hear the capitals because you know I love you.'* It doesn't make any sense, but it feels right.

I make two mugs of coffee, put some biscuits on a plate and make two trips back to the living room while I wait for Bakker to answer. On the second trip I put the note back on the table.

Bakker is not pleased when I tell her about Grace's name change. 'It would have been useful to know this earlier,' she says and then adds slightly reluctantly, 'but thank you. Can you repeat her original name again so I can make a note of it?'

'I'm sorry I didn't get to tell you, but with one thing and another I got distracted.' I am sure she gets the drift, so before she comes back with some comment, I add, 'Where was she?' I'm fully aware that she might not tell me, but today I don't care what her mood is, and I want to know what happened to Grace.

'In the lift pit, terrible place. It's down on Basement level three and only the building manager and the lift service man are supposed to have access. We've no idea how they got down there.'

I try to picture the so-called lift pit. 'Is that the space where the machinery is?'

'No, not in this case,' says Bakker, and as usual when she is explaining something, she gets nicer. It's as if she is pleased that she knows more than you, it makes her feel good about herself. I must remember to tell Benson this theory.

'This building has the machinery on the roof – the pit is like a big hollow concrete cube at the bottom of the shaft. It's damp, and there's a bit of water on the floor, but the body was in reasonable shape despite that, probably because of how cold it is down there, it's way underground.'

'So, what is the pit for?'

'There are a couple of big shock absorbers – in case all the other systems fail, I suppose, and one of those wall-mounted cabinets with circuit breakers – oh, and a big button to stop the lift in an emergency.'

'In case you're down there and forgot to turn the power to the machinery off - and it's going to come down and squash you?'

'It would hit you if you were standing up, yes – and I'm sure it would be unpleasant even if you were crouching down.'

'Thanks for telling me,' I say at the end, feeling charitable. 'Not that we ever met Grace, but we kind of feel we know her from what Linda and Mariko have told us.'

And then she surprises me. 'I know – I do too. She was obviously a good person.'

I don't tell her what Benson told us; that Grace used to work at the central police station in Auckland. It's quite possible that Bakker met her, even if her name didn't ring any bells, but I will let her find that out for herself.

I text Benson: 'Grace's body found at apartment building.' He calls nearly immediately. 'Where did they find her?'

When he hears about the lift pit, he snorts. 'Didn't they

look there to start with? Surely they searched the whole building.'

'Bakker said only the building manager and a service guy have keys – they don't know how they got in, it's down on something called basement level three. I'm not making excuses, but it sounds like a pretty inaccessible place.'

We are about to end the call when I remember my theory about how to put Bakker in a good mood, and he chuckles. 'I'll remember that if I have occasion to talk to her again.'

But things have been percolating through the back of my mind without me being aware of it and out of the blue a thought pops up and I look up Apatu's number.

'I hear you've got footage of the third guy's car. What make is it?'

'Hang on a minute,' he says and puts the phone down. I hear keys tapping and then he reads it out. 'Grey Toyota Prado 2016 model, slight dent in right hand front wing, tinted windows. Do you want the rego?'

I write it down; you never know when the information might come in handy. The more I think about what the third man or someone else might do to find the hard drive, the more urgent it feels to do everything possible to keep us safe.

After dinner, when we would usually either play chess or watch something on Netflix or read, I tell Dao about the latest developments and about the third man's car.

'I might be a bit over the top about this fortress situation.' I glance at the curtains I just pulled across the glass wall. 'A couple of people have suggested I'm obsessed, but let's face it – taking extra precautions doesn't cost anything.'

Dao shakes her head at Scruff, who is sitting at her feet with the tug-of-war toy in front of him, 'And you have thought of something else we should do – or not do?'

'Several things – we never go out on the balcony or stand just inside the windows. These curtains stay at least half pulled all the time – even in the daytime - and right across when we have lights on inside. Scruff won't play in the courtyard, we'll just let him out to pee, and call him in again. We'll not pick up any dog poo – I don't care what happens to the grass. We keep the blind down over the narrow window by the front door. Same in the garage, that window gets covered too, in case we need to go in there for something and turn the light on.'

'OK, so nobody can spot us through the windows, nobody can tell if we're home – oh, wait a minute, of course they can, they can see lights in other windows at night. Are you worried they might shoot us or something, through the windows?'

'I don't know what might happen, Dao. I'm not trying to scare you, but I want to make damn sure nothing does happen. What if they call me and say, "we have a sniper aiming at the centre of Dao's chest right now and we'll kill her unless you give us the hard drive"? Or the other way around - they threaten to kill me on the spot, if you don't tell them where it is? I have a bad feeling about this - and there's no way of proving you *don't* have something. Somebody wants that little thing, because it represents a huge amount of money, if they sell what is on it – or they want it to blackmail the people who set up this whole ghastly business.'

'Or,' says Dao, 'they know that those recordings can identify them. What if the third man is the one who killed people? Or raped them – or both? He won't want anyone to get hold of the proof of that.'

We have just set up the chess board when Dao thinks of something. 'Hunter! What about the supermarket deliveries, the third man might wait for you to open the door to take the shopping in and come charging in.'

'You didn't see the delivery yesterday – you were having a sleep. Fourteen big carrier bags – I worked out we could survive for four to six weeks if disaster struck and most of it will be used at some stage, now or later. Things that either last for ever or are frozen. Lots of tins, the freezer is full, dried things like rice and pasta, sachets and jars of various things. And toilet paper and tissues and dishwasher powder and toothpaste. So, OK – if this siege goes on, we'll not eat fresh fruit or vegetables for a while, but it won't kill us.'

'If I get desperate for a banana, I'll call Benson and ask him to deliver it in a police car – perfect!'

We play two games of chess and win one each, watch the late news and then Dao and Scruff go upstairs ahead of me. I turn off the lights, leave the little jeweller's box I bought the other day on the table beside her laptop and follow her up. We meet on the landing. 'I forgot I took Scruff's water bowl down this morning to clean it.'

I've just put my toothbrush into my mouth when she appears behind me with the box in her hand. 'Is this for me?'

'Yes, it is for you.'

'But why?' She looks genuinely puzzled.

I remove the toothbrush and turn around. 'Let's say it's the engagement ring you never got – or we could call it a two-month wedding-anniversary ring. I've been waiting for the perfect day to give it to you.'

She takes the ring out of the box and tries on her ring finger and then on her middle finger. 'It fits on that one – is that OK for an engagement ring?'

'No, I think that's the finger where you wear a 'thank God she didn't get killed in that factory' ring, you funny Little Thing.'

'You are so lovely – and on the same day that I got the only love letter I've ever had.'

'What! Who sent you a love letter?'

'You did - that note, I'm keeping it. You always say you're not romantic, but you are.'

'Well, don't tell anyone, will you? My reputation would be ruined.' I turn back to spit out toothpaste and she holds her hand up and wiggles her fingers and smiles at me in the mirror. 'Come to bed, you sexy big thing.'

I wake in the middle of the night because there is light showing in the half-open bathroom door, and Dao never bothers to turn the light on in the night. I wait for a few minutes and then I get up to investigate.

'Sorry! Did I wake you up?'

'It was worth it!'

Dao sitting naked on the loo in the middle of the night admiring her ring – perfect.

In the morning the skylight is grey, and rain flows across the glass in a strong wind. I disarm the ground floor alarm and take Scruff and the Glock down, so he can go out into the courtyard. I stand in the doorway watching him, just far enough inside so Nigel can't spot me with a pistol in my hand. Not that anyone sane would stand on a balcony today, but you never know with Nigel. I dry Scruff off and return upstairs to find that Dao has made us breakfast in bed. 'Let's not get up until we feel like it - we've only had breakfast in bed once before.'

She holds up her hand and looks at the ring. 'What about if I'm rinsing things in the kitchen? Should I take it off?'

"Don't worry, diamonds are the hardest thing in the world, I don't think you can damage it. We can buy one of those little ultrasound cleaning devices, they showed me one in the jeweller's shop.'

The rest of the day feels as if we're camping or living somewhere temporary, though it's not very different from our normal days. Of course, we don't go for a walk or to the supermarket, and some blinds are down, but we do what we always do: read, work, study, talk, eat, play.

When I mention this peculiar feeling to Dao, she says she has it too. 'But I think it's just that thing that happens when you know you can't have something; it makes you want it more. Even if I hadn't thought of a tomato for months, and you said 'you can never have a tomato again, they've gone extinct' – then I'd instantly start thinking of how nice it would be to have a tomato. I've been wanting to go for a walk all day, even though it's pouring with rain.'

'Did you send that email to Willow?' she asks when we're getting ready for bed.

'No, I'm not sending it until they get back. I checked their schedule - they'll be home tomorrow morning. I don't want her to try to read it on her phone with all those attachments. And it might ruin their last day of holiday.'

'Are you sending it to your parents?'

Now, here's a tangled web, as someone said recently. After I found Dao and she stayed with me, my domineering mother carried out a relentless campaign to convince me that Dao was after my money. In the end, I got so angry that I told her I would have no further communication with her until she accepts Dao. I said that if she changes her mind, she can email me to let me know, but I'm not taking any more calls from her. It sounds draconian, but I won't let her hurt Dao again; it's up to her to change. That was just a few months ago, and though I speak frequently to my father, and he has come for a visit since, we never talk about my mother. He loves Dao, and he knows we got married. I have not asked if he told my mother, and he hasn't mentioned it. Time will tell what happens at Christmas this year.

'I'll send it to Dad,' I say now. 'It's up to him if he tells her or not.'

While I make breakfast the next day, Dao sits at the dining table and checks the front camera footage from the last two days. She sees nobody who fits the description of the third man and no grey Prado.

To my surprise Bakker calls in the afternoon. 'I heard from Apatu that you asked about the car, the Prado. Are you concerned he could find you, if he had access to the CCTV from the factory? He would have seen your number plate, I mean – so he could have located you. I know you asked about what showed up when the girls escaped, so you're obviously thinking of that hard drive.'

'I've taken some precautions,' I say, not willing to go into details. 'I thought it would be a good idea to know, just in case he turns up.'

'You will let me know, I hope – if he turns up?' is all she says, and I say I will.

34

Life in our fortress continues quietly and without further drama. Willow, Matt and the twins return, and I send off the mega-sized email. Two hours later Willow calls and when I answer she starts to cry, which shocks me. As far as I know Willow hasn't cried since our grandfather died when she was nine.

'This is so awful,' she says when she gets her sobs under control. 'I thought you were done with these dangerous things. Why didn't you tell me earlier? Please don't even step out of the front door until everyone has been caught – or until that damn hard drive has been found. Have you told Dad? Are you all right for food and supplies?'

I assure her that we have plenty of everything and while we talk, I realise I didn't send Plum the final update, so I must send a copy of that email to her as well. Willow asks to speak to Dao, and they have a short conversation, which finishes with Dao responding to something with a giggle, 'No, he got those – he's perfect!'

'What did I get?' I ask as she picks up her book again. 'Oh, she just wanted to make sure I have tampons, but you ordered some so that's OK. Willow still feels she needs to check up and look after me, like she did after you first found me – and it's really nice, a bit like having a mother.'

I return to my laptop to send the email to Plum. As expected, this means another long phone conversation a couple of hours later, first with me and then with Dao, who goes upstairs to lie on the bed while they talk, as she always does.

'Keep my phone beside you and if Dad calls, you can talk to him,' I say, when she comes down again, 'Say I'm in the shower or asleep or something. I really can't discuss it all again, not today anyway. And he likes talking to you.'

In the evening Dao checks the cameras on the tablet and calls out, 'Come and look! Is that a Prado? It's a grey SUV type car.'

Down the street from our place, nearly out of range of the front camera, which is now on permanently, a grey car is parked. I can't see if anyone is in it, but it is a Prado. We leave the tablet between us on the bed and look at it now and then while we read, and then Dao says, 'It's gone now.'

The next day the sun shines, and life feels a bit brighter, until lunchtime when I spot the Prado again when I trawl through camera footage. It drove slowly past at five past ten, on the far side of the street and the driver looked carefully at the house. His face is only dimly visible through the tinted window, but it could be the third man, he is tall. I check the number plate against the number Apatu gave me, but it's different. I say nothing to Dao, just keep an eye on the recordings from the front camera a few times during the day.

Just after four the car is back and cruises past slowly, first on our side, so I can't see the driver, then he comes back on the other side. At this time of the day the lowering sun is behind our house, and it shines straight into his side window. The driver has a shaven head, and he is clearly focused on our house. I send a text to Bakker, telling her the plate number, so she can check if it is genuine or another fake plate, but when my phone buzzes it's not her.

A male with an American accent says, 'I want the SSD.' That's all he says, quite casually, as if it's not important. I assume it's the hard drive, but I stall for time.

'What the hell are you talking about? What's an SSD?'

'Solid state drive.'

'I don't have it.' If he can be brief, so can I.

'Your girl took it, we saw it on the CCTV, she had it in her little bag.'

This isn't going anywhere, so I go on the offensive. 'No, she damn well didn't take it. All she had in the bag was her phone, so just fuck off and leave us alone. Probably your mate who got arrested hid the thing somewhere.'

I end the call and meet Dao's anxious eyes. 'Yeah, that was him, he just cruised past. I bet it's a burner phone, but I'll forward the number to Bakker.'

While I call Bakker and leave a message, Dao starts making dinner. Knowing he is out there keeping an eye on the house is unpleasant, but we try to act as if it's a normal day; talking about it is just going to intensify Dao's anxiety. I look up SSD and find out a lot of stuff I never knew before and read it out to Dao.

'It's a very expensive kind of drive, much faster, can't get wiped accidentally by magnetism, huge capacity and has something called FDE, which means everything is encrypted.'

'Trust them to have something special,' is all she says.

We make dinner and wait to hear from Bakker, which doesn't happen until just after half past seven. 'Sorry,' she says. 'Two long meetings, one after the other, things are coming together. That plate is another fake. Did the car have a dent in the front wing?'

'I can check if you like or send you the clip – quite a good view of his face as he stares across at our house. But we know it's him, he just called me.'

We have a lengthy discussion about what he said, and if it's worth having my phone monitored, but we end by agreeing that I might was well simply tell her if anything else happens.

'I'll get a patrol car to do regular circuits in your neighbourhood tonight and tomorrow. Do you want someone parked outside?'

'No thanks – the neighbours would form a committee and force me to sell up and leave. We've had enough police activity here the last year or two.'

She seems to know about this, asks no questions and says to let her know if I change my mind. I put a loaded magazine in the Glock and leave it with the Remington in the corner by the stairs. My head is full of half-formed plans and options, but until I know what he's going to do next, it's all conjecture.

Just after dark he calls again. 'If you don't come out and hand over the SSD, I'll throw a hand grenade into the house. I've got an M67 in my hand as we speak.'

Does he really have an M67? It seems pretty far-fetched; an M67 is a ball-shaped American fragmentation grenade, roughly the size of a tennis ball. It would be easy to throw it through our first-floor window from across the street, and the damage would be horrendous. It is what's called an anti-personnel device, which is just a nicer way of saying it was designed to kill people as effectively as possible. If it detonates inside, the casing will fracture into razor-sharp fragments that fly at terrific speed through the depth of a building slashing through people. In my mind appears an image from the past of the kind of structural damage this type of grenade will do if it explodes just inside an outer wall. It takes out the wall, but the blast force also goes up and down, very damaging.

'You're bluffing,' I say. 'Where the hell would you get an M67 from? I don't believe it's real.'

'I know you've got CCTV,' he says. 'I can see the camera from here. Have a look - I'll turn the interior light on and show you.'

My mind goes into overdrive and I'm thinking of half a dozen things at the same time; assessing where the safest place in the house is, how to keep him talking, the options of lying about the hard drive, the consequences when he discovers I lied, how to take him by surprise, how to avoid a major disaster in our street. It all happens in the few seconds it takes me to open the camera view on the tablet again. And there he is on the far side of the street parked a bit closer than last time. As I watch the window rolls down, the light comes on and he rests his lower arm on the windowsill. He's holding a ball-shaped object with a thick stump pointing up and it could be an M67.

Dao is standing beside me, staring at the picture on the screen, tense as a steel spring. I call him back. 'It looks like a grenade, but it could be a training one or some kind of mock-up. I'm not making any decisions until I have enlarged the image and checked it out.'

'And don't call the cops,' he says. 'If you do, I'm launching myself out of this car with the grenade fully primed, and then we're at a deadlock. If they shoot me, the thing goes off and takes them out with me. If they don't shoot me first, I throw it.'

'Call me back in five when I've looked at it properly.'

I'm surprised he doesn't protest, all he says is, 'OK.'

I zoom in on the image and it is an M67. The US have used them all over the globe for decades and they used them in Afghanistan. I sit still for a couple of minutes while a plan compiles itself from the mass of ideas that have popped up like fireworks in my brain since he first issued his threat.

'Right,' I say to Dao and turn to look straight into her eyes, making sure she knows that this is an order. 'This is what's going to happen, so listen carefully now, Little Thing - I won't have time to repeat it. You are coming with me downstairs now. Go get Scruff and your phone and the charger from the kitchen. Both of you are going into the bathroom down there - and you are going to lock the door. We're not discussing this - it's the safest place by far if he throws the grenade at the house.'

She nods, her eyes fixed on mine.

'I'm leaving through the courtyard. And don't call the cops – this guy is dangerous. Let's see if I can deal with it first, or we might have real mayhem out there. If I want you to call the cops I'll text 'I'm OK' to you - that *doesn't* mean I'm OK, it means call the cops. If I can't text you, just wait – however long it takes, just stay in the bathroom. You'll be able to see where I am on your phone app, so you can tell the police when you get the text.'

She nods without saying anything and goes to get her phone. I put the Glock in my back pocket, and we're halfway down the stairs when he calls again.

'OK,' I say and try to sound as normal as I can. 'It looks like an M67, all right. I haven't seen one of those for a few years.' I want to buy time, keep him talking, make him wait if I can manage it. 'So, all right, you win. I'll get the damn thing out of the safe and come out and give it to you. I've just got to run upstairs - the safe is in my wardrobe. Two minutes and I'll see you outside, I'll come to the car.'

We are in the hallway to the courtyard now and time is getting short. 'Dao - listen carefully. I will let the door self-lock behind me when I leave – check the courtyard camera on your phone and set the alarm as soon as I'm safely over the wall to the lane.'

I push her into the bathroom, turn on the light and close the door as soon as Scruff is inside. I hear the bolt slide home, then I walk out into the courtyard and slam the door behind me.

<h1 style="text-align:center">35</h1>

Outside everything is quiet and still. Nearby someone is playing the piano with the window open and I have time to think how incongruous this is; the gentle piano music in the spring evening and me standing here with a loaded pistol in my pocket, possibly never to come back. I grab one of the garden chairs, climb up and look carefully up and down the lane at the back before I climb over the wall. He could have had an associate waiting at the back, but so far luck is on my side; there is nobody there. I jump down and run along the lane behind our row of houses. In seconds I am at the corner where the lane comes out on a side street. I cross to the far side and move along the sidewalk at a normal pace, try to avoid attracting attention. It's only about fifty meters to the corner of the street at the front of our house.

My heart is beating fast. I know this feeling; the taut line of tension down the back of my throat, the way things seem to be in ultra-high definition. It's the adrenaline working my mind and body, getting ready for a fight. It is like nothing else; intense focus, ready to react fast, my brain processes multiple options every second.

When I am nearly at the corner, I pull the Glock out of my

pocket and walk forward with it in my left hand, holding it down alongside my thigh. Someone seeing it and calling the cops now is the last thing we need. And there he is, the engine is running and exhaust fumes float like wisps of mist in the cool night air. His head is turned to the right, I hope he's watching our front door, not looking in the side mirror. And now I must commit to an act that could turn the situation into an immediate failure; everything depends on the door on the passenger side not being locked, so I can take him by surprise. I cross to his side of the street and run full tilt up to the car, pull the passenger door open and slide in, gun aimed at him.

He swings around fast, sees the Glock and freezes; the grenade is still in his right hand. He stares at the gun, and I stare at the grenade. He has pulled the clip off, and his thumb is holding the safety lever down. If he grabs the pull-ring with his left hand and pulls the fuse pin out – then it's only the grip of his fingers that prevents the countdown from starting. If his thumb moves off the safety lever, the thing blows up in five seconds. Shit!

'You son-of-a-bitch!' is all he says, and we sit there staring at each other in the gloomy light from the streetlights filtering in through the tinted windows.

'So, what now?' I ask after a while. My breathing has slowed to normal and now I'm here, I suddenly feel calm. 'It's your call. I don't have the hard drive, I genuinely don't have it, never did. You can accept that fact, put the safety clip back on that damn thing and drive away leaving me here – or take me with you. Nobody's going to call the cops, you'll have time to go someplace and ditch the car.'

My left hand is not my gun hand, but he doesn't know that. I decided to keep the Glock as far away from him as possible to avoid him trying to knock it aside. His eyes move from my hand with the gun to my face and then back to the Glock. I see him assess the likelihood of successfully smashing it out of my hand, against the chance that I will have time to pull the trigger.

'I'm sure you know about Glocks,' I say, keeping my tone conversational. 'No safety as such, they've got the double trigger device instead. As you can see, I have my finger inside the trigger guard and if you try anything, I'll shoot you, I'm a pretty good shot.'

The aim, now that the situation has turned into a one-on-one stand-off, is to make him believe I'm confident, calm and not scared of him; to somehow unnerve him and get the upper hand. What I don't want is some kind of knee-jerk reaction or a fight over the gun; even a verbal argument could tip this over the edge. As always when things are very dangerous and disaster is possibly imminent, things seem to slow down, time stretches, and I take in every detail. His breathing has slowed now after those fast breaths when I surprised him. He sits there staring straight ahead and thinking hard with a crease between his eyebrows. He has a wolf by the ears, as the saying goes; he can't hold on forever and neither can he let go. Now he must make a decision. Either he gives in, and I hold him at gunpoint and call the cops, or else he takes it to the bitter end and blows both of us up. There is no middle ground here, it's one extreme or the other. Even in the midst of this dilemma he seems surprisingly calm.

'And by the way,' I say, trying to sound casual, if not directly friendly, 'just in case you think you can put pressure on me by saying you will gamble on having time to throw that thing at the house before I kill you, think again. The girl as you call her – she's actually my wife – is no longer in the house. She left via the courtyard at the back, like I did, and by now she is at least a couple of kilometres away.'

He doesn't reply; he is still looking straight ahead, his forehead creased in concentration and the hand not holding the grenade has tightened on the steering wheel. It is quite possible that he might rather be dead than face the situation confronting him now; no hard drive and hunted by police. If he's going to settle for that, he can pull out the fuse pin now, roll the grenade under his seat or somewhere I can't reach it, and there will be nothing I can do. If he pulls the pin, I will have time to get out, but I would only get a couple of steps away before that damn thing detonates. My skin prickles at the thought of those sharp metal fragments slicing into my flesh.

The seconds tick by, neither of us speaks and then, without any warning he puts the car into Drive, and we move off. I have to admit that I'm reluctantly impressed by this evil man. He thinks things through and keeps his cool, no hasty reactions, no shouting. He is doing what I might have done in the same situation; drive off with the grenade handy enough to be a deterrent, so the other person won't try anything desperate, like grabbing the steering wheel. And if it was me, somewhere in a safe place I would do a very fast turn while braking hard and try to knock the gun out of the other guy's hand. So that's what he might do, but he's different from me and maybe he's worked out another solution. I knew from the start that he would never let me get out and drive away; all I can do is wait.

He drives without hesitation through the residential areas to the nearest motorway on-ramp and heads north. Just for the hell of it I start a conversation. Who knows, maybe we'll become friends, swap army experiences. For some reason there's no doubt in my mind that he's ex-army.

'Were you in Afghanistan?'

He glances at me and for a moment I think he's going to tell me to shut up, but he says, 'Yeah, three tours. You?'

'On and off for six years.'

I wait for a while as he drives at exactly the top legal speed in the left-hand lane, the grenade hand rests on the outer rim of the steering wheel. I wonder how long it will be before he gets cramp in his thumb and lets go; he's been keeping the pressure on that safety lever for a long time now.

Suddenly he says, 'I know what you do.'

He's a demon for very short sentences, this man. 'Yes?' I say and wait, two can play this game.

'Yep, you run a hire agency for mercenaries. I bet the money's good.'

'That's kind of what we do, but they're not really mercenaries – not in the real sense of the word,' I say, thinking that a normal kind of conversation might be a way of de-escalating the tension and possibly give me a chance to work out some kind of strategy. 'We don't place men in the armies of dictators or terrorists. Our guys get hired for roles like drivers doubling as bodyguards, butlers who know how to fight, personal protection squads in countries where politician get killed. You know the kind of thing.'

'I suppose, yeah,' is all he says.

We travel in silence; I drive this road to get to the cabin and I'm familiar with the various communities and the road signs. The traffic is moderate, a few cars pass us, but he is not in a hurry. He's in control of himself, sits quite relaxed in his seat now, steers with his left and rests the grenade hand lightly on the steering wheel. We have stopped talking, we're just quietly cruising northwards through the dark.

And then, for no reason, a theory appears in my mind, and I spend a couple of minutes working through it. How would this guy have seen that last CCTV recording from the factory, the one of the Dao and Mariko escaping? It is the only way he could know she had the bag, but how did he access it? Apatu said the CCTV footage was livestreamed somewhere as well as saved in that tech hub inside the container, but where was it streamed to? What if this guy is not the killer/rapist but a manager of the New Zealand branch of this evil empire? Or is he both? Does he rape and torture *and* manage the operation here? If I get out of this alive, I'll make sure Bakker knows what he said about the bag, because that is the clue.

'They get paid a lot, those guys?' he says suddenly in a conversational voice, as if we are out for a casual drive.

'They are very well paid.'

His only response is, 'Good,' and I wonder if he is thinking that maybe that's what he should have done instead of whatever his current job description is.

Suddenly he signals a left turn and I glimpse a sign saying *Woodcocks Rd.* We are heading out into the countryside, and this might be the time to push things a bit. If it doesn't work, I'll try to think of something else, but there probably isn't much time or opportunity left now. I think he has made his decision.

'Do you mind if I send a text to my wife? You can check that I'm not telling her to call the cops or where we are going or anything. I just want to tell her I'm OK. She'll be worried – she's very young.'

He doesn't know she's extraordinarily resourceful and twenty-three; he's only seen her on video. 'OK, then, write the message and pass the phone to me.'

I get my phone out, rest it on my right thigh and working one-handed, I type a text message to Dao: "I'm OK". We are driving through some kind of industrial area. He slowed down right from the time I got the phone out, possibly ready to let go of the wheel and grab the phone if necessary; he is glancing down at it while I type. He holds his left hand out and steers with the grenade hand. We are out in the country again. I pass the phone over and he slows down even more, drifts close to the edge of the seal. I watch him glance at the words and press Send, and then this strange guy hands the phone back.

I would never have done that. I would have thrown it out the window. The fact that he gave it back can only mean one thing. I was right, he has made a decision, and now I know without a doubt that he is going to blow us both up. There is no way out for him, he has been building up to this since we left the North Shore. I have a split-second chance right now when his left hand is moving back to the steering wheel, right this second before he accelerates again and crosses the little bridge just ahead of us.

I shove the door open, try to keep my grip on the Glock, clutch the phone in my right hand and roll sideways out of the car. It's not a smooth manoeuvre, not like in the movies, when someone throws themselves out and practically hits the ground running. The door swings back too soon and for a terrifying moment my right foot is caught, and then I am free. I hit hard, and before I have time to tuck my arms in, I'm rolling down a slope. I scramble to my feet while behind me I hear him braking hard, and then I am running through boggy grass and reeds. The ground gets softer with each step and my feet sink into the wet mud. The engine screams as he reverses fast off the bridge, and I know I have very little time to get away, but my left hip is hurting like hell from where I hit the ground. I try to look around me as I run, but the moon isn't quite up yet, so it's just the light from the star-studded sky to show me where I'm going. Suddenly my feet hit water instead of soggy ground and now I'm in a stream and I must make a quick decision. Do I stay here and try to conceal myself, or do I try to wade across? I decide that wading across would expose me too much, so I crouch in the middle of a clump of tall reeds, hunker down low and hope the reeds conceal my shape. I'm still clutching the phone, but my left hand is empty, the pistol is gone. I can't remember letting go of it; maybe it just flew out of my hand when I hit the ground.

I can hear him now that I've stopped moving; I try to control my breathing to hear his movements better. He seems to be to be quite a way over to the left of me and moving further away. If he can't see me, he might backtrack, perhaps walk back along the stream. I have to keep track of him. And at that moment it dawns on me that I can still hear the car. I turn my head and see its lights not far behind me, the passenger door is still open; he's jumped out and left the motor running. This is my second chance tonight; I leap to my feet and run limping back the way I came. I clamber up the bank and around the back of the Prado and cast a glance over to the side. He has seen me and he's coming towards me fast.

I fling myself into the driver's seat and thank my lucky star that we're much the same height, no problem with leg room. I move the lever to Drive and take off like a madman with the doors on both sides swinging. Through the roar of the engine and the doors vibrating against the doorframes I hear him shout. For a hideous moment I think he has somehow got into the back seat. I glance at the rear vision mirror and see his outline against the rear window. Somehow, he is clinging to the back of the car, and I accelerate hard, make tight swerves from one side of the road to the other to try to dislodge him, but he manages to hang on. Next time I look his dark shape is way over to the side. God knows what he's holding on to, but he's trying to get around the rear corner, maybe in an insane attempt to reach the rear door. I hope he's not still holding the M67. I can't stop and I have no gun, so I swerve hard again, several times, and both front doors bang shut, one after the other – and he loses his hold and falls off. As I accelerate away there is an explosion behind me, the inside of the car is lit for a second by a bright flash, the car judders and the blast seems to push me forward.

I pull over and stop on the verge and sit there breathing hard, pulling myself together. I know that the blast radius of an M67 if pretty impressive, probably ten times that of the kill radius, so there might be damage to the car. I never heard any impacts of metal on metal but decide to get out and have a look; and then I see a car coming towards me. I get out fast and step out into the middle of the road, raise both hands over my head, hope like hell they will stop in time. The car skids to a halt on the far verge and an old guy leans out the window and shouts, 'You fucking lunatic! What the hell are you doing? I could have killed you.'

I limp across and lean against the roof of his car, suddenly my legs feel as if they can only just hold me up. 'Sorry, mate.

There's been an accident just behind me, a guy blew himself up.'

He shoves the door open so fast he nearly knocks me over. 'What! I saw a big flash of light a minute ago - we were just behind those trees, I wondered what it was.' He gets out and stares into the darkness. 'I can't see anything.'

'Can you please drive forward very slowly - I'll walk alongside you,' I say and then I notice a face looking across from the passenger seat. 'Hey, have you got kids in the car?'

'Grandsons, two of them. One in the back and the older one in the front.

'This will be messy.'

He thinks for a moment, then he bends into the car and says, 'Now listen boys, there's been a bad accident. I'll leave you here, and you're *not* to get out, OK? Hand me the torch from the glove box, Rob. And do *not* get out of the car! I'll be back soon.'

I'm about to ask him to turn his headlights back on, but there's a very slight curve between us and the site of the explosion, so not much use. He gets back in the car and turns the engine off and the hazard lights on, and I cross to the other side of the road and do the same, remember my phone that I threw on the passenger seat, grab it and shove it in my back pocket.

We walk slowly along the dark road. I guess where I stopped is about three hundred metres from the explosion site, perhaps a bit more. The torch isn't much good, but at least we'll know when we're getting close, before we step on something unpleasant.

'What the hell happened? Did you hit someone?' He swings the torch from side to side ahead of us.

'No, I was taken against my will by some maniac, I don't even know his name. I managed to jump out of his car a way back, just before a little bridge and when he stopped and got out to chase me, I doubled back, got in his car and drove off, but he clung to the back.'

'Doesn't explain how he blew up.'

'He had a hand grenade, ready to blow. He'd been holding it in his hand since the North Shore.'

'You don't say!' he says. 'That's bad.' A man not given to hyperbole. And that is when we see the first shreds of flesh on the road in front of us and the old guy stops. 'Holy hell! What should we do now?'

'I'll go to the other end of the mess and stop traffic coming from that direction – I'll turn on my phone flashlight if the phone isn't busted. And I'll call the cops.'

I get the phone out of my wet jeans pocket; it lights up and seems ok.

'You take the torch and go back to your car. The key's still in the one I was driving - you can move it out to block the road if you like, leave the hazard lights on so there's plenty of warning for other drivers.'

He walks away and I'm just thinking that it's lucky there is so little traffic just now, when I see distant lights coming towards me. I start a hobbling run to get to the far side of the explosion site before they arrive and try not to think of what I'm stepping on. Somewhere here there will be a minor crater in the tar seal, and I don't want to trip and fall into this mess. I get there just before the first car arrives and stand in the middle of the road moving my phone flashlight in an arc above my head.

Two cars arrive in close succession and both drivers get out to ask what's going on. Neither turns his hazard lights on, so I tell them to do that and then I say what I said to the old guy: there's a real mess on the road up ahead where some maniac blew himself up. After a variety of exclamations and questions both drivers decide they want to see the damage and walk forward and a minute later I see the light from a cell phone swinging around and hear the sound of someone vomiting. I stay where I am, lean against one of the cars and call 111. Now all I can do is wait for someone to arrive and take over. A third car stops behind the first two and a middle-aged woman gets out, listens to my explanation and gets straight back in her car and drives back the way she came after a snappy U-turn. And eventually the red and blue lights of police cars approach at speed and I can let go and let others take charge. I feel exhausted.

36

When I finally get dropped off at home, it is long after midnight. The cops leave me on the doorstep, and I use the doorbell for the first time ever. Dao opens the door and looks as if she's going to fling herself at me in a hug, but she changes her mind when I step into the hallway.

'You are filthy! What happened? When you called you just said you were standing on that road waiting for the police.'

'I'll tell you upstairs – I need some dry clothes and a drink.'

'Benson is here – I called him, and he came over to keep me company.'

And there he is at the top of the stairs, a calm presence in our lives whenever needed: a bit tubby, shirt coming untucked and as sharp as a tack. I am very pleased to see him.

Dao comes upstairs when I'm changing into clean clothes, to ask what wine she should open and it's the perfect opportunity.

'Don't make any comments, whatever I say about the Glock, don't say anything! I'm going to let him think it was Charlie's – not a new one.'

She nods, understands the reason for this without asking

288

questions and reaches up to kiss me before she leaves. I pull on a sweater; suddenly I feel cold.

When I get down to the living room, Dao has opened the wine and there is a plate of cheese and biscuits on the coffee table along with a half-full box of chocolates.

'I found them in the pantry, so I got them out, but we've only eaten half of them.'

It seems like a replay of another couple of midnight meetings in this room with Benson drinking beer as usual and Dao eating ice cream.

'I called 111 as soon as I got your text – and I told them it was to do with Bakker's case, and then I called Benson.' She smiles fondly at Benson. 'I thought he'd like to know what was happening – but he said he'd come over and keep me company which was really nice.'

'Now then,' he says. 'I've got some news too, but you go first. What the hell happened out there?'

And now I must decide if I tell him the whole truth or only a part of it. I really want to tell him the whole story; I feel we are at a new level of trust and I want him to know. But only if he can keep it to himself.

'Well?' He fixes me with that look of his. 'Are you going to tell us?'

Dao is looking from him to me and back again, confused by the delay. I decide to confront him head-on. 'Whatever the hell it takes, you said. Did you mean it?'

I see the penny drop, and he takes only a moment to reply. 'I did – whatever it takes.'

'OK,' I say, 'let's shake on it. I'll tell you - but as far as the rest of the world is concerned the official version will do.'

He stands up and we shake hands, watched by Dao who has no idea of the significance of that handshake. The story takes a while to tell because they keep interrupting me. When I try to explain my reasons for doing what I did, Benson is at first incredulous. 'For God's sake Hunter! Why did you do a dangerous thing like that? Why didn't you call 111 straight off?'

So, I explain that the guy had an M67, and then I have to explain what an M67 is, and so it goes on. He says nothing when I say I took the pistol, but I don't tell him it was a brand new one, of course. Explaining why we bought another Glock is not on my agenda. And when I have told them in exhaustive detail why I could see no other way of dealing with the situation, if potential mayhem was to be avoided, I think both he and Dao finally understand my point of view.

'And you had very little time to plan,' says Benson. 'You did well - really well.' High praise coming from him.

'He was very calm, and he sounded rational,' I say, trying to give them a snapshot of what the situation was like in the car. 'But I think suicide was never far from his mind from the start. There was a moment when I could see his mind working through the pros and cons – just before he started driving. I had put him in a deadlock position, or rather, I had put us both in it. He could blow me up, but he'd kill himself in the process. I could shoot him, but unless I killed him outright, he could have pulled the fuse pin and let go. He told me how he had worked out what to do if the police came, how he would make sure the grenade either exploded right there and took a few officers out along with him - or he would throw it into the house before they had time to shoot him. I said that we never had the hard drive, and that I only came out and surprised him to stop him throwing the grenade into the house.'

Benson nods, but makes no comment, so I continue.

'I think it was the final straw when he realised that we truly didn't have the hard drive – and he did believe me, I could see it. He knew it was the end - the cops looking for him, lots of CCTV showing him coming and going from the factory and the thought that if that hard drive was found, he was toast. I'm sure he's on video committing murders and it's all saved on that drive – that's why he was so determined to get it back. I don't think he wanted it to sell or to blackmail someone - he wanted it so there'd be no proof against him.'

'Did he say where he was going?'

'I think he was just driving - anywhere at all, and then when the moment felt right, he would pull the fuse pin out and let go of the safety lever and blow us both sky high. He had that grenade in his right hand the whole way. Maybe he was just waiting for an empty stretch of road with no traffic.'

Benson nods again, 'And that's why you risked jumping out of the car - you thought he'd blow you both up. Jesus, Hunter – I don't know how you can be so cool about it. And I don't understand why he let you send that message to Dao – wasn't that a strange thing to do?'

I top up my glass and raise it in a toast. 'Perhaps not so strange – I appealed to his better nature, and it turns out he had one. I said that Dao is very young, and she is worried, and I'll only say that I'm OK, I promise. He might have thought of it as my final farewell message, and what harm could it do? We both knew he was going to kill the two of us anyway. It was when he slowed to a speed no faster than a man can run, that I realised I had a chance after all – for one short moment, before he speeded up again.'

Benson nods. 'You're probably right. And I am very glad you didn't get blown up, you madman. So now you've told me that you had one of Charlie's pistols – which stays between us - but what the hell did you tell them when they interviewed you?'

'I said I took a knife, a very sharp filleting knife from our kitchen. I described how I jumped into the car and had the knife at his throat in a second, because I had rehearsed in my mind exactly how I would do it, every little move was in my mind, like a learned sequence of actions. I said he was so taken by surprise that I got the advantage I wanted. They think we went on that bloody nightmare road trip with him holding the M67 and me still with the knife pricking into the side of his throat, just by the jugular.'

Now Benson laughs and shakes his head. 'Christ, Hunter! You're totally crazy – this could have gone wrong in so many ways. And where is Charlie's pistol anyway? Don't tell me you had it in you back pocket all the time you were at the station?'

'No, I lost it – truly lost it. I have no idea where it is. I might have lost my grip when I fell down that slope or when I ran through the reeds – everything happened so fast and it was a panic situation, I really don't know.'

Dao glances at Benson and then at me. 'What if they find it? Are you going to be in trouble?'

'I wouldn't think so,' says Benson. 'They'll just think our nameless friend, the third man, had it and that he dropped it – so long as they don't fingerprint it. But we don't have Hunter's prints on file anyway. And where is the fictitious knife supposed to be now?'

'They didn't actually ask me that, but I made it part of the story – I said I had no idea, couldn't think where it might be, must have dropped it. I made sure they will not be surprised if they can't locate it, if they do decide to search. I made out I had run in a different direction and then back to the car in a loop. They think he was chasing me for several minutes, not one or two.'

'Why did he bother to chase you, do you think?' asks Dao. 'I mean, he might as well just have continued driving and blown himself up somewhere.'

'I don't know – perhaps he had decided he was going to kill us both and he wasn't going to back down. Or he wanted to punish me? Maybe me jumping out of the car was the last straw, his mind might not have been super logical at the time, but who knows.'

When I get to the end of the story, we sit there for a moment just relaxing and then Dao thinks of something. 'But I don't understand how he could hold on to the back of the car, though – and with the grenade in one hand. There's nothing to hold on to, is there?'

'Roof rack,' says Benson. 'When you showed me the car on your security video, when I first got here, I noticed it. That model has those rails that run along the roof on both sides – that you can attach cross bars to. So, if he leapt up, got a foot on the bumper ledge and grabbed hold of one of those bars with one hand – that would work. Or it might have had a tow-ball he could stand on. Hard to balance but it could be done.'

The video from our front camera! I never thought of that in my desperate rush and now I'm on video running towards his car with a gun! Even though it was dark, the pistol might have been visible when I opened the car door. I used my right hand to open the door, so I could hold the gun in the left, out of his reach. What if the cops ask for the video; Bakker knows we have CCTV. Damn! And then I notice Dao smiling quietly, and she slants a sideways glance at me; it means something and maybe, just maybe, she has deleted some of it.

Benson watches our brief exchange of glances; his expression doesn't change. 'You don't normally have the camera running constantly, do you?' he asks.

'No, very rarely,' I say, taking it carefully, feeling my way. 'We did when John was staking us out last autumn.'

'And what triggers it to start recording when it's not on permanent recording?'

I'm beginning to see where this is going. 'Anything that comes closer to the front of the house than the inner edge of the sidewalk. And then it stops recording, when whatever was there, a person or a dog, goes further away - it only records for another few seconds.'

'I thought so. And some days nothing at all triggers it and nothing gets recorded.'

Dao says, 'Yes, that happens often, of course. Like today, between the time the Prado drove past the in the morning, when something triggered the camera, until you came along tonight.'

And I draw a silent breath of relief. Dao has deleted most of the day and now it looks like the camera wasn't on the permanent setting. Benson knows she has, but he is not saying it. Somewhere between "whatever the hell it takes" and openly discussing Dao tampering with what might turn out to be evidence, he draws an ethical line. Maybe not completely logical, but I'm not complaining.

So, the image Dao showed him is harmless, just the car driving past slowly and the guy staring at the house. Now we can show it to Bakker if we want to; we won't say the camera was on all the time, just that something must have triggered it. Like those ducks that kept us mystified last year.

'Talking about it has reminded me – when they interviewed me, I didn't mention that we have the car on video.'

And this is true, I deliberately didn't mention it and I tell Benson to reassure him that all the ends are neatly tied up. I never told the cops I had seen the M67 before I went out to his car either, I just told them that he said he had it in his hand when he called me, and I believed him.

'I must go if I'm going to get any sleep at all,' Benson says and yawns. 'I just want to tell you what I heard tonight. Bakker called me – she was informed first by the call centre when Dao called 111 after she got your text, and then again when you called 111, so she called me to let me know what was going on, or as far as she knew at that stage – which was a nice gesture. She didn't know that Dao had already been in touch with me. Anyway, you know how Richard saw the guy leaving the factory with that bag slung over his shoulder and we thought he probably took the hard drive? Bakker said he didn't have it when they picked him up at the airport and they have tracked him back through the airport CCTV system and they think they're on to something.'

'What kind of thing?'

'Well, they wanted to see if anyone was with him, check how he got there and follow his steps through the building – maybe he met up with someone. And the person who dropped him off is a person of interest, of course, because if they can identify that person it might make it possible to find out where he has been since he ran off from the factory that night. Maybe they are slowly closing in on that hard drive.'

And I remember my theory about the third man's role and how his knowledge of Dao's bag on the CCTV footage backs it up and tell Benson about it.

He grins, 'And you think it would be better if I mention this to Bakker, I suppose? So you don't have to risk telling her something she hasn't thought of?' We both laugh and I say, 'Of course!'

When I let him out the front door I say, 'Thank you, Benson!' and he smiles, he knows what I mean.

We go to bed exhausted. 'I feel as if I've lied and been evasive and tweaked the truth for days,' I tell Dao, when we turn the light out. 'I'm tired of trying to save the world and my own skin at the same time. This stops now.'

'I hope that's not another lie,' says Dao. 'Are we going to stay in fortress mode, or do you think it's over now?'

'Let's stay as we are – I'd like to know that hard drive is found - before we go back to normal.'

37

Once the process of statements and signing things is over, the next few days pass quietly. I refuse to go to the police station, so Bakker sends Apatu over to finish the job.

The papers are full of dramatic headlines and speculation about what went on. TV reporters stand by the damaged road and read their "at-the-scene- but-nothing to report" statements – just the usual nonsense.

A press release from Bakker is a model of brevity: "A person linked to a human trafficking ring committed suicide on a public road in Northland by detonating a hand grenade. The man's name and nationality will not be released at this time, as it might compromise an ongoing investigation. There is no indication of where the grenade came from."

There is no way of telling if they have found out his name or if they still don't know, and I don't really care. I don't expect to hear any more about it and there is no reason for Bakker to keep me informed. Videos of the explosion site and the surrounding mess appear on social media, presumably courtesy of the two drivers who couldn't resist having a look; people get their vicarious thrills in strange ways. Somehow, I managed to avoid them filming me at the scene, which one of them was intent on trying to do until I told him what I would do to him in return.

To my surprise I get a final call from Bakker a couple of day later. 'I thought you would like to know,' she says and coughs. 'Sorry, I've caught a cold. We've had some interesting news from the US about Anderson, and I would appreciate your advice about whether I should inform Mariko or not.'

Now there is a statement I never expected to hear from Bakker, and it nearly makes me laugh. Over time our relationship has progressed, but even considering how she has loosened up over time, this is the next level up from where we left off when I last talked to her.

'What's happened?'

'They've been busy over there – this darknet operation wasn't confined to New Zealand and they have pieced together what they already knew with what they have discovered after they were alerted about John Anderson's disappearance – and, of course, what we have found here. A liaison person got in touch yesterday, and it seems there are at least four other locations, two in South America. And probably more – a huge empire run from Central or South America.'

'Have they located John?'

'No - they know he left the US using his own name, but he seems to have had more than one identity set up, and they don't know where he ended up - yet. Some country the US doesn't have an extradiction treaty with, I guess, but they will probably track him down in time. But the most stunning news is that they have proof he was an active partner in the business – he wasn't just the lawyer who organised the purchase of properties and stuff like that or just got paid to stay silent. He was a partner in the business.'

I try to imagine how they found this out and fail. 'How the hell did they work that out? He seems to have been a master at covering his tracks.'

'I know, a very clever man. But in his haste to leave the US he overlooked one thing – a burner phone plugged in to charge behind his desk in his study at home. And they got into it and found enough to issue a warrant for his arrest – it is with Interpol now and I wouldn't think he can ever risk leaving the country he's in, wherever that might be.'

'Surprisingly careless to leave a phone behind – but maybe he had several burner phones and lost track when he was packing.' It makes me grin to myself, thinking of John surreptitiously packing his briefcase and pretending to go to work, but really about to flee the country and leaving a phone behind. 'And are you considering whether to tell Mariko this?

She coughs again. 'There is no reason for us to tell her, but I thought you might like to discuss it. Is it better that she knows now or finds out if it appears in media later on?'

'I honestly can't make up my mind what I think would be best,' I say cautiously, slightly surprised by her concern for Mariko. 'Is there any likelihood that Mariko's trust fund and the ownership of her apartment will somehow be clawed back?'

'No way!' says Bakker decisively and coughs hard, she sounds really unwell. 'He would have earned enough in his legitimate job to have been able to give her all that without using any crime money – and even if they could prove that they wouldn't bother anyway. No, it's not that – I just thought that if or when it appears in the press it might be a shock. What do you think?'

'I vote for not telling her,' I say and pause while she has another coughing fit. 'There is no point in telling her right now. Just let it lie and if it turns up in the media, we have a whole little support network around her now. And let's face it, she is incredibly good at coping – I base this on how she reacted when she read that email that he sent me, that last one. I think she will be OK.'

'And if it never hits the news then she will never know for sure if he is a criminal or not – do you think it matters?'

'I know, it's tricky and as I said, I can hardly make up my

mind what's best. You can always tell her after a week or two, if you think it's best.'

'Bloody cleft stick situation, as these things too often are!' says Bakker. 'I'll think about it.'

She does not mention if Benson told her my theory about the third man yet, and I don't ask.

Dao and I spend some time discussing how much we should reveal to our friends about what went on that night. 'They'll be so upset if it comes out later and you didn't tell them,' says Dao. 'I mean, it's not the sort of thing that happens very often, is it? For them it's more exciting than scary, now that it's over. I think you should tell them. Write it up as an email and send it to them.'

I think it over and decide the only way I can do this is to tell two versions. The long one with all the details, apart from the fact that I took the Glock along on the road trip, I send to Charlie, my father and Willow. A slightly shorter one goes to Plum, Simon and Tama. I say to each one that I'm telling them in confidence and not a word of it must ever appear on social media or any other kind of media, and that I'm only sharing this, so they won't feel left out if it becomes public knowledge. I add a PS to the email to Plum, who loves to share news, and say that if she so much as breathes a single word of it, I will never talk to her again.

Dao reads it and suggests that I add the part about the "I'm OK" text into both versions and that I tell them what kind of grenade it was.

I compromise by adding the bit about the text message and leaving out the make of the grenade. 'Bakker would be furious, and rightly so, if that got out. She might have a good reason not to release the details yet – I didn't like being in that cell, Dao.'

I send both versions with a promise never to get involved in anything of this kind again and say neither Dao nor I can handle any more trauma or stress; we've both had enough for a lifetime.

An hour later my phone starts buzzing. First, it's Willow, who alternates between saying I must be insane to do such a dangerous thing and telling me she can't believe anyone being brave enough to do it. It takes a lot of talking to make her understand that my decision was actually based on good reasoning; then we go over it all again.

'And yes, it was uncomfortable to know he was planning to blow us both up,' I say, 'but at least I knew all along I was doing the right thing for the right reason - and I still hoped I would think of a way to get out of it alive.'

'Uncomfortable! Hunter! I can't believe you said that – it must have been terrifying.'

'OK, it was pretty scary, but it's over now.'

'And this is really the last time?'

'God, yes! I swear – never again. Benson has promised Dao he'll arrest me if I ever take on anything like this again.'

We end the conversation with Willow laughing and me mentally apologising to Benson for taking yet another liberty with the truth.

Plum calls and I put a lid on the most rampant excitement and repeat my threat to never speak to her again if she repeats the story.

'But when it gets out, you know - in a trial or some press release or whatever – surely I can say that it was my brother who did that? Pleeease!'

'OK, but don't add any dramatic details, remember that the police have my statement, and I don't want to end up in trouble again.'

A text message from Simon makes me think. 'OK if I tell Mariko?' is all it says and I go to discuss it with Dao, who is baking a cake for the first time in her life.

'I wish I'd never started this!' she says. 'Look at all the stuff that goes into it and every single thing has to be measured or weighed – it's like some crazy science experiment! I'm only doing it because we can't go out and have coffee and nice things to eat like we normally do.'

'It's very good of you, Little Thing,' I say and survey the ingredients all neatly lined up on the bench. 'What kind of cake is it?'

'You wouldn't know it - walnut cake with orange flavoured icing. It is in your big cookery book in the section you've never used.'

'How do you know that?'

'All the pages in the cake chapter are clean.'

When I ask if she thinks I should let Simon show the email to Mariko, she doesn't hesitate for a moment. 'Of course! She knows how to keep secrets.' And I recall that look between them when they came down after showering and dressing, the day we found them.

'And it's good that they both know – so they can talk about it together.'

My Dad doesn't read emails every day, but two days later he replies with much the same sentiments as Willow's. He says nothing about telling my mother.

38

We are still at the breakfast table a couple of days later when the doorbell peels. We both reach for the tablet, and I win; it's Simon and Mariko and they apologise all the way up the stairs for disobeying instructions and coming for a visit.

'But we have to tell you what happened,' says Simon. 'And seeing it's Sunday it was perfect, with me not working, I mean. And I knew you would have said we couldn't come if I called first, wouldn't you?'

'I would.'

Mariko shakes her head, 'Simon has no manners. We could have told you over the phone.'

'Not half the fun of telling them face to face. Hi, Dao – I bet you're glad to have some visitors. How's the food holding out?'

'We've got food for weeks, but no nice things like we usually eat in cafes, so I baked a cake,' says Dao proudly. 'With icing and everything. You can have some with coffee if you like.'

'We have come straight from a meeting with Bakker,' says Mariko. 'Not an interview – just to sign some papers. Before we have coffee, we should tell you the good news. Did you know that the man, who ran away from the factory, had a little bag as well as the big one?'

'Yes, Benson told us,' I say, 'But when they arrested him at the airport, he no longer had it. Don't tell me they found it!'

'Better than that,' says Simon excitedly. 'First, they looked at footage from the cameras at the entrance to the terminal and saw him being dropped off by a young woman – and it was perfectly clear that he only had the big bag. They had no idea who the woman was, so they looked up the plates on her car, but they were stolen and didn't belong on that car at all. Then yesterday they asked Mariko to come in and have a look at the woman in the video - in case she had ever seen her at the apartments. They thought Mariko might have heard her speak – trying to get some clues about nationality and so on. They were already going back over the videos from the apartment building to see if she had been caught on camera at any stage, with or without those guys. We went in yesterday and guess what?'

Mariko grins. 'I took one look at her and said, "she lives in flat 401 on the same landing as me, I've seen her lots of times and we have shared the lift a few times. I've never really talked to her, but she is definitely a local." You should have seen their faces - it was so funny!'

'Aha, and then they decided to raid her flat to see if she had the hard drive. Maybe that's where he was hiding out until he tried to leave the country.'

'Exactly!' says Simon. 'When Mariko went in to sign things today, they told her the rest of the story. Fancy him going back to that block of flats and letting cameras record him again, as if nothing had happened. Unbelievable! And he *is* the one who suffocated that girl in front of Mariko.'

'So, it's all perfect!' says Dao and hands Simon a tray. 'If you take this, I'll bring the cake.'

But for me the crucial information is still missing. 'Did they find the hard drive?'

'They did!' says Mariko. 'The bag was in her wardrobe

and the hard drive was wrapped in clingfilm and hidden at the bottom of a box of cornflakes.'

Dao and Simon head for the living room, but Mariko delays leaving the kitchen and hands me her phone with her message folder open. The message I read stuns me; it is from an undisclosed number and reads, "Whatever you hear about me, it is probably true, but always remember that I am very proud of you and I'm sure you have a great future. J"

I hand the phone back and she gives me a wry smile. 'Kind of like a confession, isn't it? But I suppose even criminals have a right to be proud of their children.'

She puts the phone in her pocket, and we follow the smell of coffee to the living room.

MANY THANKS

We hope you've enjoyed reading this story and would consider leaving a review on your favourite review site, or with the retailer you purchased from.

These are not only much appreciated, they also help other readers discover new authors.

For more about other titles in this series, please read on.

ALSO BY TINA CLOUGH

THE GIRL WHO LIVED TWICE

What would you do if you woke up one morning and found that time had rewound exactly a year? Would you revisit your past mistakes and try to do better? Would you try to get revenge on those who had wronged you? Or would you use what you knew to get rich? When Mia finds herself in her own past, she must decide how best to use her pre-knowledge of one year's worth of events and personal issues.

When Karen's flat-mate Nick is gunned down in front of her in the street her life is turned upside-down. Everything she thought she knew about him turns out to be a lie. She becomes a suspect in the police investigation and drug bosses think she knows where Nick has hidden a large sum of money. When her life is threatened, she decides to leave town and disappear.

Karen becomes Cara and creates an anonymous existence, severs all links to her past and adopts a cash-based way of life that leaves no electronic traces. But despite her careful planning danger still stalks her and she is forced to make dramatic choices in the face of threats and brutal violence.

Can she trust the man she is attracted to, or has he been sent by the killers to gain her confidence and find the money they believe she has?

Book 1 - Hunter Grant Series

Army veteran Hunter Grant thought he had left war behind in Afghanistan – a conflict that left him with physical and psychological scars.

But finding an unconscious girl in the Northland bush and gradually untangling her story involves him in warfare of a different kind in his own country.

Hunter sets out to find and punish the man Dao calls Master, but he soon finds there is more to this story than enslavement. Before long he himself is being hunted by the overlord of a drug empire whose sole objective is to kill Dao because she knows too much.

Protecting her and waging war while trying to keep the police from stifling his enterprise takes all Hunter's ingenuity and determination and puts him in deadly jeopardy.

ONE SINGLE THING

Book 2 - Hunter Grant Series

Journalist Hope Barber disappears two weeks after returning to New Zealand from an assignment in Pakistan, leaving her front door open and her bag and phone inside. The police are tight-lipped about their reluctance to act, and Hunter Grant and Dao agree to help Hope's brother Noah find her. Details about Hope's time in Pakistan gradually emerge but only raise more questions.

Was Hope under surveillance?

Was she linked to terrorists?

And who is the man Hope called 'my stalker'?

FOLDED

Book 3 - Hunter Grant Series

First notes asking for help and folded into tiny origami shapes are found outside a city apartment building, then a physics textbook with tiny writing between the lines and then the woman who found them abruptly resigns and disappears. Are the notes asking for help real or is it a game? Hunter Grant, ex-army and with a pragmatic view of justice, reluctantly agrees to help find the missing woman.

Things get complicated when a high-powered lawyer arrives form the US, and shortly after his meeting with Hunter and Dao, a "cease and desist" letter arrives from the Cayman Islands. Inspector Bakker - a woman, who in Hunter's words "looks as if she would be useful in a brawl, provided she was on your side" - takes instant exception to his involvement and threatens to arrest him for interfering in an investigation.

Dao sets out alone on a dangerous mission, driven by a compulsive need to find out what has happened to the girl who wrote the notes, and Hunter looks death in the face when he decides to risk everything to put an end to the Darknet forces that threaten their lives.

It is 2026 and individual freedoms are severely curtailed, with state surveillance everywhere. State Security has a Watch List, and being on it means that nothing you do or say escapes the authorities, but does the Kill List really exist? And if it does, how would you know if you were on it?

Coded messages on a found burner phone, top-level government corruption and a shadowy mastermind who calls himself The Broker. In this climate of state control, three unlikely friends start quietly looking for connections and set in motion a deadly game of hide and seek that will change their lives forever.

Trying to uncover the truth means risking your life, and nothing is more dangerous than searching for evidence of government corruption.

ABOUT THE AUTHOR

Tina Clough grew up in Sweden and now lives in New Zealand; dividing her time between writing fiction and translating and editing medical research papers.

Between working and writing she looks after an acre of fruit trees, vegetable gardens and roaming hens.

Apart from reading her interests include photography, wine, growing organic vegetables, making jam and kayaking.

https://lightpoolpublishing.com